1

A
Football
Story

Mike Castronis

Independently Published
Through

Kindle Direct Publishing

ISBN 9781521726570

For 'Iron Mike' Castronis, a man who played football for the love of the game, then spent a lifetime helping boys play it well and love it as he did. In that process he turned boys into men.

Prologue

It's all Greek to me.

The story that I am going to tell you is purely fiction, but then again it's not, because it is very much a part of me. Almost everything I'm about to relate actually happened, at one time or another. The people in the story are parts, sometimes almost wholes, of the people I grew up with, playing this game called football. This story is what happened to us, or what should have happened had we lived in a better world. It is all about the greatest game, the game I was privileged to play and coach. If you happened to see yourself in this story, I hope you enjoy what you find here. I loved playing with and coaching all of you. The stories happened to me and to you over a span of fifty years; it is a shared history and to me it is sacred.

But the story predates me as well. It began with my father, the first of our family to play the greatest game. Dad was first generation Greek. That is to say while he was born in the United States, his parents were not. They came to their new home in 1910, through Ellis Island, but they did not travel together. They arrived from different areas of Greece. My grandmother, Helen Stromboulis, came from Mani, the the pinky finger of the hand that forms the larger peninsula, the Peloponnese. My grandfather, John Castrunis, came from Symi, a small island in the Dodecanese chain off the coast of Turkey.

They were here ten years before they met in Jacksonville, Florida in 1920. As was the case with most young immigrants, neither of them had any formal education, either in Greece or the United States. They taught themselves to read and write, both English and Greek. As for employment, they did as most immigrants have done through the years, whatever they could to make their way in their new country. In my grandparents' case they owned and operated restaurants. They did this for over fifty years, first in Jacksonville and later in New York City. They were very good at what they did. They never retired; both died on the job. As is the case with many immigrants they had an incredible work ethic, they were law abiding, tax paying, citizens, and through their success they made America a better place as well.

My dad, like my grandparents, accomplished a great deal in his short life of sixty four years. I am certain his parents' work ethic and positive outlook had to do with his success. I am not sure they would have agreed with my assessment, however. You see dad's chosen career path took him far from any kind of work his parents understood. He was, for all his life a football coach on the high school and later college level. Sports were about as far from my grandparents' experience as you could travel. They had never seen a game of football; they never did. Not only were they blind to his great love, along the way they did all in their power to discourage his dreams altogether.

Without going into great detail about how truly loving parents could try to prevent their son from reaching his dreams, just believe there often is a huge difference of opinion between immigrant parents and first generation children. The parents want to preserve the culture of their home country as much as possible. The children fully embrace the new culture. As far as the 'melting pot' goes; the parents do not melt while their children are like hot butter. This difference in their viewpoints inevitably led to problems in many areas of life, but the game he loved was the biggest problem of all.

My father was totally absorbed in his love of all sports, but especially football. My grandparents, on the other hand, never, until the day they died, comprehended why. Of course, they wanted him to go to school. Education was free and it opened doors of opportunity. But having never attended school themselves, they thought a high school education would be more than sufficient for him to take over their restaurant business one day. In their minds he would marry a nice Greek girl, have lots of children, and cook food in his own restaurant. It was a beautiful life, the only one they knew. It had been very good for them, but it was not what my father wanted.

To get what he wanted, he had to deceive his parents. If they had known when he began high school, that he was wasting time in the afternoon, playing sports, they'd have put a stop to it. But they were working twelve hour days, and did not understand the American school system. When he told them he was in school until five o'clock, but failed to mention that the last three hours were devoted to sports practice, the long hours did not seem too much to them, and so he managed to pull it off.

Even before the organized sports of high school there were games in the neighborhood ever every day, and dad played them all. Well, not tennis, golf or any of the rich kids' sports. He played the 'rock hard' sports of his streets. He played them all, but he loved football best. The brand of football he played as a youth, however, scarcely resembled the tamer variety of 'rec' ball we play these days in leagues around the country. First of all there was no adult supervision in dad's game. It was football in the streets with no coaches in sight. The boys ran their own teams and imposed their rough brand of discipline. In their leagues the uniform was an old cap, pulled over the ears, and jeans padded with rags. They had never heard such terms as 'two hand touch' football. They would have spurned the notion had an adult explained it to them. It was tackle the man with the ball, and their field was either someone's back yard or an unpaved alley. There was usually one kid in the group who had a football. Even if he were not much good at the game that kid was always chosen to play. This was the brand of football my father grew up with. It separated the sheep from the goats. The survivors of this brand of football were ready for the real thing when high school came along.

My dad began to play organized football the fall of his ninth grade year at Andrew Jackson High School in Jacksonville, Florida. For four years he played football, but also basketball, baseball, and he wrestled. In those four years of high school athletics, neither of his parents saw him play one single game. For the first two years, they did not know he was playing sports.

The three hour cushion with which he had padded his education resume, gave him the time needed for his practices and enough to spare for him to clean up and get to the restaurant. He was expected to serve dinner and wash dishes at the restaurant every night. When his parents finally discovered he was wasting time playing games, every coach in the school came to plead his case. With their help he reached a compromise with his strong willed mother. They all agreed that so long as he did his work at the restaurant and managed to pass his classes, he would be allowed to play sports.

Dad went on to play college football for the University of Georgia for four years, and in all that time my grandmother never saw him play. My grandfather traveled to Gainesville, Florida once to see dad's Bulldogs trounce the Gators in 1944, his junior year. Dad was captain of the Georgia team that season, and played the entire game on offense and defense. Even so I don't think granddad ever understood which one he was on the field. He didn't see well and numbers were very small in those days. From the top of the stadium where he sat, it must have looked like a can of worms to my grandfather.

When dad made All-American his senior year at Georgia, his parents did not attend the ceremony. After college and a try at professional football, Dad became a teacher and coach. Coaching football was his passion and his life long occupation. I'm not sure his mother ever understood how my dad made a living and took care of his family. She was never reconciled to the strange notion that grown men would be paid a salary for teaching young men to play a game. She had wanted him to marry a nice Greek girl and run the family business. When he opted for neither and exited her picture of what he ought to become, she just went on with her life and left dad to fend for himself. The plain truth was that when he married my non-Greek mom, she disowned him.

When I was born, my grandfather informed her that he was going to Georgia to see his grandson; she was welcome to come or not. She did not go with him, but eventually she and my dad reconciled and began to see each other again. My grandmother was a strong person, but so was my dad. He was the only one, male or female, she could not cow into doing her bidding, so she opted to leave him alone most of the time. At any rate grandmother was not 'hands on' when it came to child rearing. I can only imagine what she would think of today's helicopter parents who hover over every game, recital, even every practice their children attend. She would turn over in her grave at the idea that parents would take time off from work to coach their children's teams.

To say my dad played football for love of the game is an understatement. Nobody in his family cared if he played football; as I said, if they'd known from the start, they'd have tried to stop him. His coaches cared when he played for them, but when his eligibility ended, they did little to help him get to the next level. He went Gainesville to a tryout for the Florida team but was deemed too small by their coaches; he was only 5'11" and 185 pounds and he was a lineman. The University of Georgia had never heard of him, and so he was offered no scholarships. The local professional wrestling association in Jacksonville offered him a job, posing as the villain in their staged matches. That was his sole, post high school athletic opportunity.

So dad decided to go to college without a scholarship, but to say my dad went to get an education would be completely off the mark. When two of his friends, who had received scholarships, left for summer football at Georgia, he tagged along. But he was not just hanging out as our children today describe it. He had a plan. He told his parents he was going to take a few weeks to see Athens, the Georgia version, but that he would be back. The three of them boarded the train and rode for a day and a half to Athens. When they arrived, dad went to a local barber shop, got a shave, haircut, and took a bath (barbers offered those, back then). From the barber shop he went to the football practice fields and was issued a uniform along with about 50 other try outs. They are called walk-ons in today's college football terminology.

He must have outshone the rest of those freshmen, because at the end of summer workouts, his coaches offered him a scholarship. It was only then they discovered he had never applied for admission to Georgia. I said he had a plan. I didn't say it was perfect. Coach Quentin Lumpkin, the freshman coach, and Dean

11

William Tate, the dean of students, were from different walks of life, but shared a common goal. They wanted to beat the Hell out of Georgia Tech. The two of them walked dad through the registration lines and helped him to officially become a student at the University of Georgia. Dean Tate and Coach Lumpkin were probably about as interested in the academic side of dad's college life as he was! But he was in school, none the less, and they beat Tech two out of the three years he played.

Getting into school was a 'piece of cake' compared to the next step. Now dad had to call his mother and tell her he would not be coming back to Jacksonville quite as soon as he had promised. In fact it would not be until Christmas. When he told her the reason, she was in complete disbelief: 'Get on the train tonight and come home. I don't know what you are really doing up there, but I know nobody would pay your college tuition to watch you play a silly game.' Dad would never have convinced her, but finally, with the help of both Coach Lumpkin and Dean Tate, she was mollified for the time being. When Christmas came, there would be further discussion.

Though it is not recorded, Christmas, 1940 in Jacksonville must have gone through the storm of the century. Even so when the new year came, dad returned to Georgia. That spring, however, he was almost killed and it wasn't playing football. Oddly, it was playing for his fraternity in an intramural softball game. He was at catcher, covering home plate, when another football player crashed into his side. It took a few days to discover he had ruptured his kidney. They had no choice but to remove it. The operation was successful and he would survive.

But with only one kidney the doctors were adamant that he could never play even the least strenuous sport again. To lose the other kidney in the days before dialysis and transplants would have been a death sentence. Dad took a complete season off from all physical activity, serving as the team manager, but when he felt healthy, he began to work out. He had another doctor make him a special kidney pad and then he showed up for spring practice in 1942. Of course, he made the team. I wouldn't be relating this story to you had he not. Coach Wallace Butts was the Georgia head coach. It fell to him to make the call to Jacksonville to plead dad's case. My grandmother hit the ceiling again. Coach Butts ever quick on his feet, had a plan of attack: 'Mama Castrounis, Mike didn't get hurt playing football, it was in a game of softball.' There was complete silence on the other end of the line for a few seconds, then she said: 'Okay; he can play football, but no more of softball; that game is way too dangerous.'

The rest, as they always say, is history. You can look it up if you like. In 1943, 1944, and 1945 dad was All Southeastern Conference; he was team Captain in 1944; he was All-American in 1945. He was drafted by the Detroit Lions, but opted to try to play for the Miami Seahawks in the fledgling All America Football Conference. He had a great preseason camp, but was again deemed too small to make the team. He spent one year in an East Coast semi-pro league, playing for Greensboro, NC. That same year he and my mom were married and he took his first high school coaching job in Hartwell, Ga.

At that point he still did not have his college degree, but teachers were in such short supply after the war, you could begin to teach if you were working toward a degree. I think he finally graduated in 1951, eleven years after he had first enrolled. My mother was an honor student at Georgia. I don't think he'd have ever graduated without her help and encouragement. Dad coached at various high schools in the state of Georgia until 1961 when he went back to his alma mater to coach. He remained a coach for Georgia until his untimely death in January of 1987. Today his name is on the wall of the atrium of the University's Butt's-Mehre athletic complex, as he has been inducted into Georgia's Circle of Honor for athletes.

I could go on since I know enough stories about Iron Mike to fill several books. The stories about my dad are tough and they are heart warming, but not unique. They are no different from the stories of other sons of Ellis Island, the boys of coal miners, steel mill workers, textile laborers, and mom and pop restaurants. All these second generation boys went to college to play a game. It was a great game.

It was hard and tough, managed by men who were remorseless and relentless in their drive to win. But as hard as it was, the game was still easier than the mines and the mills. Those boys went to college to play a silly game, but in the doing of it they were changed, even educated a bit. And they changed their world as well. We sons and daughters of those players are members of the clubs and churches they could only look at through the windows. The world changed in their day and then in my day it changed again.

I played southern high school football in the mid 60's. Even at that late date, I never played with or against a black player, not even one. That all changed in the south in 1970. Some would say the change came about solely because of government mandated desegregation, but I'm not sure that is the entire picture of what happened. I think the change also had to do with our red neck coaches. One of the most red necked can serve as example. Paul 'Bear' Bryant was born and raised in

Fordyce, Arkansas. The Bear went on to star at Alabama in football. When he was hired to coach there, he put them back on the football map. By the late 60's the Bear had won more national championships than anyone of his day, but the game had begun to pass him by.

In a season opener against Southern California, Alabama was annihilated by the Trojans, principally because of the ball carrying of Sam 'Bam' Cunningham. Cunningham was African American. There were no African Americans on Alabama's team that year. After the game, the Bear asked Coach John McKay if he might bring Sam to his locker room. When they entered the quiet room, the Bear said, 'Boys, I just wanted you to see what a real football player looks like.'

Whether the story is apocryphal or not, the Bear did change the color of Alabama football. In the process he showed everyone that he was a bunch more pragmatist than he was racist. Alabama was a southern college football leader in breaking the racial barrier. Winning may not have been everything to Bear Bryant, but it certainly motivated him into change his mind about who to put on his team.

Georgia coach, Vince Dooley, for whom my dad worked, was not far behind the Bear. In 1971 Georgia signed five African Americans to football grants in aid. My dad was instrumental in signing three of them. They all were from Clarke Central high school, the Athens school just blocks from the University of Georgia campus. Some locals, including a few of my dad's friends, were not happy with his decision.

When he helped signed the black players, dad chose not to sign others in the area. I think he based his choice on whom he thought could best help Georgia win football games. I know for a fact that he took some heat for his input into the decision, but he stuck to his guns.

He had always been a keen judge of talent. The young men he did not sign in his Northeast Georgia recruiting area, never played college ball. The black players he helped sign all played and contributed to the success of Georgia football; two were stars at Georgia, and one played ten years professionally.

Dad and Coach Dooley were criticized for the decision by more than a few people, but dad never said a word about it. He was not one to complain when some people did not approve of his actions. He did what he thought best for Georgia football. I think he was happy to have some of what the Bear called football players at Georgia, because, like Coach Lumpkin and Dean Tate, he too, wanted to beat Tech. He had that drive to win that every good coach possessed and that helped make him color blind. However, for dad I think more was at work. I think it was his own story that helped him make the courageous decision to give other not so fortunate young men an opportunity in life. His desire to win was strong; his memory of the good things football did for a poor boy from the mean streets of Jacksonville, Florida, even stronger.

A few years ago my son, a Clemson student, and I were watching the Clemson-Auburn football game that opened the 2012 college season. I asked him as we watched, 'How many African Americans start for Clemson?' To his credit, he had not thought to count. But when we did it totaled 19, I think? And the best of them was their quarterback Taj Boyd. In my day, and even after, conventional wisdom was that while black athletes were made to be good running backs and receivers, they did not have the mental acuity to play either offensive line or quarterback. Thirty years later, this discussion made no sense to anyone who understood football.

In thirty more years, I wonder what other changes we will see. Certainly, there will be many, for no matter their personal predispositions, the best coaches want desperately to win and do what they need do to make that happen. The south has changed a great deal in my life time, and so far as our communal outlook on racism is concerned, I approve of every positive change. We have come from our own version of apartheid to the point that nobody's bothering to do head counts anymore, at least on football teams. Of course, there are many reasons for the change. There are some very serious reasons for the changes in the racial landscape of the south, and then there was and still remains that silly game.

CHAPTER ONE

When I was a boy of fourteen,
my father was so ignorant I could hardly stand
to have the old man around.
But when I got to be twenty-one,
I was astonished at how much he had learned in seven years.

Mark Twain

I was an English major in college, the Lord only knows
why, because I didn't. It had nothing to do with any
career trajectory. I didn't have one of those. I chose
English long before I had any idea what I would do with
my life. I suppose I chose English because I loved to read.
That love began almost almost at the same time I began.
At least I cannot remember a time I did not have some
book in front of me. I think my love of reading came from
mom, herself an avid reader, who encouraged her son to
read any book he chose. Never did she say that some book
was too adult for me. If I wanted to read it, she let me.
She was the one who taught me to read, actually; not my
first grade teacher.

Mom taught me to read when I turned five, so by the time I was in grammar school, I was reading books that were way above my grade level. While my friends were reading The Hardy Boys, I was reading Ivanhoe, The Count of Monte Cristo and many more great books. These were not required reading for school credit. They were simply fun to read. Many of those great books influenced me, but of all the authors I read in those days, no one more deeply touched my soul than Mark Twain.

He was funny, he was irreverent, but above all he was critical of his world. Though not technically a southerner, I suppose, since he was born in Hannibal, Missouri, he did grow up in a Civil War slave state. But he didn't drink the kool aid. Read Huckleberry Finn, and I think you will understand how Twain felt about slavery. He wrote against the unfairness and evil of the system when many of his contemporaries simply accepted it as the way of life.

I grew up in the deep south of the 50's and 60's. Slavery had been abolished for almost 100 years, but the unfairness left in its wake was alive. You can cut off a rattlesnake's head but the fangs are still lethal. Our Jim Crow laws, were those potent fangs. They were still the rule of our day, and their insidious nature practically reestablished slavery without us even noticing. I remember walking down the side walk in our town with my dad one day, when suddenly an old colored man coming our way stepped off the sidewalk and into the street as we passed him by.

I asked my man why the man did that, but dad could not explain it so that a five year old would understand. In my boyhood south gross racial inequality was our way of life and most of us accepted it. Face up to this historic fact now or ignore it, it was there back then. Most of us chose to live in ignorant bliss. Life was horribly unfair for almost half the people in my small world. If one were the least bit sensitive, it was painful to see. Turning a blind eye to the injustice of racism, ignoring it, was our way to live with it.

But I was a reader and Huckleberry Finn was on my bookshelf. The story Mark Twain told in that book forced me to face facts at least in the safe privacy of my room. And even though I cannot give you an exact date, at an early age I decided I would not be racist. Unfortunately, neither could I be a crusader. I was far too timid and unsure of myself. When it came to speaking out about the injustice I lived every day, I kept my mouth shut but even so I thought about it a lot. I used to lie in bed at night, pondering why I was born white and fairly privileged and not black. Just luck, or if you were Presbyterian like me, maybe God's choice. Whenever the guilt became almost too much, I consoled myself by remembering I had never heard my preacher speak on the issue either.

In the end it was my dad who spoke to me about racism. Not directly; understand. He was a man of few words, but the few he used preached at me almost every day on one topic or another. It wasn't always racism. He had opinions on just about everything. And though he did not offer his opinions to the general public, at least not oratorically, he did not hesitate to voice them to his young son. Unfortunately, it is only as I sit here years later, thinking about his words, that I am able to deeply appreciate his wisdom. Mark Twain was right. When you are fourteen or sixteen or eighteen, if you don't think your dad is an idiot at that moment, then you have no chance of appreciating him later in life! And now, I do, appreciate him.

My dad was sometimes an idiot to me, maybe, but not to the people of Central where we lived. To them he was legendary. He was the football star who made it big, but then came back home. He was the only one they had ever known who chose to come home to our small town even though he had plenty of more attractive options. He came home because he seemed genuinely to like the town and the people. And it was no illusion. He did like the town and the people. His choice to come home is what made him a hero to all those people who had no option other than to stay. He loved our town and he loved the people and they returned that love. They idolized the man.

On the good days my dad was my hero too. But on the bad days, not so much. And the not so much days definitely out numbered the good days. I am sure now, as I look back from a distance, the biggest problem I had with dad was my envy of the ease with which he did everything. Sports, school, everything came naturally, or so it seemed to me, except perhaps parenting. I do not think that came to him easily. And truthfully, though I admire him now, I don't parent like he did. His way of being my father kept me pissed at him about 90% of the time. I could write a book about him, a long book. And I may do that one day but not this time out. Though he figures prominently in this story, he is not the main character I think. You can decide for yourself if you read further.

This time, I am trying to tell another story, maybe my story, but again you can decide if it's mine. There are others in this story and it may be theirs. Before I begin, let me say I am not a novelist, whatever that word means. And here is the danger I face, that anyone who tries to write faces. Because I am an adept reader, I am tempted to think that would naturally make me a good writer. Tempted, yes, but I don't think that. I believe I am a fair story teller because I have told stories all my life. When

21

you end up a preacher, you had better be able to tell a good story, or you will not have a soul listening by the end of your sermon. They will still be there in the pews, because southerners would not dare walk out in the middle of church, on even the worst preacher. They will be there, but their minds will not. I have been writing down stories all my life, but just short essays that we preachers hope some will call sermons.

I have never attempted any extended story like this. But it is not a novel that I am writing. I am telling you what happened in my life and the life of my friends and others in our town forty years ago. I guess what I am doing is committing my memories to history. Well, my memory of the short history of one football season. But here is the problem. Even though it is my story to tell, my father, dang it, my relationship with my father, is vital to the story. Bear with me, because I don't think any story I wrote myself into would be coherent if I did not tell you a bit more about the man who raised me, the man I jokingly call 'everybody's Hero'.

Dad grew up in the small town where we now live. I am just going to call it Central, even though that is not the real name. All of my family still lives right here. Well, my sister moved to Atlanta, but she is here as much as she is there. She ought to vote in local elections; maybe she does, since this is the south. I have not asked. We are all still here, all but everybody's Hero. From the 'git go' you need to know that I will call him dad some, but more often in the story I will call him 'the Hero'. When I call him Hero, I confess, it is often envy, it is sometimes humor, but also, it is who he was. He is gone now. We only remember him. We lost him way too early in our lives, so everybody says.

He was only 63, still high school principal, with no thought of retiring. If he were alive now, he'd be, I think, eighty five and still busy-bodying somebody just by his mere presence. Probably, if he were not still high school principal, he would have gotten himself on the Board of Education, from where he could bug the heck out of the current principle. He probably does bug Ronnie Driscoll even from the grave.

After all, Ronnie was my teammate and so one of the hero's students, too. Ronnie knows the legacy, sees the picture on the school office wall, has to try to live up to it every day. That effort would bug the heck out of me. Dang it; somebody stop me; told you I wasn't a writer and here I am beginning the Hero's part in this story at the end of his life instead of the beginning, my apologies.

I said the Hero was born in our small town but technically he was not. He grew up on a farm just outside the city limits. His daddy farmed land that his daddy before him had begun to farm shortly after the war. By the way, when southerners of my generation and before say, the War, there is only one war they can mean: the one fought on our soil over one hundred years ago. Whether we are white southerners or black, we all still think about that war a lot. It was the one that made us all poor and ignorant and backward. Yankees would probably say we were poor, ignorant and backward before that war and maybe so; but if we were, that war did not help advance us to new riches or awareness. That much is certain.

So the Hero grew up in this small town and small world and I don't think he ever wanted to leave his town, but he did want to change his world. He wanted to find a way out of the ignorance and poverty, and so he made sure to go to school and not only attend, but learn as much as he could along the way. From an early age, I think he determined that he would have a better life than

23

his parents, and if possible, drag a few of us small town hicks into that life with him.

In high school the Hero played every sport, but mainly he played ball, and when I say Ball, well that is kind of like when I say the War. Around here if someone says, 'I played Ball,' everybody knows what he means, the same as if he said, 'I fought in the War.' People from here know Ball can mean only football. Our school has always had a basketball team and a baseball team, too, but Ball was just one sport. Today football is still king. In dad's day football was the king of sports, but not the king of everything like it is now, almost but not quite.

In the '40's and '50's cotton was still our king. The farm daddy grew up on had a large garden, several acres, and they raised animals for food, but cotton was the only cash crop. It was the crop that kept the farm operating. And in those days the entire family worked to bring in the cotton crop. Back in the day children started the school year August 1st, but then took all of September off, because that was the month the cotton was picked. Everybody in the family was required for that task. It went on from dawn to dusk. And so it was only after dusk that the boys gathered to practice ball. Football was important, but cotton was still king.

Cotton made the small town football players have split personalities. While the big city boys were in school in September and preparing to play on Friday, their country cousins in the small towns were picking cotton all day, and then practicing in the limited amount of time left in the evening. There was not money to turn on the field lights for night practices. Even if the lights could have been turned on, the players did not have enough energy to practice long. I don't know how they managed to pick cotton all day and practice football at night.

In August when my team held its two a day summer workouts, dad's team was in school. The boys would come in early before school and practice, then stay late after school and practice again. One bus drove them all home, and some of them did not get home until way after dark. Then when the season began in September, the boys on dad's team would pick cotton all day and wait for the coach and the local pharmacist to pick them up on the farms and take them to practice. Nobody had a car in those days; granddaddy had a tractor, but no car. There was a wagon and mule for church and other going to town events.

The most important, going to town, event in our community back then, maybe even including church, was when the football team had a home game. Everybody within walking or wagon distance was there. And on Friday nights the boys would get to play. And some of them who lived way out, when they got to playing age, had never actually seen a game. The Hero told me a story about the first game of his eighth grade year. His best friend was out of his mind excited. Of course, every player is excited for every game, and especially the season opener, but his buddy back in the day had even more reason to be worked up. My dad's friend had never actually seen a football game. He had learned to play football by practicing, but practice is not a game. The first real football game he ever saw he played in! That could not happen these days but it truly happened then!

The hero, of course, played quarterback. What else would he play? He started for Central's varsity football team from eighth grade until he graduated; in those days there were no limits to eligibility. I suppose a seventh grader could have played were he good enough. The Hero never missed a practice, never missed a game. His senior year the team won the state championship for class 'A'. By

25

the time I arrived in high school twenty years later, it was still the only championship Central high school had ever won. The Hero made All-State and was awarded a football scholarship to the nearby university.

He was the first boy from our town to earn a college scholarship and one of the first to actually go to college. Mom went with him, her family was able to pay her way. She was a town girl, her dad owned the drugstore. So the quarterback and the head cheerleader went off to the bright lights of big time college football. But after making good (they always made good), they came back. Of course, they planned it that way, because they were sadists. They planned to come back home, so their children could grow up in a very small town that did not even have a movie theater, far away and safe from the terrible influences of big city life. Can't tell you how many times we wished we could get even with them for that.

Dad first coached around the western part of the state after his illustrious college playing career, but he always knew he'd come home if he had the chance. When the head football coach at Central retired, there was only one person the school wanted to hire. Their Hero did not disappoint. He came home to be the football coach, but he also taught mathematics, not physical education, like most coaches. Mom also was a teacher. She was hired to teach English, she was yearbook adviser, and cheerleader coach, too. The Hero also coached basketball, boys and girls, and baseball. Had the two of then ever left; the Board of Education would have had to hire six teachers to fill the void. Between them, in the early days, they made about $5000 a year.

He really was a hero, I guess, and so he did not have to stay in Central. I think he had many better offers. I personally know of one. One night I sneaked out of bed and overheard an offer in the form of a phone conversation with one of his college teammates. His friend had been hired at a major college in the Southwest Conference. I could tell from my side of the conversation dad was being offered a coaching job, but not just as an assistant. He was offered the offensive coordinator job. I was heading upstairs to pack, when I heard dad say, 'Thanks, Jim; but I am going to have to turn you down. I wouldn't want to uproot my family at this time.' And I was thinking, 'Uproot me, please dad, uproot me; take me somewhere that I can see a movie on Friday night.'

That's when I knew with absolute certainty that Mark Twain was right. I was fourteen; only in junior high, but I was convinced my dad, the Hero, had completely lost his mind. He turned down the job of a lifetime, so we could stay in a town that didn't even have a Sears or JC Penny. He had the craziest ideas about how life ought to be. I was 'bright lights, big city,' and he was... well, he was not. But I'm getting ahead of myself again.

When dad originally took the Central job it was our fourth move and while he and mom were going home, it was just another move for me. When we moved back to Central it wasn't a homecoming for me like it was for them. All it meant to me was I would be new kid on the block again. I was in fourth grade, not a good age to move. The Hero had been assistant coach at a big school in a nearby city when the job opened up back home, and it was what he had always wanted. Everybody's Hero came home. It was not what I wanted. Any move is difficult for a child, but leaving my school of four years and the friends I had made was traumatic.

And in the new school, I immediately encountered that one boy all other boys fear. He was the one created by God, seemingly to make life miserable for smaller children. And that was me, small and timid. This boy with the divine calling to bully others, decided I needed to be thoroughly indoctrinated as to who was boss at his school. I'm not talking about the principal either. That's not who he had in mind. I might have been the new football coach's son, but that did not mean squat to him. If I wanted status in his eyes or if I just wanted him to leave me alone, I was just about sure that I would have to take care of that business all by myself.

Twice he beat me up good during recess. There was no one to stop him, since teachers generally did not come on the playground during our recess time. We policed ourselves, or not. Granted he was the biggest and strongest boy in our grade and mean to everybody, so the other kids might have taken pity on me, but they did not.

The herd mentality prevailed and they left me all by my lonesome to work out my own salvation, breathing a sigh of relief that it was me and not them. For me every day was like going out and having my pants taken down in front of every kid in school. The beatings hurt but the humiliation was worse. I ate a lot of lunches alone, listening to the others whisper and cut their eyes my way. I had pretty much decided my life was over at the age of ten.

Then one night the Hero called me into his den and sat me down among his trophies: 'Word is you are having some trouble with a bully.' How did he know that? Did my teacher tell him? I was pretty sure she didn't know, because she had not been on the playground, and I was not about to complain to her and ask for intervention. Maybe one of the kids told her dad, and he had brought the message to my dad. It was a small town after all and word got around. There was nothing to be gained by denying it: 'Yes sir.' I answered. His response was laconic but to the point, 'I hope you don't expect me to do anything about it, because I'm not. You have to learn to handle problems for yourself.' That was it: no

28

boxing lessons, no hug or pat on the shoulder; no commiseration.

The next day at recess, I saw my doom coming my way again. I knew it was fight or flight and if I wanted to ever eat with the other kids, flight was not an option. I had read somewhere in one of those books of mine that in street brawls the one who got in the first punch usually won. So I started running right at him. Later they said I was shouting what amounted to a rebel yell. I launched myself into the air right at him and hit him with my fist squarely on his nose. Blood, his blood, went everywhere, he ran off crying, and I was escorted to the principal's office.

In those days the punishment for fighting was a whipping and I got a good one from the principal. For a woman she could hit really hard with her paddle. Along with that I was given a note to take to my parents. I took it to mom, hoping she would understand I had to do what I had to do, and hoping that we could settle it between ourselves. But I think I knew better. She did say, 'I understand,' but she also said, 'We still have to tell your dad.' I was okay with that. He was the one who told me to take care of my own red wagon in the first place.

They went into conference that evening when he got home from football practice. My sister Mandi, always the joyful storm harbinger, came to my room with a grin on her face and said, 'Dad wants you in the den.' When I came in, I saw he had his belt off and knew pretty quickly what would happen next. He bent me over his knee and whipped my fanny. He said afterward, 'I'm glad you took care of your own business, but you are not allowed to fight in school.' He had me there, no argument, but at least when the dust settled the bully left me alone and I quickly made some friends. Turns out, everybody hated that boy and all of them were happy for me to give him his comeuppance. Everyone commented on my bravery, too, except the Hero, the one guy I'd have loved to hear from.

When I began to play youth football in Central, my coaches made me the quarterback, naturally assuming I was a chip off the old block. They would make a point to say, 'Son, how cool to have an All-American college quarterback, teaching you everything he knows.' Right! If they only had known the truth it was my mother who taught me to throw a football and shoot a basketball. When dad got home from practice, he was not interested in any more coaching duties, especially coaching a mediocre kid.

Later, the whole time I played quarterback my friends would laugh and tell me I threw like a girl, and I would say, 'Good reason for that, a girl taught me. Anyway don't worry about how I throw it; you just concentrate on catching it.' Once I asked mom why the Hero was like that, and she said, 'Don't you understand? Nobody ever taught your dad how to do anything? He watched others do things and taught himself by copying what he saw them do. He thinks everybody ought to be able to do that.

When he was five, he went down to the lake and watched the older boys swimming. Then he climbed down one of the dock poles and beat the water like an egg-beater from that pole to the next one. When he was satisfied he could manage that little bit, he swam out and joined the older boys in the deep water. He's a natural, son. He thinks everybody ought to able to do that.'

When I finished seventh grade, dad gave up football coaching to become our high school principle. It was a move up in status and the pay increase helped our family, but nobody loved playing the game of football or teaching boys to play it better than everybody's Hero. I am convinced to this day that he gave it up, because he did not want to coach his own son. In eighth grade I would begin my high school football career. It was not because I was not any good and would have embarrassed him. By that time I could play the game decently. I would not have been an embarrassment to him; that wasn't why he quit. He gave up coaching because he knew that he would have been unbearably tough on me. He would have given me double what everybody else got. He knew it and he didn't want to do it to me. He knew he would probably ruin me, and so he gave up the thing he most loved in life. If I'm right about this, it is the only time I can remember that he eased up on me in any way. I appreciated it at the time, but who knows, he might have taught me finally how to throw like a man!

That one brief concession to mercy, however, did not mean that he suddenly had mellowed and forsaken being demanding on me or my sister. My dad was the biggest name in our town. He was everybody's Hero. His mere presence placed demands on his children. People would say to us, 'We love your daddy. He is the greatest man we know.' My sister was more like our dad than I was. She, too, took no prisoners. Whenever someone would utter that nonsense about the joys of being the Hero's child, Mandi would innocently look them right in the eye and say, 'Ah, I know what you mean. I wish you could come over and live with us for a week or two. You'd have so much fun.' Nobody ever got her joke but me. When I saw it coming, I had to turn away so they wouldn't see me laughing.

Mandi would come in his den before our games in her cheerleader uniform, looking for approval. I told her not to but she never listened to me. The Hero would give her an appraising glance and say, 'Looks as if you have gained a little weight.' And she would go to her room and cry. Two days before he died we were all in the room together, and he said to her, 'You need to watch the calories after I'm gone, Mandi. Looks like you are putting on a few.' Long before that day she had learned to laugh instead of cry and so she did.

My first season of real football was 8th grade. The Hero watched our home JV football games from the press box, but he didn't travel to away games like most of the other parents. And he offered no post game evaluation of the few games he saw. After the season, however, he sat me down in his den and offered two pieces of advice. First he said, 'You have got to work on that throwing motion, you look like a girl.' My mind was going, 'Thanks, dad. I wonder why that is?' But my mouth was saying, 'Yes sir.' And then he said, 'If you don't toughen up, son, you are not going to be of much use to Coach Drucker next year.' I reminded myself of the swimming story mom had told me, swallowed the lump in my throat, and again said, 'Yes sir.' I spent that off season throwing lots of passes at the tire swing in the back yard.

During our Spring practice I was assigned the task of running the Scout Team offense, which was totally populated by 8th graders, against the varsity players. We were due for our first scrimmage and we scouts were traumatized, afraid of what the older boys were going to do to us. That day at school, however, it was raining cats and dogs and the 8th graders were ecstatic.

We thought the scrimmage would be called off and we'd have a Chalk Talk, for sure. We could not imagine going outside in this deluge. I'll tell you plenty about Coach Drucker later in my story, but for now suffice to say, our coach feared God, but he certainly was not afraid of any man I knew, including the Hero. And that afternoon though he feared his maker, he was pretty irritated with God for messing with his practice plan.

When we got to the locker room the manager said, 'Suit up'. We could not believe our ears, but suit up we did. For three hours we ran plays against the varsity defense in a monsoon. And what is that like for an eighth grader, do you think? Maybe, like diving head first into a giant meat grinder? My running backs made sure I ended up with the ball most of the time. The line couldn't block those big varsity players, so the QB, that would be me, took a beating.

That night as I was nursing my bruised body, dad walked in: 'How did it go?' I made the mistake of thinking he wanted the truth, so I innocently said, 'We did good, I think; but I'm pretty beat up.' He looked at me with a funny expression and said, 'Well, if you can't take it, boy, you had better just quit.' I wasn't about to quit. He and I both knew that. Telling me to quit was not what he meant anyway.

What he meant was, 'Quit telling him about my problems; quit complaining; quit being a cry baby.' And that was the last time I mentioned any pain of mine in his presence ever. Forrest Gregg a lineman for the great Green Bay Packers coach Vince Lombardi, once said, 'Coach has the highest tolerance to pain of any man I have ever known. Our pain does not bother him one bit.' Change the name of the principle character, the story is the same!

Now, a bit about our coach, Coach Drucker, a little history. Like the Hero, he played college ball, but he did not play at a big school like our principal. He was a lineman at one of our state's smaller colleges. He was 220 pounds but only about 5'10" tall and I swear that man had a 26" inseam, the shortest legs of a man that tall, I had ever seen. It looked like somebody had shoveled a bunch of lead in his britches and the pieces pulled his butt down to his knees.

After seniors had no eligibility left, they liked to drive by the practice field during the spring and shout, 'Give 'em Hell, 'Lead Ass'.' There is no record of an underclassman with any eligibility left ever doing that. Coach Drucker was a lineman to his core. He had played ball for a lineman who had played for Bear Bryant at Alabama. He was second generation Bear and he adhered to all the Bear's principles, especially the need to build toughness in a team.

Certainly, he understood the need for skill position players, backs and receivers, and he valued our athletic ability, but he valued physical and mental toughness much more. I don't care if you were a place kicking specialist. You competed in the tackling drills during practice like everyone else.

Coach Drucker had a special assignment for all his incoming freshmen designed to toughen us up. He assigned us all to the Suicide Squad. That's a football term for the special teams players, the ones who cover punts and kickoffs. Nobody played football for Drucker until you spent a year on the suicide squad. So when we were in ninth grade, we covered kickoffs and punts in games while the older boys took a breather. If you could not cut it on Drucker's suicide squad, even if you were a great athlete, there was a high probability you would not play much in your career. Failure on the suicide squad was the death knell of many Central high school careers.

'Little Johnny get yourself in here.' Coach said. I was in ninth grade but had never actually been in Coach's office before. Walking in there as a freshman, I understood the words Dante had inscribed over his gates of Hell: 'Abandon hope, all ye who enter here.' He sat me down and said, 'After watching you that first JV game last season, I began to wonder if you have the killer instinct. Honestly, after spring practice I still wonder.'

I said, 'Yes sir,' as if I understood my coach, but to this day, I am not sure exactly what killer instinct is. I mean I would never kill anybody and don't think I would even hurt anybody on purpose. Whatever that instinct is, that fateful day I was pretty sure he was right. At that point in my young career, about all I was sure I had was the survival instinct. When you are 5'7" and 125 pounds, playing varsity football, avoiding extinction is something you think about a great deal, killing somebody with a smash mouth tackle is a second thought, if you think it at all.

When you cover a kickoff things happen fast, mostly bad things, so survival comes in high on your to do list. He said, 'This week on the suicide squad I want you to line up here,' and he pointed to the spot right next to the kicker where the big guys usually were. Then he warned me, 'When you cover from that position, you need to watch out for that blocker over there crossing and hitting you from the blind side.'

Coach could not have cared less about my personal safety. We both knew that. He warned me about that cross over block, because he needed me alive and in my proper lane to prevent a long kickoff return. I do not know how I ended up in his office that day, but I had a suspicion the Hero had been talking to the Lead Butt. Whatever I suspected, however, I kept that thought to myself and I said, 'Yes sir.' As you probably can tell by now, I said those two words a lot in those days. We all did.

When I got home that night, I knew for sure they had been talking. Dad asked me, 'Covering kickoffs?' When I acknowledged I was, he said, 'Well, that will make you tougher or kill you, one or the other. Listen, when you go down the field somebody is going to hit you just about every time. But if you run down the field expecting to get hit, they will absolutely kill you.' Remember: 'He who hesitates is lost'.' The Hero was not clairvoyant, but he did know football enough to predict logical outcomes.

The first kickoff I ever covered in a high school game it happened. I was not going full speed, because I had my head on a 'swivel', looking from side to side for the boom to fall. And because I was expecting it to happen, it did. I got hit so hard I turned a cart wheel, no really, an actual cart wheel. I got up, looking out the ear hole of my Riddell helmet. I had to look around frantically to see where the play ended up so I could at least get close to the pile of tacklers.

The next kickoff I ran so fast, I went right past the kickoff returner by mistake, and if someone hadn't yelled at me, might have run through the goal posts. But I had made it through the gauntlet alive and that was a start. Feeling more confident, the next time down, I made the first tackle of my high school career. It was not a smash mouth, bone crusher, but I did grab the return man by the ankle and wrestle him to the ground.

That night when I got home, the Hero said, 'You looked like slop on that first kickoff; and the second one I thought you were running to the dressing room to hide, but by the third one you were not too bad.' On reflection, 'Not too bad', was the highest compliment the Hero had ever paid me regarding my football skills. In fact it was the only one he paid me, ever.

On Sunday Coach Drucker ran the film of that first kickoff play ten times. When everybody had laughed at me as much as they possibly could, he went on to point out the shortcomings of other members of the suicide squad. As I watched, I had to admit, it was kind of funny to see yourself turn a complete flip in the air and be enough removed from the action to not feel any pain. Anyway, I was now an initiate into the school of death and on my way to developing a decent killer instinct, if you can develop one of those?

I am going to skip my first three varsity years. They were normal Central high seasons, winning seasons, but not by much: 6-4, 8-2, 7-3. I am telling the story of that last season only. But before we get to the last season of my high school career, you need to know what the Hero had planned for my summer vacation, which is the real beginning to the story.

I know, you thought we would never get there! Before what I hope is all the good stuff of my story, please remember that as I write now and call my dad the Hero, my words now are not so totally sarcastic as I felt then. Now, it isn't all anger at his parenting techniques or jealousy of his ability in sports. Now, he is my hero, as much as he was everybody elses back then.

He didn't smoke, drink or curse; he never complained of pain and he had plenty. He provided for his family, though that provision was not always as palatable or extravagant as we might have wished. And he never asked anybody to do anything that he would not be willing to do himself. He led from the front. But I only see that clearly now.

And so back then, when he told me that he would decide what I would be doing the summer before my senior year, I didn't like it. In fact I hated him deciding what I would do that summer. But I knew no matter what I said, the deal was done. I figured he had his reasons, and I said, 'Yes Sir,' like I always did. Typically, he said no more just then. And so I would wait to see what wonderful job he had lined up for me that summer of 1966.

CHAPTER TWO

Winning isn't everything; it's the only thing.

Vince Lombardi

Yes, he did, believe it or not, Vince Lombardi did say it. He later tried to tone and shape its meaning by saying what his first Packers team heard that first day was not precisely what he had meant them to hear. What do you think that kind of coach speak means? Unintended consequences not withstanding, I don't know what else one might hear when a coach uses this adage as his starting point. To me it means what it says, that nothing in life is more important than winning.

But no matter what Lombardi meant, I am positive of what Coach Drucker meant when he used the quote on us: winning was all that mattered to him. Now, we sports enthusiasts haven't always thought like this. The quote, used by Lombardi, intentionally reversed Grantland Rice's much older, perhaps truer, adage: 'It matters not whether you win or lose, but how you play the game.' Apparently, in our modern times, 1966 until now at least, how you play the game is pointless unless you win it. I'm not going to sit in judgment, because I understand how much I want to win at everything. One cannot play football unless winning matters a whole lot.

Now, one more interesting thing about that quote Lombardi, used. And I say, 'Used', because that is precisely what Lombardi did. When he addressed his first team at Green Bay in 1959, Lombardi borrowed the quote from Red Sanders. Sanders was the head football coach of UCLA when he coined the famous adage in 1950. But, of course, Lombardi is more well known and so we remember him saying it and not 'Red' Sanders. After all, how many NFL Championships did Sanders win? As we are fond of pointing out in our country; when it comes to football quotes, Lombardi always wins! I'm not sure if Lombardi footnoted his quote, if in his defense he ever said, 'Wait boys, I wasn't the one who thought it up.' It is moot; Lombardi always wins. It is 'the only thing.'

Grantland Rice was the most famous sports writer of his day. And his quote captured the sentiment of that time. He wrote in a poem, 'When the Great Scorer comes to write against your name, he writes not whether you won or lost, but how you played the game.' Rice had more in mind than football. To him football was a handy metaphor to the main point which was how to play the game of life. That was in the day when God was still the Great Scorer and football was still a game, and not even the national pastime at that.

In the south of my youth God was still God, but young men were probably more passionate about football. When I was a player, we still believed in the God of Grantland Rice and in God's judgment of our lives, but where football was concerned we tended to go with Lombardi. So when Lead Butt informed our team that we would all be staying near home that summer before my senior season in order to work out together as a team, we all knew he'd been reading Lombardi's book 'Run To Daylight' again. The Bear was Coach's model, but Lombardi was his hero; he even designed the C logo on our helmets to be exactly like the Green Bay Packer G.

In our Lombardi summer there would be a weight lifting session every weekday morning at 6:00 AM and conditioning drills every evening at 8:00 PM. Whether this was legal according to the rules of our state high school association, I never knew and would not have dared to ask. Ours was not to reason why. As for those useless hours between workouts, Coach felt we should just find a job to keep us busy between the important things. Most of the boys on the team worked on farms or in town anyway. I was the only one who traveled for summer work.

I had been a camp counselor for several years. That summer I would have to find work close by. The Hero loved the camp I attended. He liked the discipline of it, knew it was a good place for me to be, and that I would come home in great shape. But he also believed very fervently that TEAM was written in much bigger letters than 'me', just like the cheap Tee shirts Coach Drucker handed out that year.

So he told me that he would find me gainful employment. That was an omen in retrospect, and should have been a clue that my summer was not going to turn out anything like I had planned. What I should have quickly said to his offer of gainful employment was, 'That is okay, dad, I will look for a job myself.' My granddad would have let me hang around the drug store, make a few home deliveries, and paid me well for doing just about nothing.

In retrospect that non conversation with my dad was a moment of temporary insanity. I simply was not thinking about that cross over, blind side block. It seemed such a trivial thing I completely forgot about it until the last weekend in May. Spring sports were over and most of us were in relax mode, warm lazy days as we ended the year and got ready for summer jobs and Drucker's insane new plan to make us into state champions in the fall.

I was rudely reminded of our earlier conversation, however, when the hero woke me up early the last Saturday of May. This alone should have raised a red flag. Saturday was his one concession to the early rising routine at our house. But instead of running for cover, I got meekly in his car. We drove out the highway to the edge of town and turned in the drive to the country club. I didn't think much of it; we weren't members, but dad sometimes played with friends and I would caddy for him.

The country club members would have given their hero a free membership, if he had wanted one, which he did not. It would have been the same as the ones they gave to our local pastors (who all had freebies). They would have given him a membership, because he was school principal. That job was almost the same as a pastor in our town. Add to all that, dad could 'forever more to kingdom come' hit a golf ball. Even though he only played three or four times a year, he could beat every member of the club. He was always first choice at the club championship, which was a member/guest affair. His team had won the championship ten years running. He was a seven handicap and would have been scratch had he cared enough to play regularly.

As his son one of the most irritating things about him was that he played every sport with no effort. Because of that he thought everybody ought to be able to do it. I wanted to play on the high school golf team, so I would not have to run track with Drucker. The only way

41

out of track for a football player was to play golf or baseball. I asked dad for some pointers, so he went out to the driving range with me. He watched me for about ten minutes, but I could sense he was quickly losing interest. So I asked what he thought of my swing. He said, 'Son, you need to relax. You are way too stiff. Just swing the club and let the ball hit it!' Great advice, don't you agree?

The Hero loved coaching, but as I reflect, I have to say that as much as he loved to coach, he wasn't all that great at it. People we call natural athletes, who seem to play with no effort, seldom are any good at coaching others. Things come so easily for them, they really cannot tell you how they do it. I, on the other hand, would have made a great coach; nothing about any sport came easy for me.

Enough griping and getting off the subject. Here we were at the country club and I was ready to caddy as usual. Turned out a day of caddying and watching the hero effortlessly move from tee to green was not in the cards. We swung around behind the manicured lawn and impressive facade of the club house and drove down a dirt road to the caddy shack. I was getting a little apprehensive.

The caddy shack was not quite so impressive as the club house. It was a ramshackle wooden affair, a combination of board and batten and lap-side construction; as if several generations of inferior carpenters had undertaken the work of building with no real plan in mind. It was a faded green affair with vertical shutter windows, held open by broken broomsticks lodged between sill and window. There was no glass in the windows. Behind the main building was an outhouse, because there was no running water in the shack.

The building itself housed all the lawn mowing equipment, two tractors, and other tools for maintaining the course. They called it the caddy shack, but the members kept their clubs in the locker room in the basement of the main building. The caddies had to go over there to clean shoes and clubs. But that was the only time caddies were allowed in the clubhouse.

The rest of their time was spent, hanging out at the shack. There was a phone to let them know they were needed. When they were not caddying, they were the maintenance personnel for the clubhouse and the golf course. And except for the boss man, they were all African Americans teenagers. I use that phrase now, but I won't be using it again in my story, because in 1966 African American had yet to be coined. Black had not even been invented. The polite word to call them was colored or Negro. There were other words, too, but I didn't use them, or tried not to anyway.

The man who ran the caddy shack was given the euphemistic title Director of Maintenance and Personnel. He was basically in charge of the caddies and the grass cutting and any other grounds keeping chore that cropped up. But also the boss man, what his staff called him, was my dad's oldest friend. His name was 'Beefy' Sizemore. Actually, it wasn't but I never knew Beefy's God given name, I'm not sure Beefy himself knew that name, at least I had never heard him use it. Maybe his mama knew.

He played football with dad and was the second best player on the state championship team. He was not just the best lineman on that team. He was the line. Dad became the Hero he was, by wisely running behind Beefy's large butt and devastating blocks. Dad also played linebacker, everybody played both ways then. He made many tackles by hiding in the shadow of Beefy's gigantic frame, only to jump out at the last second to down some hapless running back. Dad was no fool; he rode that horse all the way to the state championship.

After that game the head coach of the big university dad was about to attend was there to sign them both to scholarships. Dad signed, but Beefy said that if it were all the same, he thought he would just stay home. Well, they talked, pleaded, and cajoled and finally Beefy signed, too. He went up with dad the next year for summer practice. It was not like they traveled cross country.

The school was only an hour from our town, but Beefy couldn't take it. He was so homesick that he only lasted a week before he came on back home. He took the job at the country club and had by now been here almost twenty years. He was married, happy, and had a son on our team, a good friend of mine. Beefy's son had a real name, two in fact: Thomas Richard, but none of us called him that. We all called him Shade Tree, most of the time, just Tree for short. I will tell you later how he got his nickname.

Right now, I'm going to tell you all about the great summer job dad had lined up for me. We parked in front of the shack and I dutifully followed the Hero into the club maintenance supervisor's office, if you could call it that. The ten by ten cubbyhole was littered with pieces of lawnmowers: old wheels, spark plugs, carburetors, and who knew what the rest of it was. In the corner lay a stack of golf clubs, in various states of repair, or should I say disrepair? Behind the aging wooden desk was one picture, the 1946 high school football team picture, the one and only Central high school team that had ever won a state championship.

Our community had been waiting almost twenty years for another, but it had not happened yet. The Hero looked bigger in that picture than he did now and Beefy looked a great deal smaller. Beside that picture on the shelf was the Most Valuable Lineman trophy Beefy had received from Central in 1946 and his All State plaque. The desk was dusty and stacked with papers, weighted down by an old football helmet. There was a black phone on the far side of the desk, the rotary variety. Although push button phones had been invented, one had not yet made its way out to the caddy shack.

Dad said, 'Son, say hello to my friend Beefy Sizemore.' I did not think it was the time or place to point out that I had known Beefy for almost all my life, because this formal introduction seemed to be the Hero's way of letting me know that this was to be a real meeting, with a formal interview maybe, and wouldn't you know, I had forgotten my resume. I kept that smart alec comment to myself, stuck out my hand and said, 'Pleased to see you, sir.' Beefy grabbed me with his big old bear paw and nearly ruined my passing arm.

Dad continued, 'Beefy has been kind enough to offer you a job for the summer. You are going to be a caddy and also you will gain valuable skills working with the maintenance crew here. You will get two dollars for eighteen holes of caddying and fifty cents an hour when you are working maintenance.' Throughout this process Beefy had not said one word. I could not begin to even think about how to express my gratitude for such largesse. Nor did I know which of the two men I should thank as the Hero and not Beefy seemed to be doing all the talking.

I did some quick calculating and estimated that by August, if I were not dead of exhaustion, I would probably have netted two hundred dollars or so. Granddad would have paid me that much a week at the drug store. But that wasn't my biggest problem. I might end up having to caddy for some of my teammates' dads. And there was a bigger problem, still. Beefy was the only white person working out of the caddy shack. I wanted to shout, 'Dad, are you crazy? There are only Negroes working here.'

I could have said colored boys and gotten away with it but even in 1966 we were beginning to understand that the word boy was wrong. I had actually heard a sixteen year old friend call his seventy years old gardener, boy. Just wrong. Negro was the proper and nice word, that we used to describe our former slaves.

There were worse words, of course, redneck crap, but as I said I did not use those. Neither did I say to my dad that this was a death sentence for his son or that he was the dumbest man I'd ever met. I said, 'Yes sir,' because that is what I said to just about every adult in my life, no matter how dumb they might appear to me. And in so far as dad was concerned, I always said, 'Yes sir,' Health issues were involved; my health.

And that was that, no reference checks or drug tests (anachronisms, of course, like African-American). For the first time ever I spent the last few days of school wishing it would not end. School's end was certainly going to parallel my own, because when my friends heard about my great job, I'd be dead to them. But all things come to an end and suddenly it was the first Sunday in June.

After church the Hero said, 'You, ride home with me today.' My sister and I always chose to ride with mom, because she didn't hang around. She had cooking to do. Dad was the last one to leave church. After he had talked to everyone for an interminable length of time, he went around and checked all the doors and locked up. Riding home with dad could usually kill about half your afternoon.

On the ride home that day he was downright talkative, and that was unusual. He rarely talked when he drove, he never played the car radio, leaving any passengers in discomfort and wondering what was going on in that head of his. Sometimes we made that ten minute trip home without a word, but not today: 'Son, I sense you are not happy about your summer job.' Well, duh! 'But here's the deal. You think life has dealt you an unfair blow. I think life is pretty much what you decide to make of it. When life deals you lemons, best get out the fruit squeezer and figure how to make lemonade. And one more thing; you need to know a little bit more about life than you do right now. Open your eyes this summer and you may actually learn something.'

Well, I disagreed with the Hero in one respect, though I did not tell him. Life had not dealt me an unfair blow. He had. It was everybody's Hero who was responsible for the unfairness of it all. Which made me quick to reply only, 'Yes sir.' I knew it was end of conversation anyway. He had spoken his piece, and I did not have a piece to speak of.

My conversation with dad had ended, but my inner dialogue with myself went on for some time. I stewed about what dad said all afternoon, and I came to one conclusion. It was going to be pretty miserable all summer. But I would deal with the humiliation on my own terms, and as far as the world would see, I was just fine. And no matter how bad it was, I would never let on to that 'sum bitch' or any of his friends or mine that I was bothered. He would not have cared anyway. I would work hard, keep my mouth shut, and get through it. But I did have one bit of business to take care of first.

I was going to cover my butt where this job was concerned. I drove over to Tree's house after dinner that day. I told him about it, because I knew he would understand. I did not complain about the job, because I was working for his dad after all. He had worked for his dad a couple of summers himself, but he was real young at the time. I did tell him that I had my self respect to consider, but also the respect of my friends. We agreed that if anybody on the team so much as cracked a smile, he would beat the shit out of them for me. A quarterback has to maintain the respect of his teammates one way or the other. And the Tree was a more potent defense for my self respect than a weak armed QB would ever be himself.

And so that first Monday in June the Hero dropped me off at the shack and I started the job that would change my life. When I walked into the caddy shack, Beefy was not there, but there were about a dozen black boys from age thirteen to maybe eighteen. They were all in one corner shooting craps.

I had never seen an actual game before but I knew enough to recognize what it was. It was fast and lively. I had never heard such yelling and cussing before. Phrases like: 'Snake eyes, seven come eleven, little Joe and his slide trombone, box cars, eighta from Decata...' the older boys were rolling the dice, but the younger ones were involved, too, hanging on the outside of the circle, and they were making side bets with each other as the main action went on inside the circle. There was a stack of dollar bills on the floor, but it was coming and going so fast, I could not tell who was winning and losing.

As I watched I began to see that seven was a good number if it came on your first role, but not after that. Snake eyes and little Joe were not good ever. Eleven always seemed okay. As near as I could tell, the object was, if you rolled a nine or some other neutral number, you kept rolling until either you rolled another nine or you 'crapped out' by rolling a seven, two or three. There appeared to be two boys in charge. One was the most well muscled human being I had ever seen, and the other was one of the larger men, colored or white, on the planet. Nobody looked at me or acknowledged my presence.

The game continued as if I had not come in the building. But then suddenly, a small black boy came running in, 'He's a comin', and the game stopped in mid-roll. When Beefy walked in, everyone was sitting on a couple of benches as if they'd been that way all morning. 'Here's the week's caddy list,' He said. Since it was summer, the list for that week was longer than when school was in session. When school was in, you knew almost exactly who would be playing, depending on the day of the week.

In those days routines were more set and we had members who had days they regularly played. Wednesday afternoon's tee times were completely full, as doctors offices, lawyers offices, and the banks were closed. That was the day they always had a members only scramble. On Saturday during the school year were member/guest, best ball tournaments, and Sunday was members only. So everybody caddied on Wednesday, Saturday and Sunday afternoon.

The 'tweener' days was where the pickings were slim. Beefy managed the Wednesday, Saturday, and Sunday caddy assignments. I was about to learn that the tweener days were handled by the two boys I had seen shooting craps. Beefy handed the Monday list to those two boys and on his way into his office said to everyone in the room, 'If you don't caddy today, see me.'

So the mountain of a man and his muscular friend began to make the day's caddy list. There were about twenty or thirty people playing that day and everyone who played was required to use a club caddy; no carts; everybody walked. After the two straw bosses had picked the players for whom they would caddy, and they picked both morning and afternoon 'eighteens' for themselves.

They assigned a select few of the other older boys to caddy, probably their friends.

That was it. The rest of us were left for maintenance work. It was harder work than caddying and paid much less. On the way out the monster looked at me and said, 'Don't know what you doing here, Crack, but you ain't gonna have much work other than cut grass and dig ditches.' The boy with the muscles did not say anything. He just smirked and they walked out together.

Well, if I was not going to let my friends know how much this job sucked, I certainly was not going to let a bunch of colored guys know I was bothered by the unfairness of what they did to me. I said nothing, turned and went to the maintenance portion of the shack. That day we shoveled mud out of the creek end of the big lake that ran through the back nine holes. I left that day, covered in mud, but four dollars richer than I had come.

On Tuesday the club was closed for maintenance and repairs. That day we worked on the lake again in the morning and spent the afternoon cutting the fairways. Again, I made my four dollars without complaint, but I did notice that the big boy and his friend were not there. Apparently, they made enough from caddying and tips to not need to work on Tuesday, so they had a day off. That was more than the rest of us who would be working seven days a week that summer, six and a half, actually. We had Sunday morning off for church, of course. Nobody would have dared play golf on Sunday morning in those days. In the absence of my two new best friends, I made some inquiries about them to Beefy.

At lunch that day, I said, 'Mr Sizemore, can you tell me about the two boys who are not here today; the big one and his friend?' He laughed and said, 'You mean Jelly and Ivy? They have been working for me since they were about ten. They are your age, seniors at Birney Tech.

Birney was the separate black school on the other side of town from Central High.

It's hard for me sometimes to realize how old I have become, difficult to reconcile myself to the fact that in 2012, most of our young people have never seen a rotary phone or a phonograph. And they cannot comprehend what really ugly racism looked like, unfairness maybe, really nasty racism, no. Segregation is a word they read in their history books. But in 1966 it was our way of life. As I approached the end of my high school days we were also at the end of Jim Crow in the south. Though it most assuredly was dying, it was not going away easily or without violence. And so far, little had changed.

In 1966 negros and whites lived almost exclusively in two different worlds. We had separate churches, schools, restaurants . We did not have a theater in our town, but in places where they did, blacks were only allowed to sit in the balcony. When the fair came to town, school day for colored children was Thursday and for whites was Wednesday.

Negros were not allowed to use the same public restrooms or water fountains. Most of the negro women in town worked as domestic servants for white families. The wealthy, who could afford domestics, had a separate bathroom in their house for them, usually in the garage. Most negro men didn't have steady work and tended to drift in and out of the lives of their children. We lived right beside each other in a small town of limited geographical area, and yet we didn't even know each other.

I had grown up with these two colored boys, who obviously were good athletes, and probably played football like me, yet I didn't know who they were. Beefy interrupted my thoughts, 'You may have heard of them,

Johnny. They get in the Saturday sports page every week.' Every Saturday in the fall, the local paper would run a big article about our team. On the back of the sports page they would include a small article about Birney Tech. Beefy said, 'The big boy's real name is Bertrand Rolle and his friend is Ivory York. But nobody calls 'em that. There ain't been a colored boy born that didn't have a nickname. They call the big 'un Jelly, get it? Jelly Rolle. The othern's little cousin couldn't say Ivory. He called him Ivy, and that became his name.

Some folks over there in colored town, like to say that he is poison ivy, because he is prone to get in trouble every now and then. I never had no trouble with him, but I think it's true. He can kind of be poison if he don't like you.' Of course, I knew who they were after Beefy explained it to me. There were some people who thought they were the best black football players to ever come out of our town. In their community they were legends.

Of course, they never could have played for us. Everybody knew that coloreds did not have the discipline or smarts to play the game with white boys. We all knew that if you hit them real hard, they'd just quit. At least that was what I'd always heard. Looking at those two, man sized boys, however, I wondered.

After about two weeks I was in a decent routine: 6:00 AM at the field house for curls, military presses, bench presses, and squats, and then shower. And that's another thing modern kids have never experienced and so don't understand. We took showers together; yes, boys got 'necked' in front of other boys. I don't know exactly when or why that changed. What with cable TV and internet, boys and girls have been seeing naked bodies since they came naked out into the world.

Even with that, these children will not take a shower without a bathing suit on, unless they are behind a locked shower stall door. I don't think you have experienced life until you are in a hot shower with twelve other guys, and turn and see the guy next to you 'peeing' on your leg; get it? Hot water, body temperature pee, if you don't get it, forget it!

Anyway out of the shower, dress and drive from the school to the club and then spend the rest of the day digging ditches, cutting grass, occasionally getting a caddy assignment to break the cycle of bone-wearying work. But then, the third Wednesday I was there, Beefy assigned me to caddy with Jelly and Ivy, just the three of us. On the way to the first tee I asked Ivy who was to be our fourth caddy that day. 'Don't have one; Jelly carries two bags, Crack.'

For the uninitiated, Crack was not my special nickname. Soda Cracker was what they called white folks behind our back. Cracker for short and Crack for me, get it? Those were the first words Ivy had deigned to speak at me; I was honored. And of course, Jelly would definitely be able to carry two bags. By my reckoning he' would have been able to carry all four. I spent the next four hours listening to them making fun of their golfers and imitating their swings from behind trees. One time, looking for one of Jelly's golfer's ball in the woods, I saw him step on it and kick pine straw on top. Take that Cracker.

By the end of the day we three caddies were actually conversing and it was about a shared interest. We became warmly involved in a comparison of Central's team with Birney's. We clung tenaciously to our own opinion as to which team would prevail in a head to head contest. We were safe in our fantasy predictions, because we would never be allowed to compete against each other. But of course, in athletics there is more than one way to skin a cat or settle a difference of opinion. Though our teams would not be allowed to play each other, not ever, individuals from those teams might compete if no one knew about it.

'Tell you what, Crack,' said Ivy, 'We play a little game of ball every Sunday after we done caddying. Why don't you join us?' I was not so naïve as to miss the challenge in his words. The gauntlet had been thrown down and the honor of Central High was at stake. 'Sure, I will play. I would enjoy that.' I said, hoping my tone of voice did not betray the butterflies I felt in my stomach.

Jelly somehow sensed my uncertainty and laughed, 'We will see, Crack we will just see.' I replied, 'We will, Jelly, cannot wait.' I was becoming comfortable calling Bertrand, Jelly but it would be a while before I ventured to call Ivory, Ivy. And to this day I never even think of him as poison Ivy. Some things are just not worth the risk.

After work that next Sunday, I was mentally prepared, for what ever, but I did have one question: 'Are we going to your school's field or mine to play?' I assumed we would be on somebody's field. 'Nah,' said Jelly. 'If we went to play on our field the cops would arrest us for trespassing. If we got on your field, they'd probably shoot us on the spot. We only got a few places to play, and the best one is right across the tracks, over there. Beefy got us permission.' There was a railroad bed that ran parallel to the eighteenth hole, but all that was on the other side of the rails was a flat sandy area where the railroad company stored cross ties. There was not much grass so that I could see a fair amount of broken glass in the sandy areas.

It was only when we got to our impromptu stadium that I realized this was not a caddies only affair. There were about ten other boys waiting for us, who looked liked high school players. Obviously none from my team had been invited. I was the only Soda Cracker in sight. 'You and me doin' the choosin,' said Ivy. 'I choose first,' which meant he was going to have Jelly on his team. I was at a disadvantage because I had to choose by sight alone. I did not know how well any of these boys could play, and Ivy knew them all. I did my best but when the game started, I realized I had made a few bad picks.

Before the opening kickoff (which was a long pass down the field, not a kick) my question was 'Are we playing two hand touch, below the belt or two hands anywhere?' Ivy looked at me, 'Say what?' I wanted to know if it was to be two hand touch below the belt or anywhere? A reasonable question, I thought. Ivy laughed, 'Crack, we don't play that sissy shit; it's tackle.' And he threw the ball deep to me.

As we got toward the end of the debacle, my team was down 28-7. A couple of my ribs were sending messages to my brain that they might need serious repair. That happened on the first play when Ivy tossed me the opening kickoff. My blocking sort of evaporated and Jelly pounced. It felt like a compact car had rolled over on me. And did I now have piece of a beer bottle permanently tattooed to my butt? I knew this whole thing had been a set up, but as usual I kept my mouth shut. After I took a couple more good shots, the game settled in and I was no longer the focus of attention. My teammates had had their fun with the Cracker, but now they wanted to win as badly as I did.

That day, in my mind, all the myths were dispelled. Those guys weren't afraid of anything. They hit me and each other with savage joy. It was beautiful, really, more ballet than brutality. I had been fairly certain that Jelly was fast when I watched him move on the golf course. I found out he was as fast as me, and I was the fastest player on my team. The thing was he was 6'4" and 250 pounds.

What I found out about Ivy was that he delighted in hitting people but no one ever hit him. When you think about it, that is the mark of a great running back. They dish it out and seldom take it. Watch videos of Emmett Smith or Barry Sanders or any of the great ones. If they got hit, it was because they wanted to be hit. They rarely were taken by surprise, blindsided is the football term.

Ivy set me up twice. I thought he was going around and past me and just as I shifted my balance to get a better pursuit angle on him, he turned back into me and knocked me on my butt. He hit me twice very hard when I had the ball, but he also hit me twice equally as hard when he had it. I never hit him once, other than a glancing ineffective blow. But I got him good, anyway, right at the end of the game.

He was playing defemsove back and he was all over my wide receiver, trying to jump a short route for an easy interception and run for a touchdown. Today the term we use for that is a 'pick six'. In the huddle I told my receiver Joey; 'This time run an out. I'm going to telegraph it and he will be all over you, but I'm going to throw that one over your head so he cannot intercept it.

After the play Ivy was yelling, 'Better be glad you threw that one bad. You throw like a girl (which was true). Next play we ran the ball and Jelly smothered me. But then, on the third play, I told Joey, 'Run the short out route like before. Make it look the same, but I'm going to pump fake, and when Ivy jumps forward to intercept the ball, run the up (go deep in other words), toward the goal line. I promise, you will go right past him. Ivy never knew what was happening. When Joey caught the ball he was twenty yards behind Ivy, running to pay dirt. That was it. Game over: 28-14. When we were leaving Ivy said, 'Well, if you leave a blind hawg in the yard long enough, even he will find an acorn, Crack.' I said, 'Yeah, that may be true, but I can't believe you got suckered on the deep ball by a boy who throws like a girl?'

The rest of my summer went better than I had thought it would, for sure. That was due in large part to Beefy's son Tree. He definitely had my back with my white teammates. Once at weight lifting one of our junior running backs 'sniggered' something about caddy shack being nothing but a nigger house. I watched as Tree moseyed over to where he was standing. The big man said, 'A good friend of mine and yours works there; also, in case you did not know, my dad runs the place.' Then he jammed his fist into the boy's stomach very hard. Tree swore he only jabbed him lightly but from the way the boy doubled over and hit the floor, some might have construed it as a solid punch.

At any rate, there were no further comments about the place that employed either me or Beefy. Within the confines of the shack itself my new colored buddies had accepted me. Not long after that first football game, I was removed from field hand work and given caddying opportunities almost every day. I ate my lunch with Jelly and Ivy and realized that my dad might have been a teensy bit right about a potential learning experience for me that summer. For sure I had changed my mind about my new colored friends' ability to play football. And my thought processes were evolving beyond simple admiration for their abilities and killer instinct. I had begun to contemplate some previously unthinkable possibilities.

One day near the end of the summer over lunch I said to Jelly and Ivy, 'Have you guys ever thought about coming to our school?' It was not out of the blue. I'd been thinking about this question a long time. They looked stunned, but that did not deter me. 'We don't have a lot of colored kids at our school yet, but we do have some and they are pretty well accepted. Nobody messes with them. And I am positive nobody at school will mess with you.'

Ivy looked at me like I walked down the gangway of a space ship from Mars: 'Man you nuts. Why would I want to go to your dog ass white school?' I said, 'Well, you might be able to get a scholarship for football if you did and then you could get out of this town.' He laughed, 'Oh, so you don't just want me to come to school. You want me to play football for your team so you can maybe win a few games. I thought you just wanted me at your school, cause we friends.' I said defensively, 'We are friends and besides we haven't had a losing season in twenty years.' Jelly laughed, 'Yeah but you always beat the same six or seven teams and they ain't no good and then the good ones beat shit out of you every year. You haven't beaten Midlands in twenty years.'

They had me; if I described our team's winning tradition, the operative word would either be barely good or mediocre bad. We usually were 6-4, sometimes 7-3, very rarely 8-2, and we had not made the playoffs in five years. We always beat the other small town teams, the ones like us; but almost always lost to the city teams, the really good teams. When we played the city boys, we had already lost in our minds before the opening kickoff. These colored boys had my number. They knew more about my team than I had realized. The truth was painful.

Ivy sneered, 'I ain't joinin' up with a bunch of losers. I can lose just fine at Birney.' He was right about that. His school had not had a winning season in memory. If we were mediocre, they were just plain bad. I couldn't stop now. I continued to plead my case, 'Look guys, over this summer, I've changed my mind about lots of things.

You changed it for me. You guys can play. we don't have anybody like you.

You are right, I am sick and really tired of losing, but it's more than that. I think it would be cool to have you with us in school. I promise. I've got a few friends, who I am pretty sure would agree.' Ivy was still sneering when we left to go caddy that afternoon, but the 'J' man had become unusually silent. Jelly was a lot of things, but silent was not one of them. I wondered if he might be seriously considering my off the cuff invitation? I was not going to give up without a fight, either.

That night I got a call from Jelly. I was not sure that his family had a phone, but obviously, they did. He had never called me before, of course, and so I knew that what he had to say must be important. He did not say, 'Hello or how you doin',' or anything else. Without preamble he just said: 'First of all, I decided that I ain't calling you Cracker no more. But I sure as Hell ain't calling you Little Johnny. What kind of sissy name is that? You white boys always got two names. What's your other name?' I told him it was Jefferson; I was John Jefferson Savage. He thought about that for a minute and said, 'OK, then I'm thinking I'm gonna call you JJ, and Ivy will, too. But that ain't all, JJ. I want to come to Central and Ivy is gonna come with me.'

Wow, wow. What had begun as the worst summer of my life had morphed into a somewhat more rosy scenario. I had some new friends, even though I could not tell anybody about them yet. But if we could pull off this school transfer, my team had an outside chance at a decent season, who knew, maybe even make the playoffs. And the icing on my cake was I would not be Little Johnny any more. Maybe Big John, that would be my dad, the Hero, wasn't so dumb as I had thought, after all.

Making me caddy that summer had opened the door a crack to some real possibilities I had never dreamed of.

I told you I was not a writer. I got so excited just remembering that conversation, I completely got off the subject. The most important part of Jelly's and my phone conversation was that he and Ivy wanted to talk with me and a couple of my teammates at my house about coming to school and playing for our team. Then he actually confided in me. Up to that point neither he nor Ivy had ever told me one thing about their personal lives. In their defense, I had not disclosed anything to them about mine, either.

He said, 'You probably ain't gonna believe me, but at Birney I'm a straight A student, always have been. I don't know if I can do that at Central but I gotta come and try. If I stay at Birney, I don't have a chance of going to college and I want to be a dentist some day. If I don't get out of Birney, it will never happen. JJ, if you tell a soul I told you this, even Ivy, I swear I will kill you.'

I was pretty sure he would have, but I am a good secret keeper, threat or no threat, so Jelly had no worries from that quarter. I promised him that I would call him back in ten minutes and asked should I call Ivy. He told me Ivy did not have a phone but he'd take care of getting him to my house that night.

I hung up the phone and called Richard, aka Tree Sizemore and big Mark, Windmill Madison. They were our two tackles, the biggest guys on our team and the ones who had been watching my back since I enrolled in fourth grade. So now you know; I sometimes needed friends who could double as bodyguards and that is who they were for me. But you probably wonder how they got those nicknames?

Football players only get nicknames from teammates and coaches. They are what set us off from the other students, and even if the nicknames poke fun, we still cherish them. We wear those names to the point that most of our friends never use our real names; and sometimes, as in Beefy's case, we don't even know the real name any more.

There was something about my dad most people have never thought about, and it's pretty revealing. He never had a nickname. I think he was so serious about everything his teammates and coaches would not have thought of nick naming him. As for me, until Jelly renamed me, I'd never had one except 'Little Johnny' which totally sucked. I was little and dad was big, I was a fair to middling athlete and he was great. My nickname reminded me of my shortcomings every time I heard it. Every time somebody called me Little Johnny, I winced. Off task again; sorry.

Shade Tree got his nickname because of a big old oak tree that grew on the edge of our practice field. In summer two a day practices, he would sleep under that tree before practice. He'd get under the tree and use his helmet for a pillow and just snooze. That guy could sleep in the face of an oncoming blitzkrieg or even one of Drucker's practices. I came up with the nick name and it stuck.

The Mill's was a bit meaner, but it was funny as Hell anyway. The Mill was six feet tall, but his sleeve length was only 29". At 5'9", my sleeve length was 32". When we were in ninth grade, and on the suicide squad, we had to run down field to cover kicks and punts. One day in a film session Drucker ran one of our punt coverages about ten times on the projector.

Since we freshmen were not that important, it was unusual for him to take that long on a punt, unless there was a major screw up, but I couldn't see any. Finally, Coach said, 'Look at that arm action. It's like a tiny

61

windmill.' It was true, when the Mill ran his arms kind of went in a circle like a miniature windmill, and that was that. Windmill, or later just the Mill is what everybody called him. Funny that Coach Drucker with his lead butt would think the Mill's arms that peculiar.

Anyway, I got Tree and the Mill on the phone and at nine o'clock that night we got together at my house. The meeting was to be in dad's den with all the trophies. It was that important. Things did not begin well. Tree was easy going and relaxed as always, but the Mill, who was undeniably a redneck, was tense. Jelly spoke first: 'Me and Ivy done some more talking and we mebbe interested in joining your team.' Jelly obviously had two languages, the one he used on the phone with me in private and then this public persona.

The Mill shot up like a bottle rocket and exploded, 'Who asked you to join our team? We don't need your help.' I dived in since I was the one who asked them, 'Maybe we do, Mill. It was my bright idea to ask them to play for us. I played ball with these guys every Sunday this summer and I think they can help us.' The Mill laughed, 'Yeah? Just because somebody can play in a pasture, don't mean he can play real football.' Ivy chimed in, 'So you think what you play is real football? What you play is white man's football. Who gets to decide that is the real football?'

The conversation was not taking shape as I had envisioned. I had to steer us past this bump in the road or risk a total wreck. It came to me in a flash. I decided to use the Lombardi approach: 'Guys, look. I don't know about you, but I'd like to beat Midlands just once before I die. And I'd like to walk on the field every single Friday knowing that if we play well, we can win. It's never been that way before, but we have a chance to change that, if we can get past the personal stuff.' The Mill said, 'I don't want anybody at my school just to play football.' I almost laughed out loud. The Mill only stayed in school to play ball. If not for football, he'd have dropped out at sixteen.

That's when Ivy said something that blew me away: 'I agree with you. I can tell you, only reason Jelly wants to come to your school is so he can graduate and go to college. If he finish at Birney, he'll never get accepted nowhere. To get in your school and have a chance to make something of himself. He will play football for your team, but he don't care about football that much. Me neither really, I just want a scholarship so I can get out of this town and get me a life. I ain't no great student like Jelly, but I could get in college somewhere to play ball, only not if I play at Birney.' Well, making something of one's self was a thing that resonated with all of us, including the Mill. Knowing the limitations the small town of Central put on all of us crackers, we could imagine how much worse it was for colored people.

About that time dad and mom walked in. Mom had brought ice cream and cookies. The Hero, I suspected, as always, would be bringing his advice. I cannot think of any occasion when everybody's Hero did not have advice to lend. The man was an advice machine. Only this time I welcomed it. I suppose he had been listening to the conversation, which would not have been difficult since there had been a fair amount of shouting.

He said without preamble, 'If you two are serious about enrolling at Central, it's not too late and I can handle the administrative side of things. You can definitely come to Central. But if you are serious about playing football, I cannot help with that. You will need to take up that subject with Coach Drucker.'

He did not say it, but I knew that would be a different matter altogether. Dad was right; he could only do so much. He would never interfere with team

63

decisions. Those were the domain of the head coach. And unfortunately, I was pretty sure Drucker was a racist, far from the worst in our town for sure, but even so, did he want to win badly enough to allow colored boys on his team? Dad went on and offered a final piece of advice, 'Why don't you guys take this weekend and go up to Linger Longer' and talk this thing out some more. Come back with a plan and I'll do what I can to help.

The Linger Longer Lodge was a cabin on a lake in the mountains north of the university dad and mom had attended. He and Beefy had built it ten years ago. It was primitive, no TV or phone. It did have running water and electricity but that was about all. If we went there for the weekend, we would have to talk things out. That's about all there was to do, talk and think. It was a good place to go and think and just get away.

So that weekend the five of us took a road trip north. While we were there, we did a bit more than talk. We also did some fishing, running, some wrestling, even a little one on one blocking and tackling. One day we went over to the local junior college and got into a football game with some of their players. And that opened my white friends' eyes to the possibilities I had been seeing. Not saying we were bosom buddies when we got back to town, but we had made peace and come to a general understanding, and we had a plan. Maybe it was not the best plan, but it was a start.

CHAPTER THREE

Gentlemen, I can think of only two reasons for missing my practice: If your parents have recently died, or if you have.

Frank Leahy to his Notre Dame team

It is likely that outside of family and a few friends, no one will read this story. But on the off chance that people outside my generation read it, they will need a bit more of the social history of life in the south in 1966. The story happened almost 100 years after the War, but in that time very little had changed. I already mentioned that.

However, in the next fifty years a great deal has changed. I know because I've watched our small part of the world change for the better. But in 1966 the southern pecking order was as antebellum as ever. Here's the thing; if you cannot remember where you were when Kennedy was shot, probably because you weren't even born, you need to understand our pecking order.

There was a distinct hierarchy in the south when I was a boy. White men were on top, women, that would be white women, were just below their men, but most definitely below. White kids, boys then girls came next; seen but not heard. Jews, if there were any in your town, came next. Black women were at the bottom but definitely in the picture and black men were mostly invisible. In 1966 in southern towns and even most of the cities there was no one else, Hispanic, Muslim, zip.

Family arrangements, also, were slightly different then. For boys of my era, we were first raised and disciplined by our colored mammies, until our mothers took over. We were raised by these two sets of mothers until we became teenagers. Really I would have to say until we got to high school, about fourteen or fifteen years old. We entered into puberty and high school at the same time and that's when we actually began to be noticed by our fathers. We knew they were there before high school, because we all had heard, 'Wait 'til your daddy gets home,' about a thousand times. And we often felt our mothers' words as well.

But we were not really interesting to our dads until we took that first tentative step into our own manhood. That they finally noticed us, is not to say they spent much time with us, explaining things like the facts of life or how to prepare for college and career. My dad and I never exchanged a word about any of those things. I learned the facts of life from older boys. I planned school and career on the fly. Our dads were not much help. I guess part of our life struggle as young southern males was a quest to find male role models.

Outside the high school PE department where the coaches hung out, there might have been only two or three male teachers in the entire school and most of them were not what we were seeking. So we had three choices:

our dads who were half assed role models for lack of practice, our preachers (and we all had one of those) who we saw once a week. What they had to say made them seem too nice to be of much help. But there was salvation for those of us lucky enough to play ball, our head coach. For a ball player in the south, that man's word was the word. The head ball coach wasn't exactly a god, but godlike enough for us.

My dad was ever and always my hero, as much as I sometimes hated his guts. He was my hero, but Lead Butt Drucker was my epiphany. Now, don't misunderstand me. I am not saying I liked the man. You don't have to like your epiphany. It's just nice to have them. In my south, liking your football coach had absolutely no place in our god/mortal relationship. He was god and we were not. I would have run through a wall for him had he ever asked. For crying out loud, I served on his suicide squad my ninth grade season, tantamount to close encounters with a brick wall every Friday night.

I bled for him on any number of occasions, but I didn't like him all that much. I'm fairly certain he didn't like me either. But I took no offense because I could not tell that he liked any of his players. As Forrest Gregg once said of Lombardi, who was Coach Drucker's idol:,'He's the fairest man alive. Treats us all like dirt.'

And he of the lead butt and equally metallic head, stood directly between me and my new plans for our football team. He was the landslide I knew would fall in an effort to block my path. Bertrand Rolle and Ivory York would certainly be admitted to our school as students. That was my dad's decision and he had already stated his position. However, if they were ever going to be members of our football team, it would not be by player consensus. Coach Drucker would have absolute and final say. Even though they were potentially great players who would have tremendously helped our team, they were the wrong color so far as most people were concerned.

Though I had never discussed integration with Drucker, I saw no reason he would be different from most of the men in our town. As much as he wanted to win, if you had posed him the question, 'You can win a state championship this year, but only if you allow two colored boys to play on your team,' he might still have said, 'No.' Well, Coach Drucker was godlike, but he wasn't royalty, certainly not the potentate of our school. The Hero was above him in the academic pecking order.

You might wonder why our principal wouldn't simply overrule his teacher/coach, since technically Coach worked for dad. You might wonder that if you had grown up anywhere other than a small, football crazed town in the south. The chain of football command simply did not work in such a straight forward way in Dixie in 1966. And even if it could have been done, my dad never would have interfered. The Hero did not work that way. He did not micro-manage as we say these days. He hired teachers and left them alone to make their own decisions about how to teach or coach.

Our football team had a motto, ironically taught to us by Coach Drucker: 'If it's to be, it's up to me.' In this case no truer words were ever spoken. If I wanted Jelly and Ivy on our team, I would have to figure out a way to make it happen, it was up to me. A week before summer practice began, dad let me know that Bertrand Rolle and Ivory York were officially students of Central high school. The ball was now squarely in my court.

It was with knocking knees that I forced my knuckles to rap on the gate of Hell after evening workouts that last Monday night before summer practice began: 'Come in,' the sandpaper voice rasped harshly. When I did as commanded, Coach looked me up and down, as if trying to remember who I was. Understandable, I'd only been his starting quarterback for the past two seasons.

'What can I do for you, Little Johnny?' Drucker asked. Well, he did know who I was after all, but calling me that nickname did little to build my confidence. Trying to keep my newly acquired adult voice from cracking, I said, 'Coach, may I talk to you about the team?' Drucker raised his eyebrows a notch, not even his assistant coaches offered him opinions about his team.

'Coach, I want to talk about two potential players for this season.' He immediately wanted to know who I was talking about as he knew no families had moved into the district that summer. He made it his business to know things like that. 'Oh no, coach, these guys aren't new. They have been here all along.' He looked at me as if I had lost my senses. He knew every potential football player from first grade to eighth, and even the warm body possibles walking our halls. 'Coach (here it comes, I thought), these are a couple of guys who played at Birney, but will be in school here this year. They really are great and I wish you would consider letting them have a try-out.

He did not jump up and shout. He calmly looked me over and said, 'Let me give you three reasons why that is a bad idea, Little Johnny. First, those colored boys have their own team over at Birney. They don't need to be coming over here. Second, that colored team is terrible. If they cannot help their own sorry squad win a few games, how can they help us. Third, and this is most important, so listen to me carefully. I am the coach and you are a player. I do not need suggestions from you how to run my team. Now, unless you want me to reevaluate our quarterback situation for this year, you need to get out and let me worry about running this team.' I said, what I always said to my elders, 'Yes sir,' and beat a hasty retreat.

I had an entire speech written indelibly on my brain, all about how Ivy and Jelly could help us get our team over the top, maybe help us to state; I was going to mention what a boost a state championship would be for community morale (and the status of the coach) and how it would go a long way to improving relations between the two separate communities coexisting in our one town. I'm glad he didn't give me a chance at the speech. Had he heard it, I'm sure he'd have named my successor at QB on the spot and then thrown me out. But I need to say something before we race to judgment. Probably every man in town felt exactly like Coach Drucker did.

I was pretty discouraged when I got home that night but dad advised me to wait to call Jelly for a day or so, see if anything changed. After all, Drucker wanted to win a championship as bad or worse than any coach in the state. On Tuesday morning at weight lifting, Drucker pulled me aside and he seemed in a better bad mood than yesterday. He was never in a good mood, some were worse than others.

He said, 'Little Johnny, I've been thinking about what you said.' Since I had not been able to say anything, I wondered what he actually meant. He continued, 'I'm a reasonable man and I'm willing to make a compromise.' We both knew he was neither, but if there were a chance of my friends making our team, I was listening. 'I'll let, what are their names? Ivory and Bertrand, have an extended tryout over summer practice.'

Then I knew for sure he had investigated and found out that these two colored boys were potential scale tippers in his quest for glory. His offer was not a promise that they would be on the team come game one, but I figured it was the best offer I was getting. 'Thanks, coach,'

70

I said, 'I'll let them know to be here Monday morning.' He already had turned his back and was walking away before I opened my mouth.

That night I called Jelly and asked him and Ivy to meet me at my house. I already had invited Tree and the Mill that day at workouts. I wanted them there to corroborate what I said. There still was not a big old bucket of trust sloshing around between us five. Ivy and Jelly had heard more than enough about Coach Drucker and our fans to mistrust any promises coming from only one of Central's players. Besides they were pretty sure that Tree and I were the only ones who actually wanted them on the team. The jury was out on the Mill. I tried to put myself in their place and became discouraged pretty quickly. The deck was hugely stacked against them. Had they not been the two best players in town and, in my opinion, two of the best in the entire state, there would have been no point in this meeting.

I tried to be honest: 'I want you to understand that this is a tryout and at the end you still might not make the team; that goes for all of us.' That was the point where I fell a bit short of complete honesty. In summer practice every player was theoretically on tryout, regardless of past performance.

I said, theoretically, because there was no way the three white boys in the room were actually on trial. We would be on the team. But in a fair and just world there was no way the two black boys in the room should not be on the team as well. They were better than any of the players like us who were assured of berths on the team that year, but they were truly on trial. As good as they were, there was no guarantee they'd dress out for Central's first game of the 1966 season. Such was the world of the 1960's south.

Before they made up their minds, I wanted to be honest with them about one more detail, summer practice itself. 'Listen fellas; I have something very important to tell you. Our practices are probably harder than anything you have ever been through.' I saw their eyebrows go up and knew I was about to hear how they could take anything a white boy could, but I went on, 'We practice three hours in the morning in shorts and shoulder pads and then three hours in the afternoon in full pads. Practices are mandatory; miss one and you likely will not make the team. We never stop moving, we hit and hit and hit, and Coach likes the afternoon practice to be in the hottest part of the day. There are no water breaks. He thinks water at practice will make us soft. We never take off our helmets, even when we are not in the scrimmage.

This is the routine for two and one half weeks, that's 26 practices in 17 days. Actually, the morning practice is more difficult, because we run more than in the afternoon but somehow we manage to hit just as much. Drucker doesn't care whether you have football pants on or not. Everything is full contact. Most days I lose eight to ten pounds of water at each practice and I am skinny.

Linemen like the Mill (careful here, did not want to imply he was chubby) might lose twenty. It's hard to eat in summer practice, because you spend all your time drinking water to replenish what you lose. I believe that if I am bad in this life and get sent to Hell, Lead Butt will be standing at the gate with his whistle and I will have an eternity of two a day practices. So fellas, in a couple of days we are going to Hell, allus.'

There was complete silence in the room after I finished, until Tree said, 'Johnny, you may have understated a bit.' Where did he learn a word like understated? Finally, it was Jelly who spoke. He said, 'I'm willing to give it a try. We can always go back to Birney if we have to.' Ivy said, 'I ain't worried. Ain't nuthin' no Cracker coach can do to make me quit.' I looked at the Mill and my eyes pleaded, 'Don't say anything to piss him off. Cracker is just a word, and think about the words we use for them. You and I both know that you hate summer ball, already as much as these two soon will.'

And that one thought is probably what kept the Mill in his seat. Colored or white, we were all facing the same three weeks of Hell. So it was set that night between the five of us. Practice was at 7:00 on the coming Monday and we five would be there at 6:00 so we could help them get their equipment and find a locker. Our pads were already in our assigned lockers in the football dressing room. We white boys had our place. They would need our help finding theirs.

I do not need to tell you about all twenty six of our summer practices. Suffice to say, if you want to learn more about summer football practice in the old south, just be bad in this life and when you die, you'll learn all you need to know on the subject. I do have a few stories that will give you a flavor. To Ivy and Jelly's credit, they made all twenty six practices. I picked them up at Jelly's house (actually I met them at the road to Jelly's house, their choice) and took them home every morning and afternoon to be sure they made it.

After the first two days, there was not much said on those trips to and from practice. I could write all the conversations in a page of this story, make that a half page. Talking, like every other physical activity, is a waste of needed energy during summer practice. To Coach's credit, he didn't say the N word more than a couple of times, though it had always been a large part of his normal vocabulary. And the team also avoided using that terrible word. At least I never heard it. I guess everyone was on best behavior, trying a little.

I do have several vivid memories of those seventeen days. The first day that we held a full contact scrimmage Coach decided Jelly and Ivy needed to learn about how hard white boys could hit. He put them on the second team defense against us, his starters. He moved Jelly around during the scrimmage that day. He had him at noseman, tackle, end, and finally he put him at linebacker. Every starting lineman we had got a chance to block him and nobody could. We double teamed him with the end and the tackle, we had a running back chip him, as well, making the block a kind of triple team. It was a waste of time. Coach finally gave up and solved the dilemma by putting him at defensive end and running the opposite way.

But that didn't help much because Ivy was playing safety. Our backs got hit at the line of scrimmage so often and so hard that one of them, Ronny Driscoll, was almost in tears. They kept bitching to the lineman about crummy blocking so that finally the Mill, who didn't much like criticism from wimpy backs, said, 'If you think you can block the mother-fucker, then you drag your sorry ass over here and I'll run the fucking ball and you give it a shot.'

Once I saw Ivy run sideline to sideline, dodge three blockers and still catch Ronny for a two yard loss. In frustration Ronny took a swing at Ivy and it took Jelly and the Tree to hold Ivy back. It was the first time in my memory that the second team had held the first team without a touchdown and that scrimmage lasted two hours. We must have run a hundred plays at them. At the end Coach did not know whether to laugh or cry.

I could tell by the look on his face that he knew beyond doubt that he had the key to his success in the palm of his hand. But the question remained could he unlock the racial door, knowing what all might emerge? After all it was not just him, he had an entire town watching his every move. We had the chance for a great season, maybe the best in school history staring us in the face, and it all hung on the decision of a red neck southern ball coach.

After the offensive scrimmage we went to team defense and the scrubs, including Ivy and Jelly, put on the green scrimmage vests and ran offense against the defensive starters. Offensively, it went just about like those summer pick up games in the railroad lot. Ivy was virtually untouchable. We were able to tackle him, just because the second team O-Line was so outmanned. They couldn't block any of us and still we had a hard time getting Ivy down to the ground.

That day the best gift of the preseason was given to Tree and the Mill. When the coaches found out that Jelly was fast and that he had great hands, he became a tight end. It was like a battlefield promotion and it hugely affected our two starting tackles. Tree and the Mill had already begun to jockey for position in order to see which of them would lose their starting job.

They assumed that because Jelly was gargantuan, he'd be a tackle. That position change from tackle to end for Jelly meant for me, the QB, that we would have the biggest tight end in the state including all the colleges and universities. And the Tree and the Mill got to keep their starting tackle positions and relax. The competition between Tree and the Mill before that switch led to the worst day of my summer.

We were running a little two on one blocking drill, tight ends and wingbacks against the tackles. Tree would run a few plays, then the Mill and then Jelly. They were beating the crap out of our double team blockers, until coach got so frustrated he actually threw me in there as a wingback. With the help of my double team partners, I could sort of block Tree, nobody could block Jelly very well, but I have to say the Mill was better against the double team than any of them. He was so low to the ground that blocking him was like trying to roll a two hundred pound bowling ball out of the way. Only this bowling ball could hit you as you tried.

And coach put me in there with our second string tight end against the Mill. That boy was a one hundred thirty pound freshman and I wasn't much bigger. Our only advantage was the snap count and somehow the tight end was tipping it off. Since I was the edge blocker and he knew it, the Mill jumped right by the tight end, ignored him entirely, and hit me.

After three plays, my chinstrap was broken, my nose was bleeding and I was seeing double. And we didn't even slow him down. After the third or fourth try, the Mill squashed my face in the dirt and whispered in the ear hole of my Riddell, 'You not only throw like a girl, you damn pussy, you hit like one, too.' So much for my chances of playing blocking back on this team in this lifetime. I have never been so glad of failure in my life.

Tree also had his moment that summer. It was near the end of two-a-days. We were in the last few plays of a three hour scrimmage and everyone was exhausted. It was the first and third teams against second string and for some reason they were playing like all pros. The trick to being second string and surviving is to look as if you're giving 100%, but find a way to let the first string succeed. To live, you must lose in the end. However, some days the scrubs can be perverse, we called it 'getting a wild hair up your ass' and this was one of those wild hair days.

They were not playing the give in game. They were actually giving 100%, and we could not move the ball against them. On top of the resistance we were receiving from the scrubs, it was so hot that I had the worst case of cotton-mouth I'd ever had in my life. If you have never been truly dehydrated, then I will try to explain. I think that sputum is made up of both liquids and solids, about 50/50. In severe dehydration, the liquid in spit goes away, but the solids remain, so that you can literally rub your finger in your mouth and roll what is left of your saliva into a white sticky ball, like cotton. That's cotton-mouth. I think the next thing after that is you die, but we never got quite that far. Coach had an instinct for the edge. Anyway, we were beyond thirsty.

We had a little break as Drucker had the second string going against the threes. Us first stringers were watching the third string and trying to catch our breath when Tree grabbed a manager and sent him over to a mud puddle formed by one of the sprinklers at the edge of the field. The manager dropped a towel in the puddle, kicked it around, and brought it back. It had more grass and mud than water in it, but we passed it from player to player. First, you would hold it to the back of your neck to cool off, then you would suck as much moisture from the towel as possible. I was about eighth in line so the towel was pretty salty but still drinkable.

When it finally got to Tree, Coach happened to turn around and see him sucking on the towel. He let out a yell and came running. He grabbed Tree by his face mask and bent him over backwards to the ground. Remember, Tree was about 215 pounds and strong. When Coach Drucker got him to the ground, he put his face up to Tree's helmet mask and said, 'I hope you enjoyed that, because it's gonna cost you five gassers at the end of practice.

Five gassers would be equivalent to being kcel hauled or nailed to a wall. But Tree simply said, 'Yes sir,'

77

and he did them. Of course, we didn't confess our complicity. And he did not rat the rest of us out to save his skin. That's not how we did it. There was an honor code and so the rest of us escaped the wrath of Coach Lead Butt.

By the end of our summer practices Jelly had impressed everyone with his good nature and his athletic ability. No one could ever bait him to get angry, though a few tried. He maintained his poise through out summer practice. I thought he had a very good chance to make the team. A couple of our redneck boys even went as far as to say, 'Jelly, you could be white, almost.' I'm not sure how Jelly took that, but outwardly he laughed.

Ivy was a different story. No one would argue his ability. Clearly, he was the best football player on the field and arguably the best to come out of our town, since the great Hero, my dad. But his attitude sucked. He was never pleasant and at times he was downright awful. He didn't resist Coach openly, he just refused to acknowledge him. Drucker liked to get up close and personal with all his players. He didn't discriminate in that respect.

You might be a star or a scrub, Drucker did not care. He was mean as the devil himself, and he reveled in that attitude. I might add that he did not let his favorites off easily, except. Well, he had no favorites. He was nasty to everyone. Most of us managed to mentally ignore him while looking him in the eye and receiving the spray of his spittle in our face (eye to eye contact mattered greatly to all coaches). But when he got face to face with Ivy, that boy would stare through Coach as if he saw something behind him infinitely more interesting.

I don't think Ivy said a word to Coach Drucker for the two and one half weeks we had been practicing. Even I was beginning to wonder if Ivy had been a good idea. I knew he had character, at least I thought he did, but most of the others on our team just thought he was a sorry nigger. And for his part Ivy acted as if he didn't care that they thought that of him. He was like a finely tuned machine and that was all.

When I took him home on Wednesday of the last two-a-day practice, I felt that I had to give one more try to get him on board emotionally: 'Ivy; please listen to me. I think you are the best football player I have ever seen, but it won't matter if you never get to prove it in a game.' He looked over my head just like he did with Coach Drucker and said, 'I don't give a shit about that. I am not going to let that bastard get to me.'

I said, 'Think about what you just said, Ivy, because he already has gotten to you, or you would not be acting like you are. He's so far into your head, he's coming out your butt. Don't you know? He never wanted you on the team in the first place, and by what you have been doing you are making his job easy. He can cut you and everybody who has watched you behave, will swear it was the best thing for the team. And I'm beginning to wonder myself. You think you are winning? You, my friend, are losing. In fact, you are kicking your own butt.

The way I see it, you have one chance to prove to all the coaches that you should be on this team. You have got to make tomorrow night's scrimmage your showcase. Everyone in town will be there. Most of them are skeptical whether you and Jelly should be on this team, too. What you do on the field will decide the issue. Take the decision out of Coach's hands. Show everybody what you can do.' He paused for long enough that I knew he had heard me.

Then he said, 'Well, maybe they will see something, but I ain't never bowin' down to no Cracker white assholes, coaches, players, or fans.' When I dropped him off at the road to Jelly's house, I didn't know if he'd

79

make the team, but I thought Thursday night would be an interesting show.

I'm going to tell you all about that scrimmage, because it was the game changer for us all. But before I do, I need for you to indulge my pop psychological bent. It's probably just the preacher in me, but I really need to tell you what I think about the why's and wherefores of both Ivy and Jelly. First of all, you probably have been able to tell that Jelly managed summer practice well. Other than losing forever twenty pounds of fat, he maintained his dignity and poise throughout the ordeal.

He weighed in the day of the scrimmage at 230, and I believe that is the weight he played at all his college days. When I say Jelly managed well, he even had made some friends on the team, if only at a superficial level. Certainly, none of the guys were over to his house for dinner and he was not double dating with any of them. But even the true red necks admired his effort and general good nature.

Except for me and maybe Tree, however, there was not a player on our team who liked Ivy. Everyone recognized his talent, but most thought that his attitude would end up poisoning the team, the 'one rotten apple and the barrel,' effect. And on that, I had to admit, they were right. His present attitude would probably be a killer for us all. One bad attitude is really all it takes to ruin a team. Unless you have been there and experienced the dynamics of a team sport, this is hard to explain. Nevertheless it is true, believe me. I wanted Ivy on the team as much as ever, but unless he changed his thinking, I knew he would not help either himself or us.

Now I'm going to psycho-sort of-analyze. This may surprise you but the problem for Ivy was his keen sense of justice. He knew what was right. Unfortunately, he didn't know how to get the justice he so desperately deserved

80

and wanted. Ivy would have liked an apology from Coach Drucker and the team for two hundred years of slavery and another hundred years of mistreatment of blacks by whites. That he was not going to get, ever.

Jelly on the other hand, really didn't want an apology. He only wanted a piece of the white man's pie. And he was willing to do what he needed to get that skinny slice. My grandfather, the farmer, used to say, 'An old hog may let a new hog up to the trough, but only if the new one is humble about it.'

Most boys I knew were starting to realize that we needed to share the wealth. We were willing to think about that, but no one was going to apologize. If you think about it, Jelly was right. Perhaps the way we apologize, if at all, is not by anything we say, but simply by sliding our big ol' butt over and opening a slot at the trough. Okay, so excuse my farmer's almanac psychology. Anyway it's just my opinion.

The entire town of Central showed up for their team's preseason Thursday night scrimmage. Everyone wanted to see what our prospects were for 1966. After this scrimmage there would be debates at the barber shop and my granddad's lunch counter over what to expect, perhaps a few bets as well. This was the dress rehearsal. Next Friday night would be the real thing, so the stadium was packed. The team was evenly divided talentwise. Half the first string line and backs were on one team, half on the other. It was the same for the second and third strings. The remaining scrubs were divided equally, making it 25 or so on each side.

It would be a regular game, four quarters with referees. We would kickoff and punt. Some teams didn't have live punts and kickoffs in the preseason scrimmage for fear of injury. Coach Drucker did not care much about that. He was looking for killer instinct especially among the younger boys, and special teams were the best place to find it. I did not have Jelly or Tree on my team, but I did have the Mill. I always liked to have him, because if not, I spent half the night trying to figure out where he was, looking over my shoulder for the kill shot.

Some players would take it easy in this scrimmage as much as they could. We were teammates after all. I mean we hit each other hard, considering Coach was looking down on us from the press box. And there was the film being made, to which all of us would be subjected on Sunday. We had an adage about that film: 'You can fool the coaches sometimes, but you cannot lie to the eye in the sky.' So we knew we had to give it all we had, we had to maim, but we did not have to murder.

Unfortunately for his teammates, the Mill did not understand the phrase take it easy, not in his dictionary. He would not play dirty, but if within the rules he knocked you out or ended your season before it began, well that's the price of a ticket. Always good to know where he was, even better, to have him on your team. Also, our side had an ace in the hole, Ivy. Though he was not scheduled to start, he was returning punts and kickoffs, and I had never seen anyone do it better.

On the first kickoff of the game, he received the ball at about the ten yard line. According to the playbook he was supposed to start up the middle and then cut right behind the wall we were trying to form. It started well, with him following the wedge in the middle, but the wedge splintered quickly and broke apart; so he was looking at three defenders coming right at him. It was then he did a thing I had never seen even him do before. He completely reversed his field and ran backward twenty yards and then cut left.

Since the other team had seen our wall form to the right, and since they knew our kickoff because it was theirs, too, they naturally angled that way. When Ivy cut the opposite way, there were only two defenders left on that side of the field. In today's football terminology, he put those two defenders on an island. He set up the first would be tackler with head and shoulders feint to the outside and then cut back. That boy fell trying to make the turn and completely whiffed, but his cut threw him directly into the path of the other tackler. They were too close together for any more slick maneuvering. A head on train wreck was inevitable, so Ivy dropped his shoulder and it looked like a bull tossing the matador over his head. He completely ran under and then over the unfortunate tackler.

From there he cruised the middle of the field, casually looking back. At the ten yard line he slowed to a walk and dropped the ball in the end zone. This, of course, was all wrong to the white dominated stands. Players, no matter how talented, did not show off. What he should have done was run full speed across the end line and then carried the ball to the referee and humbly placed it in his hands. That's how we Crackers rolled in 1966. There could be no doubt about the talent we saw, but everyone there that night also saw the attitude, and that nullified all the good stuff.

We were ahead 14-7 at the half and it had been a good show by everyone, but in the locker room at half, Coach came in from the press box, unusual. I had learned to read him pretty well and he was pissed off. I knew why, so on the way out for the second half, I pulled Ivy aside for one last plea: 'Will you try to do something for me this half?' He frowned, 'What?' I said, 'Play without mocking your teammates or the fans. Just beat their pants off and show everybody what you can do.' He didn't say anything, just trotted past me onto the field. Even though he did not acknowledge my plea, I knew he heard me loud and clear.

The second half of that game was a show like nothing our town had ever seen, even and including the Hero's years. Ivy took over the game. He scored four touchdowns and he scored in every way possible, deep passes where he just outran the defensive backs. Once I threw one as far as I've ever thrown in my life. I thought he'd miss it by ten yards but he caught in stride. More important, he didn't stop at the ten and walk, though he could have. He ran over people, he outran them. On defense he probably made two thirds of our tackles from his safety position. He was twelve yards behind the line of scrimmage and he made tackles for losses. We won 42-7; the most lopsided preseason scrimmage in history.

The locker room was silent afterward. Usually it was the most boisterous time of the season, since summer practice was officially over. Even Coach Drucker didn't have much to say: 'On Monday (Labor Day; school started on Tuesday) I'll have the roster posted and the 1966 schedule.' Coach liked drama and he never told us the exact schedule until summer practice was over.

He claimed that he didn't want us thinking ahead to the games. I think he just liked to create a little tension among us. He could have saved paper. No one who went through his practices thought further ahead than the end of the practice we were then enduring. Summers with Coach Drucker were all about survival in the moment. But it was over. For me and the other seniors, it was over forever, but we still had a weekend to wait and worry about making the team.

Monday morning, I was the first to arrive at the door to the field house. I had to wait thirty minutes for the manager to arrive with the answers I had been praying about all weekend. By the time the manager posted the sheets, most of the team was there. First, the schedule:

Camden (We usually opened with them, so no surprise; they were a good warm up game)

Cesar Shoals (Another small town school we always beat)

North Fork (This was a new school on the outskirts of a nearby city; they were a building program)

Midlands (City school who we hardly ever beat. They made it to the semi's last year)

Parson's Mill (Chalk up another W)

Driscol (City school, but a toss up. Whenever we went 8-2 we usually beat them to do it)

Kerrville (Probably the best small town team we played; it was usually a brutal game)

Parnassus (We had not lost to them in twenty years)

Howard Banks (Last year's state champion in the classification above ours; virtually unbeatable by the likes of us, but at least we would not face them again, if we made the playoffs)

Royal (Our closest neighbor town; biggest rival; plenty of upsets in this series)

North Fork, Midlands, and Howard Banks were not in our classification. Whether we won or lost against them; we'd not see any of them again. We played them every year, but they had no affect on our playoff chances.

Bottom line: we had a very demanding schedule, but it always was. The best football in our state was played, year in and year out, in our area. Most seasons, if you were able to beat most of these teams, you would not see anyone better in the playoffs.

So that was to be our 1966 football schedule. There were no surprises on that page. But the other sheet contained the roster and I was far more interested in that one as was every boy in the room. The way the roster worked was Coach Drucker never allowed but 33 players on his varsity. If you were not in that elite group you faced a choice. You could quit football or play on the junior varsity team. Coach had no problem even with seniors playing on the JV, but rarely did a senior do that. Occasionally, one would, in hopes of making the varsity during the year if someone was injured. Generally though, if you did not make varsity by your junior year, you knew that your football career was over.

Sometimes there were questions among team members as to the worth of someone who made the varsity, but Coach Drucker was a fantastic judge of talent. He rarely missed picking the best 33 players, regardless of their class in school. Six of us had been on his varsity roster since our freshman year. But Coach Drucker's method of choosing his varsity is not what you want to hear, is it?

Long story short, Jelly made the team. He was assigned an 80 numbered jersey; we all knew what that meant. For example, there were three numbers in the teens: (10, 11, 12); those were the quarterbacks. I was 12 and had that number since ninth grade. There were three numbers in the 20's: All of them were left half backs, but that usually meant they played wide receiver. We only had a full house backfield on the goal line. There were three 30's who were our right half or running backs. The three 40's were blocking backs; there were three 50's for the centers. There were six in the 60's, 70's, and 80's for the linemen. Coach wasn't just 'OCD', he was 'CDO'; he even wanted the three letters in order. Anyway, every player knew by the number assigned what position he would be playing that season. Jelly's number, 80, meant that Mill and Tree were safely starters at tackle, because Jelly was going to be an end. I know I'm dragging it out but here it is: Ivy's name was not on the roster.

CHAPTER FOUR

TEAM
me

Erk Russell at Georgia may have coined this.

There were probably 40 of us crowded around the bulletin board looking at that telling piece of paper, but I only glanced at Tree, the Mill, and Jelly. I nodded to them and we went out of the locker room into the parking lot. You may wonder about the fact that Ivy was not there. I certainly did. Jelly said that he had driven in to check and he was supposed to let Ivy know. He did not explain why Ivy had not come with him. I did not ask. To this day I have always wondered if Ivy considered it beneath him to check, or if he was fearful his name might not be there? I never asked him that question the whole time we were friends.

The first thing to consider, however, was Jelly, because he was standing there. So I asked him, 'What about you? Are you going to stay?' He looked truly sorrowful when he replied: 'If Ivy is not on the team, I cannot be either, but I thought you knew that.' He looked as if he were about to cry. Everyone else just watched in pained silence.

Before going on with the story, I think you need to understand that by coming to our school and trying out for football, Jelly and Ivy made a lot of white people angry. But they had also made many in the black community angry with them as well. For certain there was an element of pride that two of theirs would be able break the color barrier. Not only that, they would have a chance to prove to the white community that blacks could compete, even excel, in the white man's chosen game. But those who felt pride were outnumbered by those who thought Ivy and Jelly were deserting them. I'm sure the words Uncle Tom had been whispered behind their backs.

Now Jelly realized they would be going home with their tails between their legs and the white folks had won again. And their community would have more fuel for the fire of their resentment. Those two boys had been under a tremendous amount of pressure from all sides, and maybe they even felt threatened physically, from both sides of the tracks.

Though I couldn't imagine them being intimidated by anyone, we all were just seventeen year old kids, after all. And we were messing around with the established order of the white dominated world. Perhaps we all ought to have felt nervous about this project we had concocted. Some people might express their anger in words, but there was another element, out there, who might be prone to act.

From what I have written about myself in this story, you can probably guess I am not cut from hero's cloth like my dad. To be a hero you have to care not one whit for the opinion of others. I worried about what everybody thought. Sure, I liked the limelight of the Friday night lights, but being Central's QB was my only venture into the spotlight. On most issues, I kept my head well below the radar. I had feelings about the injustice of southern racism, but I was not keen on making those feelings public any more than I already had.

My inclination in this particular case was to cut and run. We had done our best, but it was time to face facts. But suddenly, in the midst of this negativity, I had another epiphany, not Coach Drucker this time. It became crystal clear to me, standing in that school parking lot that I could not stop here. It had been my bright idea to invite Ivy and Jelly to join our team. And so with little risk to me and great peril to them, we had embarked on this integration campaign. I could not cut and run, not now.

With that thought, I crossed my own Rubicon. I looked at Tree and the Mill, took a big gulp of air, and I said, 'This is not right. I cannot just sit back and let Coach keep Ivy off the team. I have got to try to convince him to give Ivy one more chance. Ivy has some problems in the discipline area (talk about understatement), but everybody in that stadium Thursday night, knows he deserves to be on this team. It just isn't right.' The Mill was silent, but Tree asked, 'What are we going to do?' I cannot tell you how that little two letter word 'we' boosted my morale.

I said, 'First, I'm going to talk to dad and then I'm going to face Coach. If he doesn't change his mind and let Ivy play on the team, I will not play this season either.' You could have cut the tension in that parking lot with a knife. Finally, after what seemed like an hour of silence, the Mill said, 'Me too.' I couldn't believe that mean as dirt, red neck had an ounce of compassion in him, but then I remembered he had a serious dislike for Drucker.

He never had gotten over the nickname Lead Butt had given him. It was more than that. I knew that under the tough façade beat a good heart. He really did not like the way white folks treated colored folks in general. The Mill was mean on the football field, but he was a very decent guy in most ways. Jelly said, 'If you really mean to face Coach, I'll hang with you until we see what happens.' Tree smiled and said, 'I'm with you too, Johnny.' With that the four of us were in revolt.

I suppose it is acceptable to rebel against dictatorships. It is certainly part of our heritage in this country. Nevertheless, every boy whoever vowed to quit whatever Ball team unless he got what he wanted, even if what he wanted was fair and right, knew he was committing a serious breach of the unspoken rules, important rules. We three had not been coerced at gunpoint into serving our dictator.

We had accepted rule by dictatorship when we agreed to play football. Football is a dictatorship. In football the head coach rules and everyone, assistant coaches, players, managers obey. There can be no effective team without this agreement. I think that we in that parking lot were able to make the dangerous decision we did, because we all, at the same time, came to the realization that some things are even more important than football.

For a seventeen year old about to enter into probably the last football season of his life, this was an incredible awakening. For my entire life I had never considered there was anything more important than football. I went to church and believed in God, but was pretty sure God liked football, too. I felt like sailors about to declare a mutiny on board ship. What we were about to do could have serious repercussions. The ramifications might bear on us for the rest of our lives, especially if those lives were lived in Central. I am being absolutely serious.

If we hurt our football team for 1966, nobody in Central would ever forget, and I do mean ever. That's what football meant in any small town in the south, then and maybe even now. Taking a deep breath, I told them to meet me in an hour at my granddad's drugstore. Then I remembered Jelly could not come in the drug store, so we agreed to meet outside the store in Tree's car. The hour before we met would give me just enough time to do what I needed.

A high school principal is as busy as a one armed paper hanger the last days before the new school year begins. Of course, the teachers were getting a final day of vacation over the Labor Day weekend but I knew the hero would be at his post. I knocked on his office door and heard, 'Come in. I thought it might be you.' I asked, 'So you already know Ivy did not make the team?' He said, 'No, but I had a good idea that would be the case.' I told him I felt I had to do something. I talked about owing them both. It was my proposal that they leave their school and play for our team.

I rambled, talking about this and that, until he finally cut me short: 'Do you think what happened to Ivy is wrong, or do you just want him on the team, because you know it makes your chances for a state championship better?' I reflected that the honest answer was most likely both. But the most important thing to me was the unfairness of it: 'Dad, you know he is better than lots of guys who made the team. Actually, you know he is better than any of us.' He said, 'As a coach, that would be my assessment.' I went on, 'So then Coach Drucker is actually breaking his own hard and fast rule that the best players make the team.'

He said, 'You could see it that way, yes. But don't forget that greatness includes attitude and Ivy's has not been stellar.' He went on, 'You realize that if you try to put pressure on your coach a lot of your friends and many people in this town will be angry?' I said, 'Yes sir.' 'And,' he said, 'You also understand that if you follow through with your plan, I assume it is to threaten to quit, that you will get no help from me. You will be doing this on your own.'

I had known how that worked ever since I punched the bully in the fourth grade: 'Yes sir.' He smiled, 'Then do what you think is right.' I asked, 'Dad, do you think it's right?' He said, 'It doesn't matter what I think; it's your decision. But I will add one thing; as a coach, I would be worried that Ivy's attitude might poison the rest of the team. There is that, you know?' I said, 'Yes sir; but I don't think he will.' The Hero smiled, 'John, the jury is out on the attitude question. This one is yours to call. Do what you think is right.'

When I met the guys I told them that dad would neither intervene on our behalf nor try to stop us from confronting Coach Drucker. He said it was our decision, an honorable one, but still we could expect no help from him. This would be a battle fought within the confines of the Central football locker room. The Mill who had a sense of the tragic hero, 'us against the world', in him said, 'So fuck the bastard and the horse he rode in on.' I said, 'Thanks for that Mill, but if I am going to see Coach, you are all going with me. I'm not afraid to go by myself, but he needs to see clearly what his decision will mean for the team.'

When we got to his office that day, there were four other starters there. I was flabbergasted: 'What are you guys doing here?' They smiled, 'We are probably here for the same reason as you. So instead of three players, seven of us, all starters, walked into his office. I'm sure he knew something was up. How could he not know with a posse standing in front of his desk? Still he remained calm and

93

casual: 'Well, what brings you boys here at this time of day? Practice is not until three o'clock.' I didn't see any reason to drag this out: 'Coach, we want you to reconsider and put Ivy on the team. You don't have to cut anybody. You can give him #34 and just add one player.'

He stood up this time, and the vein in his temple was pulsing. No doubt he was angry, and from his point of view he had every reason to be angry. It was not for players to decide who got to play. We were usurping his authority. He asked, 'Is this some kind of ultimatum. What will happen if I don't let him on the team?' 'Coach,' I said, 'Please don't get mad, we aren't. We just think Ivy should have one more chance. The scrimmage proved that.'

Coach laughed and said, 'You think so? Listen to me. I let the one colored boy on the team, because he knows his place. He never caused one bit of trouble all summer. I'd have thought one would be enough for you, considering none has ever played for Central before. But no, apparently not. Too bad because the one is all you get. Because the other one is uppity and I will not have that on my team. The answer is no. He will not be on this team.' So I said, 'Then Coach, the seven of us and Jelly, will not be on the team either.' The silence of that moment was deafening and Coach said, 'Then get out of my office. The managers will collect your uniforms. I don't want to see any of you around here again.'

That afternoon I missed my first football practice since before the spring of my eighth grade year. It did not feel good at all. Then came Tuesday and school. That first week of school was a long one for the ousted eight. We ate together in the cafeteria. We spoke to no one other than each other in the halls. Even the teachers ignored us. Football was king at Central high school. Every day I rode home with Tree, straight home. Jelly was in school with us. He'd decided to come on and then wait to see what would happen. I had not seen Ivy since the Thursday night scrimmage. I heard he was back at Birney, but didn't know that for sure.

On Friday, after the sixth period pep rally which we had to attend, except we sat in the stands with the regular students, Andi DeLoach caught my eye and motioned for me to meet her in the hallway behind the gym. Andi was captain of the cheerleaders and would be homecoming queen this year for sure. I had loved that girl since I first saw her in fourth grade. But she was still dating our middle linebacker from last season, even though he was now off playing ball at a small college, trying to get noticed for big college ball. I never had the nerve to tell Andi how I felt in all those years, but if she hadn't figured it out by now, she was either blind or not half as smart as I gave her credit.

In the hallway of the gym she took my hand in hers and said, 'I am so proud of you. Don't give up on your principles. No matter what Coach Drucker does, I'm with you.' I was stunned not just by what she said, but that she had held my hand for a bit more than one second. I blushed purple and said, 'Thanks, Andi.' She said one more thing which really helped. 'A whole bunch more people agree with you than with Coach. They are just afraid to say anything.' After the week the eight of us had spent in solitary, that information was news to me.

That I did not go to the game that night, goes without even saying. None of us went. We eight gathered at my house to listen to the game on the radio. In those days every small town football team in the south had a local radio station carry its games. WLOV, the love rock, carried our games. It was AM radio, lots of static, but even with the static, it was pretty clear that we were missed. Our backups played valiantly, but to no avail.

Camden led by seven at the half. We fumbled the second half kickoff and the rout was on; final score 28-0. We had not lost to Camden in 22 seasons. I thought I heard boos in the background of the radio static, coming from the student section, probably.

Coach Drucker usually held a wrap-up interview after each game and that was the sign off moment. This night, as we waited to hear his comments, he didn't show up for the interview. Apparently, he had a long talk going in the locker room. I wish I could have been a fly on the wall to hear that one. We all had listened to the season opener with mixed emotions.

We couldn't hide the fact that we were elated to have made our point, but every one of us would have given just about anything to be on the field, and we certainly knew we had let our teammates, our friends and our town, down. Nobody said a word as we all headed home. There wasn't really anything else to say. We left with the feeling that if something did not happen really soon, it was going to be a long season.

On Saturdays some of us always met at Granddad's drugstore for breakfast. Tree, the Mill, Ronnie Driscoll, and I were regulars. Some of the men of the town would be there, too. There would be good food and a recap of the game. It was always a fun time, even if we had lost. I didn't go that morning and was told later that only a few people had showed. Either it was because it was the traitor's granddad's store or everyone was just too sick about the loss to come out that morning.

That afternoon I was cutting the grass when dad called me to the phone. It was not hard to identify that raspy voice: 'Little Johnny, get your ass over to my office; we need to talk; don't bother bringing any of your other ex-teammates, just you and me.' Okay, if he wanted to be a tough guy, I could, too: 'I'll be there just as soon as I finish cutting the grass coach.' I took my time. If he wanted to yell and threaten, he could wait.

When I arrived, I expected at least one other coach or his favorite manager to be with him in the office. He liked to have witnesses to particularly virulent conversations like this one promised to be. But it was just him. He got right to the point: 'Tell that colored boy, sorry as his attitude is, he can be on the team. I'm not cutting him any slack; he screws up one time and he's gone. You understand?' I said, 'Yes sir, but coach, I'm not sure he'll agree to play.

Coach said, 'This is my one time offer. Take it or leave it. And if he expects an apology, he can wait 'til Hell freezes over. Tell your other friends to get on out to practice and to and strap their jocks on tight. We lost last night, and I'm holding you and them personally responsible.' I started to ask, 'Did you really lose, Coach,' but prudently decided to leave well enough alone. I left coach's office knowing that only part of the battle was won. The real difficult part of the war for me still lay ahead. I already knew that it would be me and Jelly who talked to Ivy and I knew where we would meet.

Tree and the Mill were okay with me and Jelly meeting Ivy alone. Even though eight of us had stuck our necks out, Ivy would be cooler if just Jelly and me told him the story, probably. I told them that I would make sure Ivy understood who all had gone to bat for him.

As he was walking out the door, the Mill threw back over his shoulder, 'You tell the bastard we did all we are going to do. If he doesn't come back, he can kiss my ass. And he may have to if I ever see him around.' I probably was not going to use this quote in my argument to get Ivy to join the team, but it was the Mill, so I just said, 'Okay Mill, whatever you say.'

When they had left, I told Jelly to get Ivy and meet me at the caddy shack behind the country club. I drove home and told dad what had happened with coach and that we were going to talk with Ivy. He didn't say he was proud of me but he did say that we should make sure Ivy was in school Monday as he had already missed four days of class. The Hero always had his priorities in proper order, school first.

When I got to the caddy shack, all the boys were out on the course, toting bags. It was late, but the course was still full. I asked Beefy if I might use his office for an hour. Of course, he figured out what was going on but he didn't ask for details and he promised to keep the early finishers out of the shack for the time we needed. On his way out he said, 'Good luck.' And he was gone. When Ivy and Jelly came in, I could tell they had been arguing strenuously. Jelly looked at me where Ivy could not see and rolled his eyes.

Ivy looked about like my other granddad's mule when he was awakened early for plowing. The first thing he said to me, 'I ain't playing for that mother fucker, Drucker.' I had to admit that though there was poetry in his comment there was not one shred of reality. The first thing I had to do was establish the facts of life on our team: 'Ivy, Coach Drucker is the coach and that is not going to change. And he is a good coach as far as that goes. However, he is not going to be nice to you, not even once. But if you quit thinking about poor me for just a minute, I'd appreciate it.

Look around at practice and quit thinking about yourself. You will see that Coach is mean and tough to everyone. He is a racist for sure, but who isn't in the town of Central? Coach is an SOB, for sure, and that's exactly why he's a good coach. It's not personal Ivy. It's who he is. Sure he does not like you, but he does not like me either, not really. He does not even like Jelly and everybody likes Jelly.'

'You need the facts. I think they may help you decide what to do. It was not just three rebels who went to bat for you. Eight of us quit the team for you. We all are going back to practice tomorrow. Coach is going to try to kill us, almost. He has lost a good deal of face in front of the entire team. He will have his pound of flesh tomorrow. He will reestablish his authority and it will be over our nearly dead bodies.

And you know what, Ivy? We are going to let him do that, because we cannot win football games if he does not have that authority. It's not about you or me or Jelly. It's about our team. And he's our coach, so live with it.' When I started my talk, Ivy looked at Jelly and the big man nodded as if to say, 'I will be back out there at practice tomorrow.'

I went on, 'Now I want to tell you about the eight guys who stood up for you, Ivy.' You know four of us: Me, Jelly, Tree, and the Mill, three others are preachers' sons. You can understand that they would be concerned about unfairness. But you will never guess the last guy, Ivy, unless I tell you. Do you want to know?' He kind of mumbled, 'I guess.' I said, 'It was Ronnie Driscoll. You don't like him and he does not particularly like you, either, yet. Does it surprise you that Ronnie would be in your corner? When I saw him with the others when we went in to talk to coach, it surprised the heck out of me.

'If you come back, you will eventually take his job. He thought he might be a star this year at running back. Now he probably won't. But some things are more important to good football players, Ivy. With Jelly and you on our team, we have a chance to be great and that is what we all want. In the process we may all get something personal from that, but first we want to be great.

However, one of us will not be as great. A real man gave up his chance for you, Ivy. So you can worry about Coach Drucker, but he is only the coach, not the team. We are and we want you to play for the team. Your teammates want you out there. I got to go.'

With that, I took a deep breath and stood up. I left the room to Jelly and Ivy. I said a prayer as I was leaving, 'Lord, let him have heard me and let him hear Jelly. Amen.' That night I waited near the phone but Jelly didn't call. I didn't hear from him on Sunday either, and I was dying to call him, but we had agreed that I would wait for his call.

On Monday most of the team was hanging out in the breezeway where the school buses unloaded the kids who came from the country. This was our usual preschool hangout, and typically there was plenty of joking. Today it was different. The tension was palpable, like static electricity before a thunderstorm. Finally, Jelly's bus pulled up and he got out, Ivy was right behind him. Nobody said a word but you could hear the cheering anyway.

It was not until twenty years later that I found out what had happened to change Drucker's mind, and it was not my dad who did it. But he knew the story and he finally talked to me about what had happened that Saturday in 1966. It was on his deathbed that he revealed the truth. Of course, he had not intervened with Coach Drucker. I was not surprised. It would have shocked me if dad had intervened. It was the mayor and three of the most important business men in town who intervened.

The gist of the conversation was Drucker promising that no uppity colored boy was going to tell him how to run his team and not the principal's son, either. And then after he finished his tirade, the mayor responded, 'That is your business, Coach, it's your team.

And if your team goes to state this year, and if you win it all, we will buy you a new car and call you the best coach in the state.

On the other hand, if you don't go to state, this will not be your team next year. You will be out. As much as all of us may not like it Coach, times are changing. Colored boys are starting to play at other places in the state and they are making a difference. We want colored boys to play on our team, too. And we have the opportunity to start the ball rolling with two great ones but it's your decision.' And they got up and walked out. That's what happens when racism is trumped by pragmatism. Go team go!

CHAPTER FIVE

You gotta be a football hero
To get along with the beautiful girls.

(Song circa 1950's)

All day Monday as we passed each other in the halls the Fated Eight, would grin and wink. We were no longer the Ousted Eight as Drucker had reinstated us. We had now renamed ourselves. We were fated because we were going to all experience near death at practice, or afterward, at our special practice. We were pretty sure about that. As we passed in the halls we would laugh and say, 'I can't wait until this afternoon.'

In the era in which we played football, our coaches generally used Monday practice to correct the mistakes of the previous game. For example, if a team's tackling had been poor, the players on that team could count on every tackling drill from Eye Opener to Eye Closer during Monday's practice. If it was pass protection, there would be a passing scrimmage with the Statue of Liberty rule in effect. That rule was as follows: 'If your man sacked the QB, you were given the ball, and you stood in the classic passing pose, arm extended, ball in throwing position.

The coach would blow his whistle and every lineman on defense tackled you simultaneously If you moved, you were made to stand in there and do it again! And so on.'

I think all these toughness drills stemmed from Bear Bryant, the supremely successful Alabama coach. Once after a loss as he was being interviewed by the sports writers, he said, 'This loss is on me only. I take complete responsibility.' As we were watching on TV, dad turned to me and said, 'His team is dead Monday. When he takes responsibility for a loss, the Bear means he will coach next week so as to insure it will not happen again. That means his team is dead and they know it.'

Coach Drucker hated to lose and he had been whacked Friday not by an out of town opponent, actually, but by eight of his own players. He hated subversion worse than losing, and the fated eight had totally subverted his authority. Practice for the entire team would be brutal on Monday. What happened to the eight of us after practice was going to be unspeakable.

At lunch that day, there was a free space beside Andi DeLoach. I remembered one of my dad's favorite sports expressions: 'He who hesitates is lost.' So I sat down beside her without my usual inner debate about whether that would be a good thing for me to do or not. I seized the moment. My snap judgment must have been okay because she gave me that knockout Ipana smile and said, 'Little Johnny, I'm so glad everything has worked out.'

I wanted to tell her that it was not going to be worked out until about 8:00 that evening, but she didn't need to hear about my problems. More importantly I needed to work with Andi on the JJ thing. 'Andi, did you hear that Ivy and Jelly gave me a new nickname? They are calling me JJ, since my two names are John Jefferson.' Please take the bait, I was thinking. She did,

'That's very cool. JJ hmm, well I like that. Would it be okay if I started calling you JJ?'

I was beginning to feel like a really smooth operator. If Andi DeLoach started calling me JJ, it would be as if it were mentioned in the morning school announcements on the intercom. By the end of the day every girl in school would be using my new nickname, and the snowball would roll. I said, 'Yeah, I guess Ivy and Jelly wouldn't mind if you joined them.'

But now the slick operator had something much more important to ask Andi, and I knew I was on shaky ground. I was going to ask her for a date. If she said, 'No,' I'd be crushed. If she said, 'Yes,' I'd probably be crushed by Thad the first time he came home from college. 'Andi, since Thad is away, I was wondering if it would be okay for you to go with me to the Sock Hop after the game this Friday?' After every home game we had a dance in the school gym. There wasn't even a pause. She said, 'I'd really like that Li... I mean JJ.' Well, I might be dead in a few hours but I was in heaven already. I don't remember if I ate anything for lunch that day or not.

Life is filled with highs and lows. I'd just had the high of my life. I had a date with Andi DeLoach. But the low was coming like a thunderhead peaking over the horizon. I had a prior date with Lead Butt Drucker and that might mean that I'd never live to have my date with Andi. Lunch was over, school was out, time to batten down the hatches and tighten the jockstrap. When I got to the locker room, the Mill said, 'Well, if it isn't JJ, itsy bitsy JJ. Aren't you a cutie pie? Tell me who you have a date with Friday. No, let me tell you that you are a dead man when Thad comes home.' Crap, that was fast. I said, 'How'd you know?'

The Mill laughed, 'It's all over the school. I think it'll be in the paper tomorrow morning. But don't worry about Thad killing you, because Drucker's about to do that right now for him.' The Mill would crack a joke at the gate of Hell, which is about what he'd done. He absolutely had no fear. When Thad came home, I was going to ask the Mill to be my date for the entire weekend.

We all dressed and jogged over to the practice field. Many coaches would never let a player walk, once on the practice field. Coach Drucker had that rule, of course, but he also had the rule that you never even walked to the field. When we left the locker room, we ran everywhere. After calisthenics, we headed over to the chutes.

The chutes were a metal pipe affair with seven slots, one for each lineman and even for the tight end and split end. Everybody got to share the joy. The chute slots were three feet wide and four feet high; there were metal pipes on both the entrance and exit. A lineman had to fire out under the first bar, stay low enough to get under the second. Then he hit a practice dummy held by a scrub and drove it down an eighteen inch wide board for twelve feet. At that point he'd release and run twenty yards down field, hit another dummy and roll three times, then get up and sprint back to the huddle. Meanwhile the backs ran either power sweep right or power sweep left around the edge of the chute and down field twenty yards where we roll blocked a dummy, also three rolls, and back to the huddle.

Normally, we ran three plays and the second string ran three, and then the third string. Then we did it all over again. But three can be a deceptive number, because the play had to be perfectly executed. A fumble, two rolls instead of three, one poor block, or someone not running full speed, meant that particular repetition didn't count. So we would all run that play again. Three plays could quickly morph into 23. It all depended on Drucker's mood, because there was a mistake of some kind on every play. If Coach were in a mediocre mood, he might overlook a minor miscue. On this day his mood would be most foul.

And so we started. The first string ran about eight reps before Coach was satisfied. Then the second string ran ten. Of course, we eight miscreants had been relegated to third string for our insubordination. After we ran our thirteenth play the Mill threw up but that was not abnormal. He had thrown up at every Monday practice in my memory. After the fourteenth play Tree raised up too soon and stunned himself on the second bar of the chute. 'Dong', it sounded like a bell.

Unfazed, Coach Drucker said, 'Move his ass out of the way, and get in the huddle.' It wasn't a bad concussion, as they go. Tree was back in the huddle after a few more plays, a little woozy, but that's what a concussion will do. He swears to this day he cannot remember the rest of that practice. I think he was lying. You would have had to be dead to not remember that practice. All in all we third stringers ran twenty three chutes. Then all three strings did it again. It was not as bad the second time. Coach was ready to get on to other things.

Next, we ran a drill we all called Double Reverse. But it had nothing to do with the play of that name. The reverse in this drill was the roles of backs and linemen. In the drill the linemen carried the ball and the backs tackled them. The big hogs would start at the fifteen yard line on the hash mark. Then they would run side ways to within a yard or two of the sideline. At that point they would turn and head downhill for the poor little backs who were waiting between two dummies at the three yard line. The dummies were the boundary. The collisions at the three yard line on this drill were legendary. Teeth were lost, noses broken. If the lineman scored, the backs had to go against the next lineman again and again, until they made a stop. If they stopped the lineman, he had to run the ball again.

Ronnie and I were going up against the Mill. He loved this drill. He'd be out there snorting and pawing the ground like a bull, yelling, 'Fresh meat!' As he rounded the corner, picking up speed, the ground started to undulate. I yelled over to Ronnie, 'Take him low,' and then it was too late for conversation. The Mill hit us like a runaway train, and of course he scored. But as Ronnie grabbed his knees, I punched the ball out of his arms at the one. His body had crossed the goal line, but not the ball. We won;. He had to go again. He came at us cursing and swinging and we ran, of course! But success was short lived. Drucker had us run this drill until I was seeing stars.

Finally, we finished all the fundamental drills that Coach Drucker had planned for the day. It was time to scrimmage, but this form of scrimmage was what was called an Inside Drill. This particular version of a scrimmage was conducted on the goal line. It was man on man. Even the sissy wide receivers had to come into the drill and be blocking backs and linebackers. Again we played inside narrow boundaries, two dummies uncomfortably close together. There were nine on defense: five linemen, two linebackers, and two safeties; everybody stood within five yards of the line of scrimmage. On offense we were in the Power I, full backfield.

Coach had sent the managers to the lower end of the practice field, which was always muddy anyway, but today he had them water it with a hose to turn the mud into a shallow lake. It was worse than a mud hole, it was dangerous. On one play, I ended up on the bottom of a pile of bodies. Everybody was so tired that by now, they could hardly get up, and I was buried in the watery mud. I actually thought for a moment that I was going to drown. I literally had to fight with all my might to get my nose and mouth up out of the mud. The last man up was Tree, because the Mill was holding him down, and he got up swinging at anything close to him. My life passed before my eyes. It would not be the last time it happened that day.

After fun in the mud we ran an open scrimmage for an hour. It was not pretty. We were so tired by then it was difficult to remember our plays and assignments. Nobody was able to do anything that pleased Drucker. Our two new players, Ivy and Jelly, had never seen Coach at his finest. Neither had been through anything like this at Birney, I'm sure. At first they were running full speed, but one never ran full speed at one of these corrective practices. To do so would have made survival impossible. We knew it, the coaches knew it. We all did our best, but nobody was fooling anybody. We were conserving energy and our lives. Ivy was first to catch on to the fact that nobody on the field that day cared whether he scored or not. Jelly caught on to, and they got into the survival swing.

After three hours, Coach Drucker blew his whistle. He growled, 'That's it. Hit the showers.' But as we were running off the field, thinking we had survived, he said, 'Except for the dream team. You eight stay here with me. Ivy you stay, too.' When everyone was safely out of earshot but us nine, Drucker said, 'I guess you are starting to think you are in charge of this team. We are about to correct that misperception. This is my team, so you eight get over there. Ivy you are just here to observe.'

We started our private practice with a fun little ditty called saddle up. Each of us had to take one of the others piggy-back and jog them to the other end of the field, 100 yards. Then we switched positions and the other one carried back. We did this six times each, until I was so dizzy and out of breath I could hardly stand. Ivy watched, eyes as big as saucers. Then we crabbed on all fours, the length of the field six times.

Then we drove the seven man sled the length of the field twice. Anyone who has ever driven a seven man sled knows that it moves unevenly. If one side got behind, Drucker would make them push the sled in a circle until it was even again. After twenty yards of this sled work, your thighs were on fire. The last eighty yards were sheer agony. At the end, we were hanging onto the sled dummies and struggling to breath. Snot was pouring out of our noses and a few were crying. Crying in this case is just a bodily reaction. It is as unintentional as a running nose but embarrassing all the same.

That was it. We couldn't have done any more even if Coach had wanted us to. He turned to Ivy and said, 'Did you watch what just happened very carefully? Know what? You are responsible for what just happened.' And he walked off and left us on the ground, gasping like catfish on a dock.

It was 30 minutes before any of us could get off the ground. We still had 500 yards to the locker room and Drucker was standing at the door watching, to make sure we jogged off the practice field. Tree and Jelly were the last ones in, took them an hour. When they came in, each was leaning on one of Ivy's shoulders. He was crying and his tears were intentional.

So that was it. Coach Drucker was again the coach and we were just a few of his dog assed players. And so all was again right with our football world, no really. But, I reflected, we were alive and I had a date Friday night!

And, God bless us, Ivy was on our team. It had not been in vain, any of it.

The next morning at school if you had not been on the field with us the night before, you could not have told that we had walked back from Hell. Teen-aged athletes have incredibly resilient bodies. We recovered quickly from our ordeal. In addition, we had no visible scars. Football coaches were masters at inflicting significant trauma on their charges without leaving a single telltale physical mark. Andi cornered me on the breezeway and asked how bad it had been. I said, 'What? Oh, you mean practice yesterday? It was not as bad as we thought it would be.'

She said, 'No, I'm asking about the extra, special practice for the eight rebels.' I said, 'You aren't supposed to know about that practice. As far as I am concerned, it never happened, so no comment.' She laughed. I added, 'Besides you would have had to be there to understand.' There was really no way I could begin to explain to the uninitiated the pain of a regular football practice, let alone the special one we had that day.

I have taken a stab at it in a few paragraphs, but unless you have been through it, you cannot appreciate the agony of this kind of physical carnage. When asked about the difficulty of football practices, football players mostly say, 'It was okay.' In other words, 'If you have never been there and I have to explain it to you, you would not understand anyway.'

The thing that saves football players from worse travail is the simple expedient of time. There is never enough time for coaches to get everything done in preparation for the next opponent. So as much as they might be inclined to spend a lot of time punishing failure, they still have to plan for the next potential success. Ultimately, practice is to get ready for the game coming up. Therefore, we all knew Tuesday would be a normal practice. Coach Drucker wanted to win and so he had to move on. He had made his point, and now he had to get us ready for Cesar Shoal.

When Jelly and Ivy asked me what practice would be like today, I told them not to worry, all past sin would be forgotten, not forgotten exactly. All would be swept under the rug of necessary preparation. The great goddess of victory, Nike, demanded that bygones be bygones.

We had to worry about the spread formation and an even front defense. Most of the teams we played ran a tight T formation and employed a noseman, which meant an odd defense. Cesar Shoal spread the field and ran a 4-3, which is an even defense. So, have you got all that? Never mind. Just understand this. They were the only team we faced who ran the spread and passed as much as they ran.

As QB I typically threw the ball ten to twelve times a game and sometimes much less. If we were winning by running the ball, Coach might not call for any pass plays at all. Cesar Shoal threw 25 passes per game, every week. This proclivity to pass presented problems for any defense normally geared to stop the run. And their defense was equally difficult to deal with because they had three linebackers instead of two and they loved to stunt. That is just 'footballese' for they moved around a lot. So Coach Drucker had to set aside any further thoughts of retribution. We had lots to do in preparation for these guys. Sorry about all that football jargon. I put it in to show you our team had lots to do. Really, it's not a game for dummies like many people think.

Most uninitiates perceive football to be eleven big dumb guys running into eleven other big dumb guys, doing mayhem on a grand scale, pushing and pulling each other down a field, flying wedges and all that crap. It is havoc and mayhem to a degree, as you can tell from my stories about practice, but it is havoc and mayhem with a plan. There is strategy, much strategy, in fact. I don't want to bore you with esoteric details of game plans, but I do want to give you an outline of a season. If you take some time to read this particular sketch, you will hopefully see there really is a plan to football.

It begins with spring practice. In some ways those twenty practice days of spring are like the NFL combine today. The coaches have just said good-bye to eleven or twelve starters. Spring practice is a search of the talent pool, lots of contact work to see who will hit. But also it's a look at the various skills new players bring to the table.

Spring practice is the time coaches get to know those boys who will be next years team. I don't mean to make it sound easy. It's more brutal than most practice times because injuries don't matter. If a player is hurt, he has four months to recover. During the season time for recovery is more like six days. Spring Practice was my least favorite part of football. The Mill liked it but I've already told you that he's touched in the head.

Summer practice comes next. It lasts most of the month of August. It is a combination of conditioning, individual skill training and team building. A team that cannot perform the individual skills of blocking and tackling will be a poor performer regardless of player talent or sophistication of offense and defense. High school teams do lots of fundamental drills early in summer practice.

As the team gets closer to the first kickoff, however, the punishing individual drills evolve into more hours of team play. The time the entire team spends practicing together is called scrimmaging. There are lots of scrimmages near the end of summer practice. Usually, coaches ease up the last week to allow the players legs to recover their bounce. The scrimmages become full speed with no tackling. Every player knows that these final practices are cake compared to spring practice and early summer practices.

When the season begins in earnest, there is a regular routine: Monday, as previously mentioned, is the day to correct the mistakes of the last game. It is the hardest practice of the week and the longest.

Tuesday is day one of preparation for the next opponent. Usually there is plenty of contact on Tuesday but the session is shorter. On Tuesday every drill and scrimmage focuses on the game plan for the coming opponent.

Wednesday is almost totally devoted to team work, including the special teams. Deep into a season, especially if things are going well, it's not unheard of to go in shells on Wednesday Shells simply means practice in shorts, shoulder pads, and helmets.

Thursday's practice is shorts, Tee shirts, and helmets, no pads at all. It is situation day. The team is on the sideline and the coaches call out all the possible game type situations that occur. We run on the field and line up for punts, kickoffs, returns, goal line play, extra points, etc.

Usually, we are on the field for an hour on Thursday. If football practice is ever fun, then it is fun on Thursday. There is plenty of joking and talk about what we are going to do to our opponent. If things are going well, even the coaches join in the fun. That would be the assistant coaches, not Drucker.

Thursday was the day Drucker posted the starting lineups for the game on Friday, but I always knew from Tuesday's practice what to expect. On this second Tuesday of the young season everybody was back to their starting positions except Jelly. Ivy had never been considered a starter. so he wasn't with the first team, either. The reason Tuesday tells all, is that it would have made no sense to start people in practice on Tuesday who were not going to play Friday night. And by the second set of snaps on Tuesday, Jelly was at tight end. So I knew he would be in the game quickly. Drucker would not have practiced him on Tuesday had he not intended to use him Friday night.

Something noteworthy occurred in the middle of Tuesday's practice. During the scrimmage Ronnie fumbled on a running play. This usually called for some shouting and threats from Coach, but this time he inserted Ivy with the starters and he stayed with us the rest of the scrimmage. I really felt sorry for Ronnie. When something like that happens, the rest of the team moves away from the guilty party, as if not to be tainted by his misfortune. Ronnie stood on the sideline alone for the rest of the scrimmage, a picture of dejection.

In the defensive part of practice our corners and safeties were having a difficult time with the pass routes the scouts were throwing at them. To deal with this, Coach took the drastic step of putting Ivy and me at safety to shore up the problem. Ivy was a good choice but I figured Coach must have been really desperate to use me. I hadn't played defense since my sophomore year and not well then.

Although we only had 34 players on the varsity, about twenty eight of them could really play well, so we two platooned, that means we had different teams for offense and defense. We used this system unless the situation became desperate. I was the quarterback and Coach Drucker's quarterbacks did not play defense. I was comfortable being left out of the defensive plans, so I hoped practice today was not a foreshadowing of things to come.

On offense, Tree and the Mill both missed pass blocks on the same play. Two of our scout team linebackers shot the gaps and clobbered me, before I could even set my feet to pass. In lieu of statue of liberty coach made them hold hands and jog around the practice field together. It was hilarious and effective. I wasn't hit again all day. In the end I felt we were making progress and Cesar Shoal was not the toughest team on our schedule by far. Maybe we'd get our first win Friday.

Wednesday's practice was a surprise. Coach sent us out in shells even though we had not done anything to deserve this kindness. Perhaps he was throwing us a bone in hopeful anticipation of a good game Friday. On Thursday practice was almost festive. We were scampering around the field before practice and even had a touch football game, backs verses linemen. We killed them, of course, because it was two hands touch, my favorite! The starting lineup was posted and as I expected, the fated eight were all playing again. Ivy was not starting, but he was returning punts and kickoffs. It was not much, but one had to start somewhere.

Friday is a special day in high schools around the south. It's the day the cheerleaders take charge. When I opened my locker there was a big bag of candy from my secret cheerleader. I had been getting these every game day for four years, but it was nice to know who my secret cheerleader was to be this year. There was no name but I recognized the handwriting and all the i's were dotted with little hearts.

Nice touch! The quarterback got the cheerleader captain for his secret admirer. I usually gave most of the candy in my bag away but I liked the Snickers bars. There was also a note: 'Go JJ, Swamp the Shoal.' The metaphor was a bit odd, since a shoal is already filled with water, but it's the thought that counts, I suppose.

At lunch the Pep band was playing in the corner of the cafeteria and the central table was reserved for the team. We each got a small steak, baked potato and salad. Given the gruel usually served in our slop house, this was uptown fare. The rest of the students ate the usual: two over cooked vegetables and mystery meat, sloshed down with warm milk. At seventh period, the entire school filed into the gymnasium. The team was already there, because we all had seventh period PE, a perk of football players. We never actually did PE. It was just a time to relax before practice.

At the Pep Rally the 34 team members sat together on the first two rows of the left side bleachers and the students were arranged around the gym by their class: freshman, sophomore, junior, and senior. There was a cheering contest, which the freshman usually won, because theirs was the largest class and they were just happy to be in high school.

Then the pep band played and the cheerleaders did a skit about the game and led cheers to get us fired up. We sat with our game faces on (a game face is no smiling or laughing, deadpan as they say). Our coaches sat directly opposite us watching while we acted as if we could not hear the shouts and cheers. I know, it sounds lame but that is how we did it in those days.

When the rally ended, all the students went home, and the team started our pregame meetings. There was a break from offensive and defensive meetings for a light supper and then everyone went to the training room to be taped. The principal taping was ankles and the reason for ankle taping was simple. Ankle sprains were always a danger and if severe, could nag a player throughout an entire season.

So if you sprained an ankle in the game and had not come to the training room to be taped, you'd be punished as soon as you could run again. During the week we wore high top football cleats, so we did not tape, but we wore low cuts for games and the tape was protection for exposed ankles. The team doctor was also available to check out injuries from the week before and he would give painkilling shots to those who needed one.

I probably shouldn't tell this part, but players with nagging injuries: shoulders, ankles, hips, etc, could get a painkiller injected just prior to the game. The Tree usually had his knee drained on Friday as well. He had a chronic problem that caused the knee to gradually swell during the week. I think there must have been some loose cartilage in there floating around. We never knew for sure. There were no MRI's then and X-Rays were often inconclusive. Surgery would mean the end of Tree's senior season. Better to drain it weekly and take the pain killers.

Sometimes, Tree's knee would lock during a game, and he'd get one of us to slam it open, no, really. That knee slam usually got the floating cartilage loose, and the knee moving again. I probably shouldn't be telling this, either. None of it was legal, but it was a long time ago and the team doctor is dead, so...

As you have walked with me through a Friday in preparation for the football game, how could you not think football players were the most pampered boys in their high school? But we were also the most brutalized. We were a study in contrast. Our peers loved us, our coaches tried to pulverize us. This bipolarity created both an attitude of entitlement and servitude.

But in either case there could be no doubt that we seventeen years old boy/men carried the banner for our community. This meant that the adults in our town, especially the men, valued us very highly for the little we did on Friday nights. All this attention, the candy, the steaks, the cheering was new for Ivy and Jelly. Their side of the tracks did not value the sport as did the white side. While all this silliness was going on, their eyes were often big as saucers. But they learned quickly not to ask questions and soon they joined the insanity and came to take for granted the adulation just as the rest of us did.

As much as they had learned by this time, Jelly and Ivy still had a great deal more to learn about Soda Cracker football as they jokingly called it. I still remember the chill that ran down my spine that first game night in the locker room. Jelly and Ivy were laughing loudly and joking about the havoc they were about to wreak on Cesar Shoals. They even had a transistor radio playing. With my spine tingling, I ran to the corner where they were dressing: 'Hey guys, shut up and turn off the radio.' They looked as if I had lost my mind. This was how they got mentally prepared to play ball.

But in the white boy's locker room, I suppose you could say the southern white coach's locker room, nobody spoke a word and few dared crack a smile. There were only the sounds of tape being torn as ankles were wrapped and the incense of analgesic balm. In white boy football you were theoretically not ready to play unless you had your game face on. Behind that somber façade you could be thinking about going parking with your girl after the dance.

So long as your game face was suitably on, no coach cared to find out what was going on in your pea brain. That night, when I finally convinced them to turn off the radio, Ivy sneered, 'That may be what you white boys do, but it ain't the way we do it.' I said, 'Well, you are in Rome now, so best act like a Roman.' Ivy had no idea what I meant, but Jelly did and he said, 'Cool it, Ivy; we got to get serious like the rest of the team.' Ivy chuckled, 'What's up Jelly, you getting' white on me or something.' Jelly said, 'No I ain't getting' white but I do want to play with these crackers tonight.'

When our quiet time was over, we headed out to warm up. It was exactly 7:15, 45 minutes and no seconds before the kickoff. Anyone who needed could set his watch by Drucker's warm up schedule. And why we called it warming up, I don't know. After his regimen of drills, it took the team the last ten minutes before kickoff to recover enough of their wind in order to play the game. We did everything full speed in warmups, including tackling. It was nutty, but it was how we did it.

Back in the dressing room, among his gasping players, Drucker called out the starting lineup, as if anyone had forgotten since he posted it on Thursday. This time, however, there was a change, first time ever. Ivy was to be the starting safety on defense. I heard him muttering, 'Don't give no shit about defense.' But I also heard, 'Shut up man, and just be glad you getting a chance to play,' and I thought, 'Maybe Jelly is getting white.'

So then we went out the door of our locker room and took that final walk (and it's the only time we did, walk) out of the locker room and down the path to our field. The name of our field was Banks Field after the most successful coach we ever had, our only Coach of the Year. It was the only award my dad didn't win. Coach Banks coached my dad when the team won state. I guess the Hero helped Coach Banks win the award even though he didn't win it himself. The stadium, however, was Henley Stadium, named after a man who never played a down of football in his life. He owned the bank in Central and his money paid for the stands. So if you want a stadium named for you you can either play or you can pay.

When we got to the gate outside the track, I could see our cheerleaders standing in the shadow of our goal post holding up a huge, two-story, run through banner. It was so big that the two smallest cheerleaders were standing on the shoulders of the two largest ones to keep it from toppling over onto the field. The cheerleaders spent all Thursday night painting it and it lasted two seconds. I think they liked to get out of the house and stay up half the night talking, so the run through banner kept getting bigger and bigger. The team captains for the week had the honor of leading us through the banner and bursting it into shreds.

The Mill was standing beside me and said out of the corner of his mouth, 'I'm gonna bust that fucker myself.' Of course we weren't captains this week, since we didn't play last week. On our team players were chosen to be captain based on the previous week's performance. I said in alarm, 'You can't Mill. Coach'll kill you. You know it's the captains who get to do it.' The Mill sneered, 'None of them pussies deserve to do it. They played like shit, all of em.' But I know he's joking about a banner bust. After last Monday, I am dead certain he isn't about to piss Drucker off again, at least not this soon.

Two quick funnies about banner bustin,' that happened to our team. Run through banners started during our high school era, and of course they originated with the city teams, not us country bumpkins. When we visited Midlands our junior year and our cheerleaders saw their big beautiful sign, it would not do but we had to have one the very next week. Nobody could tell them how to construct a banner like that, except maybe the Midlands cheerleaders, and they weren't about to look like rubes by asking the city slickers from Midlands how to do it.

I remember we had an elaborate planning meeting with Drucker, my dad, and everybody from the mayor down giving input but none of them knew how to make one either. That first banner night our cheerleaders were so excited they were about to wet their pants for us to run through it. Ronnie and Tree were captains that fateful night.

When they hit the run through at full speed, it didn't break. Ronnie and Tree looked like one of those test cars, slamming into a concrete wall. They bounced back ten feet and the banner started to wobble back and forth until it finally fell in a heap of paper on top of the cheerleaders and our captains. It was the funniest thing I'd ever seen and yet not a soul laughed. Coach Drucker would have killed us. What a relief. I had almost been captain that night.

Next week we did call the Midlands cheerleader advisor and she told us that a banner with paper that thick needed to have several slits through the middle in long lines in order to shred properly. Otherwise, a car could not have cracked that thing. Nobody told us country bumpkins that. I could hear them laughing all the way to Midlands high.

One other funny story: one night we were playing an away game. The visiting team never had a run through. It would have been too difficult to transport. But our opponents had quite a large one set up. As we were running on the field first, the Mill pealed off and ran through the Parnassus banner, bursting it into a million shreds. The crowd went nuts but the Mill acted as if nothing untoward had happened. I asked him why he did it after the game. He said, 'None of them pussies could have broke it anyway.' Probably, he was right. We beat them four touchdowns that night.

We ran through our banner without incident and over to our sidelines. The band was playing the Central fight song, the student section was wild as usual, alcohol probably had something to do with that, and the parents section was even more noisy and full than usual. Jelly and Ivy probably had a little something to do with that.

There was even a contingent of black folks standing between the track and the end zone. There were at least six thousand people, counting about a thousand from Cesar Shoals, who traveled well. An interesting fact, the last census numbered the town of Central at five thousand inhabitants. I told you everybody came to our games.

The place was lively, but then silent for the only time all night as one of our local preachers opened with prayer. After that we took off our helmets for the only time all night as the band played the Star Spangled Banner. Then we knelt for the Lord's Prayer: 'Our Father... and the power and the glory forever, Amen.' After 'Amen', the Mill shot up like a sky rocket and shouted, 'Now, let's kill the mother fuckers!' Yes siree, Another night of football in Dixie: God's country, God's game and we all fight like Hell!

(So now, for all my church members and church members everywhere. There's going to be bad language in this book, you already noticed? I know I'm a preacher, but I grew up in a locker room from the time I could walk. A locker room is not a sanctuary and the fellas in there are not choirboys. I could have left all the swear words out, but it would not have seemed true to me. The worst offender was the Mill, and yet he probably had the best heart of us all. The cover of a book is not the story, the language a boy may use, is not necessarily the boy. If the language offends, sorry. Read some other book.)

We won the toss, so our captains proved to be good for something in spite of Mill's opinion of them! Our kick return team, unlike most of our opponents, sometimes featured our starting linemen. Tree and the Mill were next to our center, our guards stood outside them on the front five. The theory was our guards, who pulled a lot could run further. What we did was crisscross the four lineman to develop blocking angles and if you timed it right, the cover guys never saw the blocks coming. Tree and the Mill were pretty good at this; our center doubled with Mill and Tree took his guy alone. We left the kicker for our three man wedge. The return man, Ivy in this case, was supposed to read the three blocks of our wedge.

But tonight it did not work quite as drawn up on the board. Ivy took the opening kickoff out ran the wedge, made the kicker miss him and then ran 92 yards for a touchdown right through the heart of their team. I thought sadly, 'Probably the last one of those we will see all year. When this film circulates to all our opponents, Ivy will never have the ball kicked to him again.' But it was a good start for us and set the tone for the entire game.

I went 9/10 passing, two were touchdowns and ran for forty yards on six carries. I had never had a performance like that. Of course, the yardage was made running behind the Mill and Jelly and the TD passes were to Jelly and Ivy. The one to Jelly was what we called 32-Slip (Don't fret the terminology, just footballese to say, Jelly sneaked out and I threw him a short pass.) It looked like the fullback got the ball but it was a fake. If it was a good fake, the linebacker froze and the tight end would be open on a little slip route. It looked as if he were blocking the defensive end and then he just slipped past him. The passing window was minuscule, but if I timed it right Jelly was good for ten yards until the safety could get him.

The timing was perfect and when the safety came over and up to hit Jelly, it looked like another of those car commercials where an unfortunate test Volvo hit one of those brick walls and the manikins shatter into small pieces. This time it was a real person and Jelly just splattered him around the landscape and out ran the corner to the end zone, 55 yards. The end of that touchdown looked like a dog chasing a horse and the little safety never got close. Ivy's catch came on an out and up that was supposed to be only an out. (Again footballese. An out is a short pass and an out and up is a long pass. The real point is, Drucker wanted his play called, not mine and Ivy's)

Coach Drucker called the plays from the sideline and he wanted an out, but it was ten seconds to half. Ivy said, 'JJ, you throw whatever you want to, but I'm running an out and up.' I blanched, 'No, Ivy, you can't do that. Coach wants the out. He'll kill me if I call a play other than the one he signaled.' Ivy said, 'Tell him you misread the signal. Tell him anything you want to. I'm going deep.'

Of course the defensive back wasn't fooled. With ten seconds in the half, he was not about to give up a deep pass. I threw the ball as high and deep as I possibly could and Ivy just went up and took the ball away. The corner gave it his best, but he fell in the attempt and Ivy ran the final sixty yards uncontested. To his credit he ran all out, all the way to the end zone this time. It was the first time I had thrown a touchdown and left the field feeling guilty. I'd never disobeyed the coach; well just that one other time.

It was 28-0 at the half. Coach played the starters one series in the second half and then put in the second team. Ivy scored three touchdowns and we beat Cesar Shoals 49-14. So now the entire town of Central and a thousand other people had seen the team we truly had for 1966. I can tell you nobody went home disappointed that night. There were chants in the student section at the end of the game: 'State, State, State.'

In the locker room Drucker finally got around to asking me about the last play of the first half: 'Sorry coach, I guess I just misread your signal.' He looked at me with his 'don't bullshit me' look, but let it pass. When he addressed the team, he said, 'You can put that crap about the playoffs out of your head. If you commit that many turn overs in the games down the road, you won't be going anywhere but home in November. I'm sure every boy in the room was thinking like me: 'Gee thanks, Coach. Good game to you, too!'

Now, let's dance, except I don't. I am the worst dancer I know. Ivy and Jelly can dance. I saw them playing around at the caddy shack when certain songs came on the radio. Believe it or not the Mill is a good dancer, too. I think it's because he doesn't care what anybody else thinks about him. Whenever I tried to dance, I could see myself through the eyes of everyone else in the gym. What I saw was all of them laughing, at me!

I knew Andi liked to dance. And I knew that girl could dance. I had watched her too many times to mention. I had gotten to watch her dance so often, because she had never danced with me. I was excited to be going to the dance with the best looking girl in school and shaking in my boots at the same time.

So out the door of the locker room we heroes went, and all the steady girls and the dates for the evening were waiting. There were hugs and even a few kisses, and then there were the awkward exchanges from the other players

125

like me, who just had a date, maybe even a first date. Not knowing the protocol, I reached out my hand as if to shake hers?

I knew it was lame but it was all I could think to do on the spur of the moment. Andi saved my day, of course. She rushed right by my outstretched hand and gave me a big hug and peck on the cheek. I must have turned beet red, because I could feel the heat from my head to my toes. 'Great game, JJ,' she said so everybody could hear. 'It was your best ever.'

I was on at least cloud ten, the one above nine. It was a real compliment because unlike most of the girls, Andi knew football. Her dad, like mine, played in college, and she enjoyed watching games on TV with him. He even taught her how to throw a pass so she passed like a boy, unlike others who shall remain unnamed. Then she really showed off her football knowledge: 'You timed the pass to Jelly perfectly on that touchdown.' It was a really nice thing to say because we both know it was Jelly who did the heavy lifting. But thanks Andi for not mentioning the last part. As we made the short walk from locker room to gym, my whole world had changed.

And the gym had changed as well, from sweat and bouncing balls to pastels and party lights and even a band, not a great band, but a real live band, not that DJ stuff they do now. I was trying to think how to get out of dancing, at least for the time being, when Andi said, 'JJ, I bet you are tired. Why don't we sit for a while and just talk?' Now here was a woman who understood me. I said, 'Thanks, and then we can dance some,' and I meant to try, just not yet.

I looked for Jelly and Ivy and they were there, but over in the corner with the few colored students at our school. Nobody was bothering them. Nobody was even acting as if they were in the gym. This was before mandated consolidation of schools, by four years. Integration had begun but only a trickle. There were about 40 colored kids in our high school of the 400 students, one in ten. There was no overt animosity between students. There were too few colored kids for the white kids to feel threatened. The animosity would come in four years.

Right now, there was just mutual ignore-ance. We were in one area of the gym and they were off by themselves in another area. This had never been a problem for me before, but now I had two friends, well not exactly friends yet, but 'getting to be' friends standing over there. We had never been to each others' houses. I forgot, they did come to mine once. I didn't even know where they lived.

But we had worked together and now we were teammates. I didn't feel that I could play ball with them and then act as if they didn't exist after the game. I took the plunge: 'Andi, if you don't mind, I'd like to go over there and talk to Jelly and Ivy. I haven't had a chance to tell them what good games they played yet. Would you excuse me for a minute?' Andi laughed, 'No JJ. I won't excuse you. If you are going over to talk with them, I'm coming, too.' And so the quarterback and the head cheerleader went over to the nonexistent people in the corner. It's not the same as when I tried to dance, but at that moment I was sure everyone in the gym, including the teachers, were looking directly at the two of us. This time it was not my imagination.

And then I danced but not with Andi first. First, that idiot Mill grabbed me and started to jitterbug around the floor, holding my hand. Since it was the Mill, I danced with him. Then Jelly and Ivy joined us, and that's okay in our world because no white girls were involved in the dancing.

127

Then Tree and Ronnie came over, and pretty soon the whole team was dancing at half court. You know what? I was dancing pretty good with the Mill and the boys. When it ended we all got our dates and danced again. I was looser than usual, with Andi it was easy. She almost led me, and I was so busy looking at her, I could not think of anyone looking at me. So it went well.

When I took her home and walked her to the door, again, I was at a loss. I figured a hug and a peck on the cheek were okay, since she'd done that to me already. As I went to kiss her cheek, she turned her head and kissed me on the lips. She said, 'You probably don't know, but I've been waiting a long time to do that.' Well, sister, guess what? Me, too!

I asked, 'What about Thad?' She said, 'Don't spoil the moment, JJ. I haven't told anyone yet, so you are the first. Thad and I broke up the day he left for school. So that is taken care of. He will be mad when he gets home, but let's cross that bridge when we get to it.' I was pretty sure that bridge was out there in my future. And pretty sure I'd be walking across it all by myself. But after tonight I was ready, at least, to give it a shot, I think.

CHAPTER SIX

Show me a good loser,
and I'll show you a loser.

Lead Butt Drucker (et, al)

Monday is the first day of most people's week. When I was in high school, my week, at least in the fall, began Saturday. That was because my week ended in the wee hours of the morning after our Friday night game. I'd come home after my date and I'd still be so high on adrenaline from the game that I could not sleep. My mother, ever ready to help her baby boy, stepped in to my aid at that point. She would sit in my room with me and listen patiently as I rehashed every single play of the game, the highs but also every low.

I would finish this monologue about six o'clock on Saturday morning. She would go on off to bed, joining the hero who'd been asleep since thirty minutes after the game. He was not prone to recapitulation especially concerning my exploits. Trying not to wake my sister, Mandi, in the next room. I would dress and go to granddad's drugstore for our Saturday morning ritual.

Before he opened for business, he'd let me in and we would have a cup of coffee together. Then he would go through his routine of opening the drug store. While he did that I'd read the morning sports page about our game and others around the state. When the store opened at eight, Tree and Ronnie would already be waiting to come in. The Mill usually arrived about 8:30 still groggy from sleep.

We'd all four have breakfast at the short order counter as the good citizens of our town started to drift in to take their seats in the booths behind us. All morning we would talk about the game, and as it drew near lunch time a few of us would go to my house to watch the college game that was on TV that day. This was way pre ESPN so there was only one or, at most, two games on television any given Saturday. Didn't matter who was playing, we'd watch it.

Our Saturday was a slice of heaven. It was the only day of the week that there was no school, no football practice, and absolutely, positively, no Drucker. Since we watched film on Sunday and practiced and played Monday through Friday, Coach Drucker was a near permanent fixture in our lives. He even attended the Presbyterian church where my family went, one advantage to being Baptist, I suppose. But he did not invade our sacred Saturday time. After four hours of watching football and lazing on the couch came Saturday night which was for dating. All in all, it was a grand day to be alive, especially if we had won on Friday night.

On this particular Saturday Andi and some of the other cheerleaders stopped by the drug store before lunch. They were going swimming out at her folks' farm and invited us to join them. We had planned to watch the 4:00 game that day, an ACC/SEC rivalry game, so swimming was a perfect prelude. Honestly, even if they had been planning to swim at 4:00, I'd have forgone the game. How often do you get to see Andi DeLoach in a two piece bathing suit?

Before we left we decided to call Jelly and see if he wanted to go with us. Hindsight is 20/20 and if I'd been thinking, I'd probably not have called him. After some hesitation, Jelly said he'd meet us on the highway going out to Andi's farm, still no invitation to come by his house and pick him up. As we were pulling up to the lake, Jelly dropped a bomb on us, told us he did not know how to swim. Well, I sort of had a suspicion that was the case. It was part of the reason I had invited him. I had been a swimming instructor at my camp for three years so I offered to give him some pointers. The girls were already on the floating dock in the middle of the lake, but I had invited Jelly to swim with us, so I had to take care of him first.

While we were still in my dad's car, Jelly said, 'JJ, dem be white girls out on that dock.' Whenever he was nervous, Jelly reverted to colored, street English. As his words sunk in, I had a feeling that we were close to making a huge mistake. Thank goodness Jelly was thinking, because I was not. Jelly said, 'Mebbe it be mo bettah if you just drive up to the house over der and park under dat shade tree. Think I'll take me a nap.' And so I did, as the wave of nausea that had crept over me began to subside. Jelly's caution prevented what would have been a catastrophic mistake.

It was 1966 in the south. The last colored boy had been lynched in our county by the KKK shortly before I was born, twenty-five years ago. I knew as well as anybody that colored boys simply did not dance, talk, or swim with white girls. In fact, they had better not be seen to smile at one. We left Jelly in the car and swam out to the dock. When I got her where no one else could overhear, I told Andi what was going on. She said she'd think of a way to get the other girls and boys to leave early. I swam over to the bank of the lake and acted if I were leaving. And true to her word, before too long, the girls and boys said their goodbyes, leaving Andi alone on the dock. And so I went to get Jelly.

Swimming was as simple to learn as anything I knew of, unless you are 230 pounds and deathly afraid of the water. But I was determined to teach him and Jelly was willing. We started out by splashing and playing around in the shallow water. Then I worked on getting Jelly to put his head under water and blow bubbles. A five-year-old can do this in two tries. It took Jelly about ten minutes to completely immerse his head.

On those first aborted attempts he barely got his face wet before he came up rubbing his eyes and nose as if he were drowning. When he finally submerged his whole head, it was for about two seconds. Then he shot up spouting water out of his nose like a whale and the water in his hair beaded up on the follicles. I'd never seen hair do that before.

When the coast was completely clear, Andi swam over to the shallow water where we were practicing. I was okay with her being at the lesson. I knew she would not tell anyone about it. She knew the potential repercussions if anyone heard she had been swimming with Jelly. She would never do anything to get him in trouble. Also, her dad was an okay guy. He knew if she was with me nothing bad would ever happen.

Still, she didn't actually get in the water but she offered much encouragement from the bank. Finally, I got Jelly floating on his back. I thought that was enough for one lesson. Jelly looked as tired as he had last Monday at Drucker's special workout. 'Next week we will work on kicking and going forward like a torpedo,' I said. He looked decidedly doubtful, but I could tell he really wanted to learn. As we were getting ready to leave, Andi said, 'Some of us are going to the drive in tonight. Would you like to come?' Had I died? I was sure I was at heaven's door. I said, 'Sure, can Tree and Ronnie come, too?' It wasn't a date, but it was close enough for government work.

Dating in the south of those days was a ritualized and serious activity. The boy asked the girl out. He might do so in the school hall during a break, something like that, face to face. Usually however, a date was arranged by phone. If it were a first date, the dad met you at the door. You were given the once over and then the curfew time. About then the girl came in the room with her mom. You both said goodbye to her mom and dad and beat a hasty retreat to the car.

But since Andi had invited me to go with her friends, it meant that it was not a formal date. In those days girls did not ask guys out, ever. But if a girl had friends and if she invited you and you included a few of your friends, the ritual was circumvented.

There were other perks to non dates. On dates the boy drove, in my case my mom's station wagon would have to be used. I didn't have a car. Most of my friends did, but the Hero didn't believe in a free ride. Since it was not a date, Mandi would be able to drive her car. That would be much more fun, because she had a 1962 Chevrolet Impala SS convertible. As I look back that car now seems as big as a small motor home. We could have filled the inside with water and had a swim lesson with Jelly.

In 1966 there were even bigger cars, like Buicks and Cadillacs, but that Impala could carry eight people, at least, ten at a pinch. With the three of us and five girls, it would be a tight fit but the drive in movie theater was only twenty miles away in the next town. So we all piled in, making sure to sit next to a girl. The last thing I wanted was Tree's thigh pushing into mine all the way to the drive in. Andi was driving and I didn't want to make it too obvious so I sat in the back between Sally Jamison and Rhonda Hadley. They were cheerleaders and I had been on a date with both of them so we were all friends. They seemed to be okay with being squashed between me and the Tree.

The drive in was a notorious, heavenly place where steady couples went to do some serious petting and other stuff I had only heard of or talked about with my friends. Also, it was a place to drink if you could find an older person to buy beer for you. I'd never had a beer in my life but most of my friends had. They told me that's what you had to do at the drive in if you had the money and if someone looked old enough to buy the beer. So it was a potential den of iniquity on many counts.

On the other hand, the drive in could also be just a place to have great fun if you went with a group of friends. Usually we brought lawn chairs and sat outside the car, careful to remember bug spray as the drive in lights attracted clouds of mosquitoes.

When we got to the road turning into the drive in Andi asked, 'How much money do we have,' which meant how much money do you boys have? Even on a non-date in 1966 girls did not pay. Between us we had a grand total of six dollars. Andi said, 'Okay, four of you get in the trunk. That way we have two dollars left for cokes.' It was one dollar for admission and cokes were twenty five cents. Tree, Ronnie, and two of the girls got in the trunk. You could just about stand up and dance in the trunk of a '62 Impala so it wasn't too bad for them.

When we got to the ticket booth the girl looked at us suspiciously as if to say, 'One guy and three girls? You are either a great stud or something is wrong with this picture.' In spite of her skepticism she took the four dollars and in we went. We pulled over to the darkest part of the drive in lot and they hopped out of the trunk. Then we drove back to the open seating section near the concession stand and got out our chairs. Ronnie and I went to get the drinks.

Somehow I ended up sitting next to Andi with the other girls spreading out around Tree and Ronnie. I think everybody was beginning to figure out what was happening with Andi and me except me, of course. I still had no clue what were her intentions. But even with my naïveté on Monday it'd be all over school that Andi DeLoach and JJ Savage had been to the drive in on their second date or non date. And soon the news would make its way down to the coast to the ears of a certain crazed linebacker. Oh well, 'In for a penny, in for a pound,' as we like to say in jolly ole England.

About half way through the movie, I reached over and took her hand. It must have been temporary insanity. My heart which had relocated itself somewhere in my larynx, was racing ninety miles per hour. Would she take it? Would she move away? She took my hand and held it for the rest of the movie. 'Okay, so what?' you are thinking. Let me tell you, in 1966 where I lived hand holding was a big deal. You know to this day I cannot remember the movie we saw that night, but that's not why we went to the drive in picture show anyway.

A southern Sunday morning meant two things only: Sunday school and church. Though my friends and I went to different churches on Sunday, we all went. In those days the choices were much more limited than today: Baptist, Methodist, Presbyterian, Episcopal, and Catholic in order of size and attendance. Most of my friends, of course, were Baptist or Methodist.

135

I was a black sheep Presbyterian. Ronnie and Rhonda were the only ones of my immediate group who came to church with me. It was boring as heck, but it was only two hours and kept the folks happy. We Presbyterians were number three in size, but probably number one in per capita income. Well no, the tiny Episcopal Church had the richest members of all.

The oddest thing, you'd never believe me but the mighty Mill was Catholic. Catholics were such a rare breed in the south of those days that the nearest Catholic church was ten miles away. Yes siree, the Mill was a mackerel snapper, but no-one ever called him that to his face, at least not more than once.

The most liberal church in town was probably a toss up between us and the Episcopalians. That was why it was a total mystery to me that Lead Butt Drucker was Presbyterian. He was the most conservative red neck I knew, and yet he taught adult Sunday school for the Presbyterians, go figure. I saw him every Sunday of my life, and every other day of my life except Saturday, yet he never spoke to me in passing at church.

I really didn't care much for church or Sunday school, but attendance was not an option. My parents were Christian and they knew what needed to be done to avoid the hot breath of Hell. It was to have them, my sister, and me in church every Sunday. Most people thought I was a nice guy and I liked being thought of in that way so I kept my feelings about church attendance to myself. I was squarely on the fence when it came to religion. I'd have enjoyed the extra sleep on Sunday, but my dad, was all in. He was an elder and also taught Sunday school and mom played piano in church. Sunday mornings were just a part of life for us in those days, a necessary thing to be tolerated.

If Sunday mornings were a boring ordeal to be endured, Sunday afternoons were another, higher level of pain altogether. They were also to be endured. They could be painful, but one thing for sure, they were seldom boring. At three o'clock the team gathered in the field house to watch game films from the previous Friday. Another way to put it would be to say we lambs gathered for the slaughter. We sat and watched the 16 millimeter horror show in which we had starred.

The show was directed by Count Druckula. Lots of blood was lost. Film sessions for players were no win. If you won the game, Drucker raised Hell with the style in which you had won. If you lost, he raised more Hell because you had no style at all. He had never handed out a compliment to anyone in the four years I had sat in the darkened locker room and flinched through the show.

Every film was a sequel. It was Stupid Football I, II, III, etc, down to Stupid Football X. The vituperation never ceased. The only variation was the recipient. The start of that day's film critique looked like it was going to be our guards who were the recipients. They were both juniors and thus the expected targets. Coach didn't rag on the seniors quite as much as the underclassmen.

This day it was Tommy Jones' moment to shine. The spotlight was on him. Drucker did not like a single block he attempted all night. At one point came Jones' piece de resistance. It didn't often happen but poor Jonesy threw a genuine, honest to God, lookout block. That's the block where the lineman completely whiffs his defender. And to prepare his running back for the coming annihilation all he can do is turn his head from his spot on the ground and shout, 'Look out!' to the hapless back.

After this inexcusable mistake Drucker finally exploded, 'Jones, do you know what you are? You are bird shit. All you do is hit and splatter.' The entire room, except for Jones, fell out of their chairs laughing. We laughed to ease the tension and we laughed in relief that it was Jonesy and not us who came in for Drucker's attention.

I finally received my recognition which I had known was inevitable. It was on the TD pass to Ivy. 'Little Johnny, (I was resigned to the fact he would never call me by my new nick name. The old one was too degrading for him to drop.) show me the hand signal for an out route.' All plays were relayed to me by Coach from the sideline. He called all plays, not me. It was an elaborate system but after three years, it was engraved on my heart. And here's the important thing to remember. His call was the only call. There were no audible-options.

When I made the proper hand motion, he then asked, 'What is the signal for the out and up?' And I showed him that one, also. He then said, 'Why would I ever call for an out and up from a quarterback who throws like his sister?' 'Thanks coach, and you have a blessed and holy Sunday, too, you jerk.' Never mind the quotes. This was only what I was thinking. My mouth was saying, 'Yes sir.'

During the course of that year, every player would come in for their share of the rag from Drucker, whose highest praise came when Tree threw the most awesome pancake block I'd ever seen. He turned off the film projector and said, 'Tree, shit, that was not half bad.' Every player got the rag except Ivy and Jelly. Not once did Drucker say a word in films or on the field in criticism of either of them. It's funny how a redneck like him, could not actually say a bad thing to the source of his prejudice publicly. As to what he said in private, I was not privy but I imagine it was a different matter altogether.

As horrible as Drucker could make the game seem in a film session, the big eye in the sky as we called the film, the 'big eye did not lie'. We made mistakes in that game, for sure. Every team makes a lot of them early in the season. But even with the errors, it was apparent we were going to be the best Central team since the days of everybody's Hero.

And, as for me personally, I realized that my statistics were going to be significantly inflated in my final season. As poorly as I threw the ball, I had too much talent at my disposal to fail. Basically, I could throw the ball down the field and one of my teammates would be there to catch it. Our new tight end and that other guy, who could play any position on the field, were going to be a huge asset to Central football and its QB.

I felt sorry for Ronnie. He was a good friend, and I knew that pretty soon he'd be replaced at running back by Ivy. But that is football. Coaches play the best people whether they like them or not. Eventually the cream rises to the top. I suspected the change would be made this Friday or if not then, definitely by the next. We had no hope of beating Midlands without Ivy running the ball and Jelly catching passes. Even though Drucker would not openly admit it, with them playing for Central there was a chance a complete asshole would be Coach of the Year in 1966.

When Monday morning arrived, the pending game with North Fork was on everyone's mind. They were sort of a wild card on our schedule. We were not sure what to expect. They were a new city school and had only played football for the first time last season. We beat them easily in that game last year but most of their players were only sophomores. This year they had a junior class but no seniors. That would make them better but probably not up to our level yet.

Still, they were a city school with plenty of talent, including a flashy running back of their own. We were not going to overlook them. Drucker, like every good coach, would remind us all week: 'Play 'em one game at a time.' North Fork, therefore, was on every football player's mind. But they were not the topic of conversation in the school halls that week.

The hot topic had to do with the pending engagement of Andi DeLoach to JJ Savage. As I walked the halls between classes it felt as if every eye was on me and I heard the whispers and giggles. I guess that is the price of new found fame and a very small school. I was praying fervently that my new fame as quarterback and lover had not yet reached the state's coastal areas, particularly the institution of semi-higher learning down there where an ex-Central linebacker was playing college ball.

Monday's practice was a walk in the park compared to the previous Monday. What a difference a week makes. Ivy was at running back more but when he ran the ball, Ronnie was not taken out altogether. He was now playing wide receiver when Ivy was at tail back. Even though not tailback, Ronnie had a home. I promised myself that I would make sure I threw the ball to him every chance I had, that is, if Drucker even called any pass plays that week.

One of our linebackers had hurt his knee in the last game and when it came time for defense, Jelly was inserted into that slot. It looked to me as if Drucker was thinking, 'If I cannot keep them off my team, I am damn well going to use them until they drop.' I was all for his change of mind.

On Tuesday I sat down by Andi at lunch, the place beside her seemed to be vacant a lot these days. She looked happy to see me, so I didn't beat around the bush: 'Since everyone has us married, I was wondering if you'd like to go on a date with me Saturday?' Friday was out, because our game was away and we would not be back home until late. She said, 'Well, let me just check my schedule. Oh, dear me, it seems that I am available.' I said, 'Great, thanks for being so nice. What time should I pick you up?' She pursed her lips, 'I said I didn't have anything on my schedule. I didn't say I wanted to insert your name in the blank space.' Can a living, breathing human actually deflate like a balloon with a hole in it? Everybody at the table was laughing. Of course, they'd been listening. But then she said, 'I'm only kidding, JJ. Of course, I'd like to go with you.'

I'll take 'em how I can get 'em, easy or hard, so with that item checked off of my to do list, I could focus on North Fork. Our preparation would not be tricky. They were a mirror to our team, because their head coach had been an assistant to Coach Drucker for four years before his big break. He had been my quarterback coach for the first two years and I really liked him. It would be good to see him Friday. The week went well and to me it felt as if we were ready. After four years a player can sense where the team is mentally, and mental can be even more important that our physical condition. There would be no mental letdown after our first win. I felt confident about that.

On Thursday Drucker posted his starting lineup and Ronnie was still the tailback, but under his name in parentheses was Ivy's. Jelly was starting at line backer as well as tight end. When Drucker addressed the team that day he said, 'Their coach used to coach for us.' (No kidding Coach. What a great memory you have and what's his name?) He went on, 'I guess some of you like him, but I don't want any fraternizing before or after the game. Just get your business done and we can go home. I suppose I could read into this that Drucker didn't like our former coach, but why was that news? He didn't like anybody.

North Fork turned out to be more of a challenge than any of us had dreamed. At the half we were tied 14-14. They took the opening kickoff and drove 73 yards for a touchdown. Their tailback, also a colored boy, had slashed and crashed the last nine yards. He and Ivy met head to head at the goal line. I thought Ivy stopped him, but the referees thought not. They squibbed the kickoff to prevent Ivy from using his return skill. As I had thought, we were going to see a lot of squib kickoffs this season.

But the advantage for us was that the shorter kick gave us good field position and we worked our way down the field, just as they had, yard by bloody yard. We faced two crucial third downs, and on one, a third and eight, Coach called for a roll out option, a pass play. I would take the snap and roll to my right and look for either the wide receiver on a deep route or the tight end curling underneath him. They were both covered so I shouted to Ivy who was protecting me, 'Get the end,' and he upended the hapless defender. As I started up field but before I crossed the line of scrimmage, the linebacker gave up coverage to tackle me. I lobbed a wounded duck to Jelly, who caught it and ran for the first down. My pass violated the cardinal rule of quarterbacking: 'Never throw across your body.' But Jelly was as big as a barn. How could I miss hitting that.

Finally, Ivy took a pitch, outran the entire defense, and dived over the right pylon to score. He made a move on that run I'd never seen before. We see it in every game now a days but when he did it, it was a first. He looked like he was going out of bounds but at the last minute he extended the ball to his left over the pylon. The rule is a touchdown is decided, not by where the player is, but by where the ball is, so touchdown. We scored again and it looked like things were going our way but our fullback fumbled on the fifteen yard line. For their offense it was a walk to the end zone from there, so we left the field at half tied 14-14.

North Fork received the second half kickoff and something happened that had not happened to us in the four years I'd been on the team. Their stud back ran it all the way for a touchdown, ninety yards. On the ensuing drive we committed a turnover but not a run of the mill turn over, a pick six. I threw the interception but I don't think it was on me. I was throwing a simple out route to Ronnie but he slipped on his cut and fell. The defender was behind him and my pass hit him square in the chest. He was so surprised he almost dropped it but he managed to secure it and it was an easy jog for thirty yards to the end zone. So we were down 28-14, with three minutes left in the third quarter. Since high school games have twelve minute quarters, we only had fifteen minutes left to play.

Fifteen minutes in a high school game is a heartbeat if you are behind two touchdowns. We were likely to get the ball only two or three times for the rest of the game, so we were in deep doo-doo. They kicked to us and of course squibbed it along the ground again. It bounced toward the center man in the wedge. He did a very smart though unconventional thing. He turned and flipped it back to Ivy, standing behind him. Everyone in North Fork's coverage was converging on the wedge when Ivy started away from them to his left. It was as if we drew it up on the chalk board. With his speed it was no contest, seventy two yards for a touchdown.

After our kickoff North Fork started on their twenty eight. Their drive was a thing of beauty: six yard run, two yard run, three yards and first down. Six first downs and eight minutes later they were on our twelve yard line. With four minutes left, even if we stopped them

143

we had 90 yards to go the other way. They were not taking any chances. They ran a simple wide sweep to our left. I thought their back was free and then Ivy came from nowhere and hit him as hard as I've ever seen anyone hit. The ball popped straight up and Jelly grabbed it on the dead run.

When they finally caught him, he was on their nine-yard line. There were less than two minutes to go. In the huddle Ivy said, 'Give me the ball.' Drucker was screaming at me from the sideline. I looked and he signaled 25 Isolation. It was a straight dive play with the full back leading Ivy, good old Mr. Imagination. Everyone in the stadium knew we would run that play.

(Alright, hit pause. There is more to this book than football games. But the games matter. I apologize to those who have no understanding of the terminology I use in the games. So, a crash course, Football 101. We lined up in the I Formation. That meant, the center, the quarterback, fullback, and tailback were in a straight line. If we'd had drones in those days and you could take a picture, the four of us formed an I. Ivy was in the back of the I and he generally got the ball on a handoff from me. When I say 25 Iso, forevermore, from now on, all I mean is Ivy got the ball and the fullback blocked in front of him. We would isolate one hapless defender and he was in a no-win situation. If he went left, Ivy went right and vice-versa. It's a wonderful plan, if you have a back like Ivy. Now, if I say 25-Iso, Boot, all I am saying is I fake to Ivy and go the opposite way to throw a pass. Since everyone would be chasing Ivy, I was left free to throw the ball to Jelly or Ronnie. That's it, class dismissed. If you run into other problems with my football speak, use your imagination.)

When our two backs hit the line of scrimmage, one following the other, there was no hole to be seen. Ivy was not going to let that stop him. He bounced out of two tacklers' arms and danced sideways to his right. They had him hemmed in but he cut back ninety degrees to his left and split two defenders. Then he hit their star on the two yard line. This time it was not close. Ivy rolled him over on his back like a tumble bug and walked over the top of him into the end zone. I had not seen that many different moves on a nine-yard run in my life. I think all eleven players on defense took one shot at Ivy, and except for the poor back, they all whiffed. He probably wished he had as well.

Now we faced a choice. There was a new rule being tried out in high school football called the two point conversion. The team that scored had the option to kick for one point or run/pass the ball for two points. Not every region in our state had this option. The new rule was on trial and we were one of the experimental regions where it was in effect. We used our last time out to talk about what to do. Drucker was thinking about kicking and going home with a tie. That was the old Central way of doing it. But we were not the old Central, so I said, 'Coach, if we line up to run, everybody in the stadium is going to think Ivy will get the ball. Why don't we run 25 Iso Boot?'

What happened on that play was I faked to Ivy going right behind the fullback on the isolation play. Then I bootlegged back to the left. The book on me was I could not run or throw to my left. My old coach, who was watching from across the field, knew this better than anyone. On that timeout he prepared his team for every eventuality but a left bootleg! The rest of the play was for Jelly to line up on the right and run a crossing route. If he were open, it would be an easy conversion.

Surprise of all surprises Drucker agreed to my idea. As we ran the play, everyone but their outside linebacker was fooled. I was running practically alone to the left except for the one linebacker who somehow had sniffed out the subterfuge. He had me dead in his sights, when out of nowhere he went down. The Mill, who had pulled to lead me, saw the problem and peeled back and erased him. Now there was only the corner back and he was faced with a tough choice. He could cover Jelly coming across, or come up and tackle me. I was the weak link so he chose me and it was really his only chance. But as he came toward me, I dumped the pass over his outstretched hands into Jelly's bread basket and the good guys pulled off the win: 29-28.

They did get the kickoff and then attempted two desperation passes but Ivy intercepted the second one to seal the win. All my life up 'til then I had been a football traditionalist, don't change the rules, the rules are sacred. That night I became a revisionist. Thank God in heaven for the two point conversion.

After the post game remarks from Drucker and our showers, we loaded the bus to head for our team meal. We rode a charter Greyhound bus to out of town games. Our band and the students, who followed us to the games, rode what we, the pampered few, derisively called Yellow Hounds (school buses). The football team rode first class, no yellow hound for us. But like the friendly skies, we flew by assigned spots. OCD Drucker had a seating chart for traveling to the game: coaches in the first two rows either side of the aisle, then quarterbacks and tail backs, and on through the backs to the linemen. In the way back sat the managers and scrubs, lucky enough to make the travel squad.

But if we won, Drucker threw out his seating chart and let us sit where we wanted on the way home. I usually sat with the Mill because he was so funny. His jokes made the trip home go quickly. Tonight I sat with Jelly man and

146

the Mill sat across from us with Ivy. We sat in the front of the bus, right behind the coaches. Bus wars were being fought all over south in the sixties for the right to sit in the front or to only have a seat at all in the back.

But football teams were solving the problem with a merit system. On the team, the best players got first choice of seats, a pretty good way to do things I thought. On our bus there was no quibbling about it. If you were a good player you sat in the front. And since our two best players were colored, they got to sit where they chose. Nobody on our bus cared about the color of your skin. It was all about the level of your skill.

While the yellow hounds made their way home, the grey hound stopped at a local restaurant, more perks. We ate a post game meal, steak and potatoes, all the trimmings. When we arrived at the restaurant for the post game meal, our cheerleaders were at our tables waiting on us. They were always included, win or lose.

This must have been a tradition before Coach Drucker came on the scene. I could not imagine it had been his idea. Andi had saved a seat beside her but I sat at another table where I could see her. She was not happy, I thought. Then I got up and walked to her table: 'Just kidding. May I sit here?' Well my dad always said, 'Sauce for the goose is sauce for the gander.' At least, I think that was the way he said it. Anyway she let me sit down. The meal was tasty, the trip home relaxing, and God's other day, the day God allotted to ball players all over the south, lay just over the horizon. Go Hornets, go!

CHAPTER SEVEN

*Golf is a game played on a six-inch fairway
between the ears.*

Ben Hogan

'The Central Hornets are about to face their toughest test
of a very young season,' and that was how the Saturday
morning paper wrote it up. We weren't getting any love
for our narrow victory over North Fork. The sports editor
of our paper was of the opinion that last night's game
would not be much of a springboard to vault us over
Midlands, next week's opponent.

In response, I could only think that the editor of
the sports section of our local newspaper had not played
last night against North Fork and I had. I knew they were
a better team than they were being given credit. I would
not be surprised to see them make the playoffs at the end
of this year. But then I was probably prejudiced since we
had just barely beaten them, and I do mean barely!

On one point, however, I was in full accord with
our local pundit. We were facing an uphill battle this

week. I thought our team was as good as Midlands and, with the addition of Ivy and Jelly, perhaps even a shade better. But I also knew that as much as I thought that it was possible for us to win, I probably did not yet actually believe that we would beat them.

We were going on the field this week carrying a heavy burden, twenty straight years of mostly losing to Midlands. The mental barrier all those losses created was huge. I was going to do my best to overcome it in my own mind and then try to help my teammates over the hurdle as well. Ivy and Jelly were going to help me, even though I had not yet asked them. But, first things first, it was Saturday. I had a date with the prettiest girl in school and a Druckerless day ahead of me. Midlands was for Sunday and that would begin with films but that was to worry about later.

I did my usual that morning. After keeping mom up most of the night, I arose early and went over to my granddad's drugstore for the breakfast and game rehash with the local hindsight know it alls. You know about hindsight? Anyone can call a perfect game in hindsight! Hindsight vision is always 20/20. After the rehash Tree and I picked up Jelly, as usual, on the side of the highway. We were, as I promised him, having another swim lesson at the Deloach's farm.

This time we got his head underwater quickly, did some jelly fish floating, and ended with him pushing off the bottom of the dock and kicking as hard as he could through the shallow water. He was pretty confident and relaxed as long as we were in shallow water. I was also confident because Tree was there to help me pull him out if there were trouble. There was no way I could have managed by myself as Jelly outweighed me sixty pounds.

Tree was alert and ready because even in shallow water a neophyte swimmer can quickly get in trouble.

And if that novice happens to be 6'4" tall and weighs 230 pounds, it can be serious trouble. If Jelly had ever panicked, he and I were both goners, thanks that Tree was there.

When we were going back to town, Jelly asked me the question I had been waiting for and praying for: 'Mom wanted to know if you'd like to come and have dinner with us tonight?' Well, talk about being caught on the horns of a dilemma. I had been hoping and praying for a chance to meet Jelly's family but I had been praying about my dating Andi, too.

I told him I'd come but knew I'd better call Andi pretty quickly. When Tree and I got back to my house I called her and she said I absolutely could not go unless I took her with me. So I got on the phone again and called Jelly. Of course, his mom was fine with both of us coming. It would be an interesting evening. I was pumped for it but also nervous. To tell the truth I'd lived with colored people my whole life, been practically raised by one until I started school, but had never been inside a colored person's home.

When I picked up Andi, the first thing I asked her was did her mom and dad know where she was going. She said, 'Sure JJ, I told them I was going out to dinner with you.' I said, 'Andi, you are going to eat with me, but...' and she asked with a look of total innocence, 'But what, JJ?' And flashed me that million dollar smile. I said, 'But if you don't finish those kinds of sentences with your parents and tell them where we are going to eat our dinner, you will get me in trouble one day.' She laughed, 'I think I already have gotten you in trouble, but in another way.

Did you know Thad is coming home this next weekend? You don't need to worry. I can take care of him.' I knew she could take care of Thad for herself but would I be able to take care of Thad for myself? What the heck was I thinking about to ever ask her out? It just wasn't like me at all to be taking risks. Generally, I'm a cautious individual. But here my senior year I had gotten myself kicked off the football team, probably was on some KKK hit list, and now was going to get my butt kicked by Andi DeLoach's enraged ex-boyfriend, linebacker, stone-cold killer.

Well, Thad had been kicking my butt for years in every sport we played. One more butt kicking wasn't going to kill me, I hoped. As we drove I was still chewing on the honesty thing, so I said, 'Andi, just because you tell your parents we are going out to eat, doesn't mean you have told them the truth. A little bit of truth is not necessarily the truth, you know.'

She said, 'Let me ask you a question and will you tell me the truth?' I said I would. She went on, 'Are you happy I am going to dinner with you?' And I told her, of course I was, and she said, 'Then let's just drop the subject right now.' I have always gotten the last word with her, just like with my parents. It was, 'Yes Ma'am'. Thus ended the ethics lesson on truth telling by Professor Savage.

Not only had I never been to Jelly's house, I had no idea where it was. It tells you a lot about the southern culture of the '60's that in a town as small as ours no white people even knew where any of the colored people lived exactly. I knew there was a colored neighborhood somewhere behind the junior high school out on the east side but that was the extent of my knowledge. Jelly's instructions were to drive down Main Street past the junior high and he'd be waiting on the right side of the road. When we saw him, I realized he was standing on the edge of a dirt road. I had passed that road a thousand times and never really noticed.

He got in the car and we drove down that deeply rutted dirt road. We passed a few trailers and some small shacks that looked as if they might have been abandoned. He told us to go slowly and I could understand why. There were children playing along the side of the road and in the road.

There were alleys meandering off in both directions from that dirt road, and through the woods I could see other houses at the end of each lane. There were old cars on blocks in front yards. There were even wells with buckets and hand cranks that appeared to be in use. I thought that by now everyone in our small town had running water. The houses all had front porches, often with old couches and washing machines on them, and an occasional refrigerator.

This world we were seeing for the first time was difficult for a white boy and girl to conceive. I noticed that Andi was uncharacteristically quiet as her wide-eyed stare took in the surroundings. Jelly must have seen us staring open mouthed but he did not mention it.

Finally, he said, 'Turn here,' and we went down a fairly long gravel drive and into a neatly mowed yard with lots of flowers. In the middle sat a small but very well kept house. In the bed in front of the house were every kind of flowering plant I'd ever seen, some I'd no idea what they were. On the right of the house was the remnant of last summer's garden. On the left side of the house was a pickup truck and an older Ford, a '61 Fairlane, I thought.

I parked my dad's Buick behind them and we got out. On the front porch were three small children, eyes as big as saucers, fingers in mouths. They looked at us as if we were Martians, recently landed on their planet. Apparently, white folks did not drop by often. They were as much at a loss for words as we were. Jelly said, 'These

152

are my sisters (who I thought might be twins), and my cousin who stays with us.' With that brief introduction we all went inside.

Once we were inside I realized the Rolle's home was larger than it looked from the front facade. It was what southern whites derisively called a shotgun house. It was narrow but long, there was a central hallway that ran from front door to back door, hence the description shotgun, meaning you could stand at the front door and fire a shotgun out the back door without hitting anything. To the right was a den, behind it the kitchen, and behind that a bathroom and bedroom. On the left side there seemed to be three other bedrooms. As late as the '60's white folk's homes often had only one bathroom and perhaps a half bath, as it was called back then. So the one bathroom was not an unusual thing.

What I was beginning to understand was unusual about the Rolle's home was that it had a bathroom at all. On my trip down the dirt road to Jelly's house I had noticed that most of the houses we passed still had an outhouse in the back yard. All told, the Rolle's home was a very warm and comfortable place. I could tell that the back portion had been added later. Originally it must have been two bedrooms, den and kitchen, with outhouse in back.

The house, by design, was meant to appear small if approached from the front. Maybe the Rolle's liked to maintain a low profile. For whatever reason, I did not know. Their kitchen was large and I knew we would be eating in there but we did the same in our home. Our formal dining room was used at Thanksgiving and Christmas only when the whole family gathered. Other than then we ate in our kitchen, too. Everybody I knew ate in the kitchen.

When I met Bertrand senior, I was very surprised, because he was as small as me. Judging by Jelly, I had thought he would have been a big man. Then when Miss Janine came into the den from the kitchen, I understood from whom Jelly got his size. She was the epitome of an African queen, full bosom, ample hips. Miss Janine was a big woman, not fat, big. She made two of Andi and Andi was not small. She had the most serene and jolly expression on her face and I began to see the source of Jelly's personality, too.

His dad was a nervous sort, hands constantly moving and he was up and down from chair to chair. Miss Janine was the Queen Mary to his harbor tug. He seemed to circle her as she moved majestically around the room. She had the most beautiful mocha-colored skin while Mr. Rolle was almost ebony. They were quite a contrasting couple and Jelly was his mama's boy.

The children were standing tentatively on the periphery of the room, eyeing us nervously. As I was trying to think what to say to them, Andi came through with her usual poise. She grabbed the hands of the two smallest children smiled at the other one and the four of them headed to the back of the house. I suppose to look at toys and the things that girls have in their rooms.

Andi could talk to anybody but I had noticed over the years that she was completely at ease with children. That was a talent I sorely lacked. At camp the director had always put me with the older campers. Any child under twelve was a mystery to me. Miss Janine also left. She went into the kitchen to finish dinner and the three of us went out to the front porch where there were four very comfortable rocking chairs.

Mr. Rolle was a pipe smoker and getting a bowl packed and lit takes time. We sat quietly until he was pleasantly puffing. When he seemed comfortable, I asked him about his property. He said, 'This here house sits on six acres which my daddy owned before me. He farmed a good bit, mostly. But I'se only got me a garden. I work as a carpenter over to Sanderson Construction. We 'heritated the house from my daddy, but I'se done added a few rooms.'

About that time Miss Janine called him to the kitchen to set the table, leaving Jelly and me on the porch. I could hear squeals and laughter in the back of the house. Andi, the pied piper, was working her charm. That's when I found out a good deal about the Rolles. I didn't pry.

Jelly just started talking: 'Our family has lived here since the civil war. This land was given to us by the Rolles who owned the plantation up the road. Naturally, we took their last name, since we were slaves and didn't have any last name before.' 'It's nice land,' and I added, 'A nice house, too, Jelly.'

He said, 'Thanks, but we really don't want anyone to know much about it. White folks always tend to get nervous if colored folks do too good. In fact, colored folk around us get that way, too. When daddy added the back of the house, he kept it narrow like the front and from the road in it looks real skinny and small so you can't tell what all is back here. No white folks come back here anyway, which is good. But daddy is a careful man.

He told you he was a carpenter but he's more than that. It's like this. When the architect designs it and the builder doesn't quite know how to make it work by the design, he asks my daddy and daddy just knows how to do it. He can read a flat blueprint and see the three dimensional house. He has never had any training. His vision is a gift, pure and simple. Daddy has worked for the Sandersons since he was fifteen and he's 45 now.'

155

I reflected that Mr. Rolle looked more like 65, but probably from all the hard outdoor work. Jelly continued, 'He doesn't make the minimum 75 cents, like most colored men. He gets a hundred dollars a week, flat.' I did the math and $5000 was a lot of money for 1966.

Jelly went on, 'I have an older brother who's a sergeant in the army. He's in Vietnam right now. He is small like daddy, not like me and mom. You met my two baby sisters and my cousin and that's us. Daddy always worked hard and he keeps quiet. Plus, the Sandersons take good care of him. Momma works, too. She's a nurse's aide at County,' (our small local clinic/hospital).

I was beginning to understand Jelly's drive. The word had been spreading around school that Jelly was very smart. He started out in the mid level classes at school but after three weeks, he suddenly appeared in all my classes. My dad told me he was wasting time in mid levels. He needed the challenge of advanced classes. He was the only colored student in the high level classes. I was beginning to see how he came to be so smart. His mamma and daddy were smart and they had encouraged him to study and develop his mental skills. What he told me made me start to wonder if there weren't probably a lot more colored folks like Jelly than most white folks wanted to admit.

About that time I heard Miss Janine shout, 'Come and get it.' We all sat down at a round table way too big to have been store bought. I suspected Mr. Rolle might have been the finish carpenter who wrought that beautiful piece of furniture. There was a lazy Susan the size of most tables in the middle and it was loaded: cob corn, lima beans, mashed potatoes, string beans, cornbread and the biggest pile of fried chicken I'd ever seen. Probably those legs, wings, and breasts had been on the hoof yesterday!

156

There was no way I was getting to sit by Andi. The girls had her surrounded so I sat beside Miss Janine. We joined hands and Bertrand Senior returned thanks: 'Gracious heavenly father, we thanks you for good food and friends and the chance to share them both together. Amen' Just like I liked prayers, short and to the point.

The lazy Susan began to spin and pretty soon we all had some of everything and when we did, we began to eat. My favorite Sunday of our church, my only favorite, was third Sunday, because we had a pot luck luncheon after the worship service. But it was hardly pot luck. The women of our church only brought their best dish and plenty of it.

This meal at the Rolles was a third Sunday type meal and then some. We ate until I thought I might not be able to get up from the table and then Miss Janine said, 'Save room for dessert, apple cobbler.' We didn't have ice cream with it but that would have probably adulterated that pie.

After dinner we went out to the porch and sat. Besides the rockers, there was a porch swing which went to Andi and the girls. This time they let me join them. It might have been romantic without three little girls crawling all over us. It was cozy, though.

After a while Jelly said to Andi and me, 'Ivy was thinking that you would maybe like to go out and see where he stays?' This was quickly turning into the cheapest date of my life. Free dinner and now the evening entertainment would be free, too. And I say that earnestly, because there was nothing I'd rather do than uncover some of the mystery of Ivory York. Andi was good to go, so we said thanks to the Rolles, hugged the babies, and got in my car.

Jelly directed me back to the paved road and then to the left which led us out of town. We must have gone six miles at least when Jelly directed me down another dirt road, this time to the left. The house we came to eventually was not like the Rolles at all. It was a two room shack with an outhouse behind it. There was a small, ramshackle barn that had seen much better days. The Rolles had a small garden beside their house but this was a real farm. Probably they grew cotton. Most farmers in our area did.

Two men were sitting on the front porch. When we got out of the car, I could see one was Ivy and the other was one of the oldest men I'd ever seen. Probably, he'd been one of those servants Abraham left behind that day when he took Isaac up the mountain to sacrifice him to God. Ivy said, 'This be my gran, he be called Yorky. This be his farm and I stay with him.'

We stayed on that front porch for two hours, talking about the game last Friday, the new school, the intricacies of cheerleading. In that time Yorky never said a word, not one. No exaggerating, didn't open his mouth. But I could tell he was taking in every word the four of us said.

From what I could see of his fields from closer up, he was principally a cotton farmer. I could still see the stalks of the recently harvested plants. There were the remains of a summer garden, too. And there were pigs and chickens somewhere. I could hear them. Clearly, this was a working farm. They ate what they grew and sold cotton for needed cash, the old way of life on small southern farms, colored or white. I never found out how old Yorky was but he must have been in his eighties and still farming. When it finally was dark, we took our leave and headed back to Jelly's house.

On the way Jelly told us a little more about Ivy: 'Yorky is Ivy's granddad but Ivy told you that. He's lived on that farm all his life. He's pretty good at growing cotton. He had two sons but one was killed in Korea. He was Ivy's daddy. The other one got in some trouble and got killed by some white folks a few years before that, maybe ten years or so.' A gaping hole opened in the pit of my stomach. I was afraid to ask, but wondered if he'd been that last black man lynched in our county. Whatever actually happened to Ivy's uncle, white folks were involved.

That's when I realized why Ivy had little reason to want to associate with the likes of me. I'm not sure Andi understood all that Jelly was talking about and so she didn't say much. But I did not understand it all either. We both let Jelly talk: 'Yorky got his name from the Yorks who gave his daddy that land. He hardly ever leaves the property. It's as if he's afraid someone will take it if he's not there. Ivy takes care of him, does all the shopping and housework.

'And those days he wasn't at the country club last summer, remember? He was not loafing like you may have thought. He was on the farm helping his gran get the cotton in. If not for him, the old man would have died a long time ago. I appreciate you not letting him know I told you all this. I thought it would help you understand Ivy if you knew a bit of his story.

'Also, but you probably have figured it out. It was my idea for you to come out to the farm, not Ivy's. I talked him into it. Just so you know, it was not an easy thing for him to do.' Suddenly, in my mind, all Ivy's tough talk just washed off him like dirt from a good soap bath. I was seeing Ivy as I'd never seen him before. And the more I thought, the more I knew I'd do anything I could to help him. He and Jelly were special people.

At the film session Sunday afternoon Drucker was almost subdued. I said almost. A thunderstorm is relatively subdued compared to a tornado. It's all relative.

159

I should have said, 'Drucker was less angry than usual.' Partly, I think it was because his mind was already focused on our nemesis coming up Friday. But also it was about the fact that we played a darn good ball game.

North Fork would have other teams scratching their collective heads before this season was over. But as yet they were an enigma to those who had not played them. I for one was glad to have played them early and solve the riddle. They would be really difficult in a few more weeks. But the close game was not a bad thing for us since we had survived it. A win is always a win whether by one or by 51.

I actually was glad it was so close in one respect. I thought our close encounter Friday night would only lend a sense of overconfidence to Midlands and I'd take any edge I could get. I still was trying to work out how to overcome the collective inferiority complex our team bore in relation to them. I thought that, as outsiders, Jelly and Ivy might be the key to us getting inside our own heads and correcting the problem we always had this week of the season.

I was right about Drucker being focused ahead. Monday's practice was not about last week's mistakes. We were a day ahead of the normal routine. This Monday practice was all about preparing for Midlands. I thought it was a good thing, this early start on gaming Midlands, because we needed every minute we could squeeze out of the week to be prepared.

On Tuesday morning I spread the word to the team that we were going to meet in the back corner of the cafeteria during lunch. It had to be an informal private team meeting. Drucker was too much of a control freak to allow any such thing as a players only meeting on his watch. The other students knew something important was up, so they left us alone.

I began, 'Guys, listen. I just want to get some things out on the table. I know and you know that we have not beaten Midlands in twenty years. We need to be honest about that, first of all. Every one of those years they were better than us, bigger, stronger, faster. Some years we were close but we have never been better than them as a team until this year. This year they are not better than us. They graduated 18 seniors last year so they are young. We have them early in the schedule and they will be better down the line. But right now, they can be had. And we have two players who are better than anybody on their team and you know who they are. So if we are ever going to beat them, this is the year.'

Jelly just said one thing, 'I'm happy to be playing with you guys and I am gonna do my best in the game.' As always, Ivy was more blunt and let's cut him some slack. I will name his attitude optimistic instead of bragging. He flat out said, 'I am going to score three touchdowns in this game, I guarantee it. If our defense hold 'em under three, we will win.' Well, there certainly was no humble pie in Ivy's talk.

It was time to finish the meeting before a coach happened to walk into the lunch room. So I said, 'It doesn't matter if we win or not as far as state is concerned. They are a class above us. But I'd like us to be the first Central team in a long time to beat them. Think about our status around here if we do but the heck with status. What I really want is for us to just relax and have fun.' End of meeting, could not linger, Drucker's ears were large.

The rest of the week everybody was loosey goosey. Sometimes being loose means lack of focus but when playing a big game, being loose is usually an asset. The somewhat jocular atmosphere didn't worry me at all and Drucker seemed okay with it, too.

161

Thursday's final practice was as upbeat as any I'd been to. There was no sense of impending doom that I could detect. That seemed a good thing to me but still God only knew if we were ready to beat Midlands. If some coach could ever come up with a hard and fast formula to get a team mentally ready to play a game, that coach would be an over night millionaire. Every other coach in the country would buy that blueprint. There does not seem to be a formula. It's a nebulous thing. But I thought we were ready to go out and play.

Friday's steak lunch was lighthearted, nobody was tense, so now I began to worry that maybe we were a bit too loose. I told you I was a worrier. The pep rally was the best I've been to in my four years. Everything was too good so now I was beginning to wonder if I had set us up to fail? By the time we took the field I may have been the only doubter left on the team. How do I do this to myself?

Midlands won the toss and elected to receive. They started from their own 33 after a decent return. Ivy was playing corner because they had the best wide receiver in the state and a quarterback who could throw it a mile. They knew how aggressive Ivy played so they went for the home run on the first play. The receiver ran an out, pretty safe route, except it wasn't an out, and on the pump fake Ivy jumped the out route.

But it was an out and up, just like I beat him with on the sandlot. My heart sunk and so did my head, did he never learn? He was fooled again, but when I looked up, Ivy was running stride for stride with their stud receiver. Apparently his jump of the out route had been a feint and he was ready. As the ball sailed down the field I was hoping for a breakup and second down and ten. Ivy had other ideas. They went up for the ball together. Now, this guy was 6'3" and Ivy about 6', but Ivy out jumped him about a foot and took the ball right out of his hands.

162

The receiver had his wits about him, however, and had Ivy wrapped up for the tackle. As I was trotting on the field, I heard a shout and stopped, because somehow Ivy had broken the tackle and was heading back up field. It looked as if he were going to try and outrun them to the left, but at the side line he reversed field and in so doing, picked up a convoy of blockers. Midlands players were cart wheeling ass over teacups as our boys hit them from the blind side. It was a walk off pick six.

After the kickoff we held them three and out. As we lined up for the return, Ivy sneaked up to the outside right linebacker spot and Ronnie moved to the return safety position. We had watched their film over and over. Their punter was a three stepper rather than two stepper. You can punt it farther with three steps, but it takes more time to get the punt off. Tree and Jelly crossed each other from tackle and end and Ivy poured through the hole they created. He hit the kicker on his second step. The ball popped straight up and he caught it on the dead run and never slowed down, touchdown.

He came running off the field shouting, 'That's two!' I yelled back, 'That doesn't count. It's a defensive touchdown.' He laughed, 'OK, I'll get two more! And of course, he did. He caught a little swing pass from me and just outran the corner to the end zone.

The half time score was 21-0. Everything was going right for us and wrong for them. Late in the third, Ivy hit up in the line on the 25-Iso and the Mill practically lifted the tackle up in the air, knocked him into the linebacker and Ivy didn't break stride, 80 yards.

With a quarter to play, Drucker kept the starters on defense but played the second string on offense and the game ended 28-0. It was Midland's worst loss in five years. It was our best game in my memory, all the way back to fourth grade pee-wee ball when our family had come home to Central. The individual play by Ivy was the best since everybody's hero had been the QB.

When Drucker ended his post-game talk, he opened the locker room as always. That's when I saw him. Crap, he was bigger than when he played for us last year. Thad came directly to me without preamble: 'Little Johnny, good game. Got a date tonight?' I mumbled, 'Yeah, Thad.' He grimaced, 'With who, Little Shit?' Thad knew very well who my date was that night.

He turned to leave but stopped and threw over his shoulder: 'I'll be waiting out behind the Rib-Shack but you're probably too chicken shit to show up.' He didn't wait for my answer. Tree and the Mill had been watching. Tree said, 'I'll go with you JJ.' Mill said, 'I wouldn't miss it, Johnny boy. You're gonna get your ass kicked.'

That night at the party Andi could tell I was bothered about something. I'm not the strong silent type, but at least I wasn't crying. She asked, 'What's wrong, JJ?' I said, 'Thad stopped in the locker room after the game. Seems he thinks you are still his girl friend. He wants me to meet him at the Rib Shack after I take you home.'

She blanched, 'You aren't going are you?' So even this girl who is my friend, not my girl friend, thinks I'm going to get my ass kicked. I said sarcastically, 'Of course not Andi. Then everyone in town will know I'm chicken shit, just like Thad said.' She said, 'I could talk to him.' I thought then everyone could say I got my new girl who is my friend, only, to do my fighting for me. But I didn't say it, I'm not that stupid. I was hoping she might be my girl friend one day, but only if I did not die tonight. The rest of the dance in the gym that night was down, down, down. When I took Andi home, I didn't have the energy to even kiss her goodnight.

When I got to the Rib Shack, Tree and the Mill were there already, but so were Jelly and Ivy. I had no idea that they'd be there. Man, was I glad to see the four of them waiting for me. I'd probably get my head pounded in but at least I was not going to die. They wouldn't let him kill me. Mill, maybe, but surely the other three would intervene and toss in the towel. Somebody had to hand the ball off and throw girlish type passes at them next Friday.

Thad was there, too, with three of his redneck friends from last year's team. He looked at Ivy and Jelly and said, 'No niggers allowed in there', pointing at the Rib Shack. Ivy said, 'We didn't come here to eat your stinking red neck ribs. We're just going out back and watch JJ kick your red neck ass.' Thanks Ivy, why not make him even madder, good strategy.

We went around the back and Tree, who had appointed himself ring master, said, 'This is gonna be fair. No foreign objects, fists only. No wrestling, three and out.' What he said meant that we'd fight three rounds, each three minutes long, then it was over. That may sound short to you but nine minutes with a bruiser like Thad could be a lifetime, a short painful one, but a lifetime all the same.

All seven of the spectators circled around us to form the boundary. If I got knocked out of the ring, they'd throw me back. The Mill said, 'Hold it. I need a word with JJ.' It was the first time he'd used my new nick name, a good omen? Thad said, 'What the Hell for, Mill, you gonna coach him up real quick?' The Mill said, 'Shut your fucking mouth Thad, or it'll be me instead of JJ.' That got his attention. Even Thad would think twice about three and out with the Mill.

My friend whispered in my ear, 'Remember fourth grade?' I nodded. He said, 'The only way you won that fight was you hit me first, you stinking little sneak. (I don't think I ever mentioned that my fourth grade

165

tormentor, later my good friend, was one Mark Madison, aka the Mill?) The mighty Mill said, 'Remember; the one who gets in the first and the hardest usually wins.' So for coaching tips, time to fight.

Tree was timing, and he said, 'Go.' Thad let out a roar and charged me. I stood as if frozen, but I actually had a plan, based on the Mill's advice. At the last second I ducked left and swung my right fist as hard as I could right at his nose. Somehow I connected squarely and broke his nose. Blood went everywhere and kept running and running, down his face on his shirt, everywhere.

In the first three minutes I hit him two more times in the face and he never touched me. I can be very shifty when I am scared witless. Besides that, I don't think he could see me through the blood and I was back pedaling like Hell around the ring.

As we progressed, I realized Thad knew less about fighting than I did. As we started round two, Thad managed to push me into one of his friends and he grabbed me. Then Thad hit me so hard in the stomach I thought I was going to throw up. Before he could hit me again, Ivy had tackled the other boy and Tree jumped between us: 'We'll just take a little break from that sucker punch you threw, Thad.' When Ivy let the other guy up, I was pretty sure that boy would not interfere again.

So we started back and Thad tried to tackle me, not fair of course, because we were supposed to be boxing. Two could play dirty, so as he came in head down, my knee accidentally slipped up and made contact with that tomato-like nose of his. That was it. He slumped to his knees and did not get up. I was so tired and scared I thanked God we did not have a round three.

I beat Thad like we beat Midlands. We hit them early and hard and time ran out before they even realized what had happened. And we acted as if it was supposed to happen, so I acted like it was supposed to happen behind the Rib Shack, too.

As we were leaving the Mill said, 'I'm disappointed it not go three.' Jelly asked him why and he said, 'If it had gone three, I'm pretty sure Thad would've recovered and kicked JJ's ass!' You could never tell when the Mill was kidding and when he was serious.

When I got home, I called Andi. She had been crying, I could tell. 'What happened,' she sobbed. I said, 'Well, I'm still here, and though I haven't checked all over, I'm pretty sure I'm healthy enough so we can go out tomorrow night.' I didn't give her the details.

By Monday everybody in school would know anyway, and it would be way better in the telling of this tale to let others do the talking. By Monday evening that fight would have achieved mythic proportions. I was not about to spoil a great story with the truth. And the truth was I have never been so glad to be alive as I was that night. I was beginning to think I might be a head hunter after all. You remember I told you. I'd always wanted to be one of those guys with killer instinct. The Mill would probably laugh at my pretensions, but one could always dream.

CHAPTER EIGHT

Potential is just a fancy word for, 'ain't worth a Damn, yet'

Jeff van Note, Atlanta Falcons Center

Saturday dawned brightly and I was up early. It was a sweet day to be alive. The Breakfast Club, as I had now named it in my mind, was about to convene. The club had now grown to include any of my teammates who could get up early enough to come and get a free breakfast provided by my granddad. He didn't mind since the growing number of paying customers more than compensated him.

My teammates had been joined by all of the men in town who were interested in cussin' and discussin' Friday night's game. The thing I most enjoyed about the discussion was those old players' critique of Drucker. I acted disinterested, of course. It was in the best interest of my health that I act disinterested. Behind the bland facade, however, I marveled at a big old world outside of my very small one that was not dictated by Drucker's every whim. Those men could not have cared less what Drucker thought of their criticism.

This morning the drugstore was packed. It was small wonder, considering what had transpired last night. There was the smell of fresh coffee, the sound of bacon frying, and there would be eggs and grits. The air was already blue with the cigarette smoke. It was 1966, remember? Everybody smoked everywhere, put out their butts in what was left of their grits.

In addition to all the sights, sounds and smells of a southern breakfast, there also was the smell of sweet, sweet victory. Almost every man in the room had played for Central in the last twenty years, meaning not a man in that room other than me and my teammates had ever beaten Midlands. Our athletic stock had doubled at least since last night.The unspoken question on everyones' minds that morning was: 'Did that nigger really promise he would score four touchdowns?'

The Mill, who was not intimidated by adults at all, was the first to speak: 'I know you heard the rumor and I know what you are wondering. Hell no, the colored boy didn't say he'd score four touchdowns. He only promised us three.'

You could hear the intake of breath around the room. Promising touchdowns before they were on the board was blatant heresy in the religion of southern, white football. The 'aw shucks, twern't nuthin' mantra was what we recited every day of our careers. You might believe you could score three touchdowns against the second best team on your schedule but you kept your mouth shut about it. And if you did score three, your response was, 'Aw shucks...'

Not a man in that room could abide Cassius Clay, for example. They knew he could fight but the nickname they used for him was The Louisville Lip. And they still called him by his God and mama given name in Central even though officially he now was Muhammad Ali.

169

Crackers were raised up by our folks to appear humble about any success that came our way even when we thought we had done it for ourselves. What Ivy had said before the game, just was not said in our circles.

I knew I needed to say a few words in his defense so I immediately chimed in to emend Mill's remarks, 'But he did exactly what he said he would do, right? And when he blocked the punt and scored the second one, he shouted to me, 'That's two.' But when I shouted back, 'Defensive TD's don't count,' he said, 'So I'll get four tonight.' That's what finally was said and what he did.'

There was no argument about my statement of the facts. Everyone in the room had been at the game. No one had ever seen a performance like that and lots of men there had seen Big John play. At that point Granddad intervened: 'Fellas, you can say nigger anywhere you want outside of here, I guess, but you may no longer use that term it in my store, OK?' Wow! The times, maybe they really were changing.

Then someone asked, 'Why can't we have them ni.., them colored boys come to breakfast so's we can meet them face to face?' Granddad answered that one decisively, 'You know the law. If I opened my store to coloreds, I would be closed down by the authorities. How about this instead? Why don't we call this the Central High Breakfast Club (I may have mentioned that name to Granddad) and move the meeting next week to the school cafeteria? I'm sure 'Big John' would let us meet there. The school is open to everybody so Bertrand and Ivory could join us.'

After a brief discussion, it was agreed that hence forth, with the Hero's permission, of course, we'd meet on Saturday morning at the school cafeteria. Some things change because some things never change. What would never change was the southern male's interest in the game of football. What did change was the venue for our next breakfast because of the southern male's interest in all the ones who play in the games on Friday night. Next week our entire team would be able to attend the Breakfast Club. It now had that official name. We were the Central High Saturday Morning Breakfast Club, or just Breakfast Club for short. And no longer would anyone be excluded.

There are laws that if you break them you get in trouble and then there are laws that no longer matter. In the south we still had lots of laws on the books that weren't enforced. They were called Blue Laws. There were laws for example, about stores being closed on Sunday but these were starting to be ignored in our large cities. As long as stores didn't open until after church, the enforcers were willing to look turn a blind eye. But in the small towns of the south, Jim Crow was largely still in effect.

Of course, the integration of Little Rock schools in 1954 began to change those laws, slowly. My granddad was absolutely right in saying that had he allowed coloreds in through his front door, his drug store would likely be closed. And even had our local authorities turned a blind eye, people might have taken their business elsewhere.

Granddad had always served food and filled prescriptions out of his back door for the Negro community. That was the way good men and women of small southern communities in 1966 tried to not discriminate. It was tough in small towns. However, in the cities things were changing.

Rumor had it that in Midlands Negros had begun sitting floor level with whites in the movie house. Forever, the balcony was the only place Negros could sit. Since we were feeling pretty good about ourselves, we decided to push the envelope. Win a few ball games and a fight or two and you begin to think you are bullet proof. We were going to the picture show in Midlands.

That night Andi and I, Tree and his date, Ronnie and his date, and the Mill with no date piled in my mom's Chevrolet Bel Aire station wagon. It held nine so we had room for two more, Ivy and Jelly. We didn't really give our parents the entire picture. I blame Andi again for the partial picture truth, her forte it seemed. We told them some of us were going to the city to see the new movie Little Big Man, starring Dustin Hoffman, Faye Dunaway, and Chief Dan George. We just didn't give them all the passengers on the flight manifest.

When we got to the theater there was a long line. As we were waiting, a couple of football players with dates got in line a few behind us. There was no mistaking that red letterman's jacket with white leather sleeves, a big M on the left breast. We had on our jackets, too. They actually waved and came over to talk. Nice guys really, they were very complimentary of our play against them the night before and were interested to meet the chief cause of their defeat. It was true, no denying it. Without Ivy and Jelly we'd not have won that game.

One of them said something that meant a lot to me: 'I know we usually beat you but we never take you for granted. You are one of the toughest games on our schedule every year. It's just hard for you to beat a team with more students in their school. We have more athletes to choose from.' Having never really talked to an opponent before, Drucker would not have it, it was interesting to hear about our team from their perspective. They wished us well the rest of the season and predicted we'd make it deep into the playoffs.

The movie was fantastic even though I was nervous that someone would make a scene about Ivy and Jelly.

Obviously, things were changing in the city. Everything was going smoothly until on the big screen Hoffman tried to explain the Civil War to Chief Dan George. He called it 'The war the white man fought to free the black man.' As soon as the words were ought of Hoffman's mouth, Ivy shouted, Sheee-it. There was dead silence for a second. You could have heard a pin drop. And then Andi, of course, began to laugh. It was funny, after all, and pretty soon everyone in the cinema was cracking up. When we got back in the car, the Mill said, 'Dammit Ivy you racist, I can't take you anywhere.' Ivy said, 'Sheee-it.'

Church was more interesting than usual because the preacher, for once, allowed himself to get a bit topical. He used our win over Midlands as an example of the power of thinking positively. Was he quoting from the letters of St Paul or the letters of St Peale? But it was nice to know that he followed our football team. After church when we finally got the Hero off the front steps and home, we had a nice lunch and then it was time for game films.

Each Sunday Tree, the Mill, Ronnie and I, and now Jelly, played a game related to the film. We each threw a buck in the hat and ventured a guess as to what would be Drucker's demeanor that day and what tack he would take during the film session. After attending these horror movies for four years, we had begun to recognize tactics Drucker used that had nothing to do with whether we won or lost.

One of Vince Lombardi's players once remarked that the most painful film sessions with him were after a really big win, not a loss. It was the same with Drucker. He used the film sessions to manipulate us so as to finagle the attitude he considered proper for the next game. He might correct mistakes, or not. In football there are always plenty of mistakes to point out, win or lose. But he didn't need to point them out. Every boy in that room was painfully aware of his screw ups. Remember, 'the big eye in the sky, blah, blah, blah.'

In the sweepstakes pool that Sunday I guessed Drucker would be pointing out mistakes with the intention of bringing us down off of our cloud. It would be brutal even though we had won the game big time. I won the money that day, enough to cover my date next weekend. As we watched ourselves dismantle Midlands, Lead Butt was at his caustic best dismantling us. He particularly needled the Mill but I came in for more than my share as well. So I collected everybody's dollar but it didn't make the pain entirely go away.

Drucker could get under your skin. Even when you knew what he was doing, it still rankled. But try as he might, Drucker was not going to make any of us believe there was a chance in Hell we could lose against Parson's Mill. They were a town team, like us, but their school was smaller, and they had a new coach and young team. Besides, they had not beaten us in years.

This week Ivy was named to be one of our captains. It would have been hypocritical for Drucker to ignore the fact that he had scored four times against one of the best defenses in our part of the state. Of course, this would be a first. All of us wondered how our fans would react to a colored boy going out for the coin toss. It was an away game but not far, and most of our town would follow us half way across the state. So they would all be there. First time a colored boy was captain, history being made in Central. There were lots of firsts that year and plenty of logistical problems as well. For the first away game that year we'd been in a big city, so we had gone to our usual restaurant for our pregame meal, no problem.

This week we were in the sticks, stickier than even Central, really small. As we began to seat ourselves, the owner walked over to Coach and whispered, 'I can't serve them here.' Ivy and Jelly had to eat in the kitchen so about ten of us joined them in there. After that, our coaches decided that we needed to be prepared in advance for potential turn downs. If we could not find a restaurant at our away games that would serve our entire team, we'd eat in the cafeteria before we left. Then we'd have box lunches on the bus on the way home.

In 1966 nothing was easy when it came to negro and white relationships. It didn't bother us as much as it did the adults. It led to funny situations, too. One restaurant owner timidly asked Ivy if he were a negro. Ivy said, 'No sir. I am 'eye-tailian'. What seems strange to us now was our way of life then. There just was very little social interaction between negros and whites in those days, actually there was none. So including Ivy and Jelly in our activities was always an effort in planning. And even with the best laid plains, you never knew.

Practice that week was long and brutal. Drucker was determined to bring us off our high from the Midlands victory. At least the weather had begun to cool. October had arrived and with it weather change. But the change did not help our performance.

Drucker didn't need to bring us down from the clouds. We had begun to feel a natural low following Friday's high. Football teams cycle just as people do. Nobody can stay high all the time and teams can't, either. We went through the motions at practice. It was a very lackluster week which only served to make Drucker more angry. That meant harder practices and a downward spiral of pain.

By Wednesday it was as if summer practice had resumed. Tempers were growing shorter. We were pissed at Drucker but the only outlet was each other. That's how it happened. On Wednesday the Mill and Tree got into it.

We had been running the same play over and over because the Mill kept screwing up the double team. One time he knocked his own end down, another he just whiffed. Finally, he hit the defensive tackle so hard the boy went back about five yards and the Mill landed flat on his face and on it went. In the huddle Tree muttered, 'Get it right dumb ass. We're tired and you're the problem.'

The Mill didn't even grace the comment with a reply. He went after Tree with his arms flailing. When the bigs go at it, everybody bails, teammates, managers, and coaches. Let the pit bulls get it out of their systems. You might lose a hand intervening. Jelly, who might have been able to stop it, was stepping forward, when I grabbed him: 'Let 'em go Jelly man. How can they get hurt with all that equipment on.'

It was actually funny, if you backed off and took the larger view. They looked like two bears in the circus. They kept cuffing each other in the helmet until they were so tired they finally just gave up and got back in the huddle, huffing and puffing. Drucker said, 'If you girls are through hugging each other, we need to run this play again and get it right.' And so it went.

Since fall was upon us, Jelly had his last swimming lesson and actually used his arms and kicked his legs and went about ten yards completely on his own. Next spring I'd teach him how to breath as he swam and my work would be done. Then he would be able to move forward on his own. Swimming could be marked off my to do list, but there were other pressing issues to be addressed, such as the question of my letterman's jacket.

These days my son, who plays for Central, has to buy his own shoes, socks, etc. Meaning, I have to buy them. We buy supplemental insurance and pay a fee for the meals the team provides. In my day we paid for nothing, not even a jock strap, which I don't believe they wear anymore. We also received a team jacket every year we played enough of the requisite quarters of the game. If you lettered, the jacket, like everything else, was free. These days the kids get the C from the school but then they must buy the jacket themselves. Their parents buy, but you already know that.

To earn that coveted Central jacket back in the day you needed to play in half the quarters during the season, 20/40. If you were a senior and played nineteen quarters, nineteem, Drucker would not give you a letterman's jacket, and no jacket, no glory.

I had already lettered three times and so in my closet hung three identical jackets, except my C had a bar for each additional year I had lettered. The jackets were all wool, Kelly green with two stripes circling the shoulders. This year, if I didn't get hurt, I'd be a letterman after the Parson's Mill game and at the end of the season I'd receive a wool jacket, green, like the others but with yellow leather sleeves, the most coveted senior jacket.

That was in the future. Right now I had those other jackets to deal with. Or, at least one of them. So here's the decision. Cheerleaders liked to wear a football letterman's jacket over their uniform when the weather became cool. Every year a cheerleader had worn one of mine, but they weren't my girl friends. No strings were attached. This year I faced a slightly different situation. I had a friend who definitely was a girl, but not my girl friend. Would she want to wear my jacket?

Thursday was the day to take care of this business. I was sitting with Andi at lunch, which was by now a regular thing. I casually mentioned to her that she could wear my letterman's jacket at the game if she wanted to. She said, 'Thanks, but Tree already gave me his.' My face fell off a cliff, and she laughed and said, 'I'm just teasing,

JJ. Are you ever going to learn? Whose jacket would I wear but yours? I'd love to wear it.'

So ever more casually, I said, (and this was a huge step) 'If you want to, you can keep it for a while it and wear it to school.' Most cheerleaders only got the jacket for game night and then returned it. If a girl wore a jacket to school, she was making a statement about herself and the donor, sort of.

Now the ball was in her court. It was her turn to flounder around speechless. It was a treat for me to see Andi DeLoach at a loss for words, it was a rare thing. What we had here was a next level offer. If she wore my jacket to the game, no big. All the cheerleaders had a jacket from someone and they returned it immediately after the game. The moment she stepped across the threshold of school with my jacket on, she'd be saying, 'If you need a date, don't bother calling me.' She finally said, 'I'll let you know tomorrow night after the game.' Dang it, she had fired that old ball back across the net right at me but I wasn't in the mood to beg. I hated these dating games. I needed to think about the real game at hand and now Andi was in my head, so what's new?

Before we get into the game itself, I almost forgot to tell you the one troubling thing about Parson's Mill. They ran the Wing T offense. This was the closest thing to the triple option out there before Darryl Royal unleashed his potent wishbone attack out at Texas. In the Wing T the quarterback had only one back behind him, the full back. The other two backs were flanked just outside their ends. One went in motion every play. The quarterback could hand the ball off to his fullback, he could keep the ball himself, or he could toss it out to the wingback who was circling through the backfield, just behind him.

To stop this offense you had to be prepared to stop all three options every play because you never knew which player would end up with the ball. I loved this offense and promised myself that if I ever coached, this would be my offense. It is exciting to watch and the devil to try and defense. The twist this year was their quarterback was a pretty good passer and if you lined up to stop the three run variations, he could throw passes off of the identical backfield action. So really, every play promised four different options and they all started off looking like the same one play. It was very confusing and if you let them get rolling, they could march the ball right down the field.

Friday night, as we were getting ready to break the run through banner, the Mill, who was standing next to me, said, 'I got a funny feeling about this one, Johnny boy. I think it may come down to you so don't choke it. If you get the job done, I promise I'll never call you Little Johnny again'. The Mill should have been a coach. Now I was ready for anything!

Parson's Mill took the kickoff and marched down the field just like I knew they could. Their quarterback was masterful. He out guessed our defense every time. We'd converge on his fullback and he'd keep the ball. We put two on him and he pitched to his wingback, right, left, left, up the middle, 80 yards, TD.

We received their kick and started a drive of our own, all runs. Ivy was gamely running but his blocking was all but nonexistent. To his credit he never complained about lack of blocking. He liked to brag, true, but he never complained about his teammates. He liked to do the thing they now call trash talk but he never trashed a teammate, not once in all the time I played with him.

Finally, facing a fourth and seven on the sixteen yard line, Coach wisely opted for a field goal: 3-7. The game was up and down the field, mostly them going up and down the field and us whiffing. But we both managed to score once more so the half time score was 10-14. We narrowly avoided letting them score again. The clock expired as they lined up on our seven yard line.

At the half Drucker spoke first and then divided the team into offense and defense and let his assistants work on second half strategy. On the rare occasion he was stumped in his play calling, he'd consult his quarterback. This night I was waiting and hoping because even with a bright idea, you did not approach him first. So, here he came, 'JJ (what the hay, JJ?), any ideas?' Very carefully, I said, 'Well we haven't thrown many passes,' he interrupted, 'In case your counting, we haven't thrown any.' So I said, 'I guess since they run so much, it's easy to get in a head to head contest, running at them as much as they run at us.'

Here goes, ' I think we can run bootlegs on them. Their ends are not staying home. And I think play action off of Ivy's runs will freeze the linebackers, especially the one on our left.' He said, 'But you don't throw well to your left.' I answered, 'And they know that, Coach, so they won't expect it.' Finally, my biggest risk of all: 'Maybe we could throw a few on first down?' It was hard to get that one out of my mouth. It ran counter to the honor of a southern coach in those days to start any offensive series with a pass. It was downright unmanly but he said, 'I'll think about it.'

After the kickoff, we had the ball on our thirty six. Drucker signaled me 25 Iso Boot. Which meant I was faking a 25 Isolation to Ivy going right and bootlegging with the ball hidden on my hip back left to throw a pass. Jelly was lined up on the right side of our line and was crossing the field to the left, mirroring me. Ronnie was running waggle, which was a zig in and a zag out, in and back out, and then deep. You can just remember deep.

The fake to Ivy froze the linebackers in place, just as I thought so Jelly got past them. This left the defensive back with a choice. He could go with Ronnie deep or pick up Jelly. A twenty yard gain is preferable to a touchdown so he wisely ran with Ronnie and I hit Jelly for twenty and change. Next play I gave the ball to Ivy on 25 Lead and he ran for twelve yards. Next we ran another pass, and I hit Ronnie for a touchdown. That poor defensive back didn't know what to do. So now that I've bored you with details and made you know, I know a little bit about football... enough silly details anyway.

The game went back and forth: 17-14, 17-21, 24-21, and with three minutes left we were down again, 24-28. Jelly had caught four passes and Ronnie three, two for touchdowns, sweet vindication for the man who unselfishly gave up his spot to Ivy. I was proud of Ronnie. He'd played a great game, but still we were down, and on our own 22 yard line with two minutes fifteen left in the game.

Coach called a drop back pass. They were my least favorite, but at least it was a pass so there I stood with the pocket collapsing on top of me like a tsunami. At 5'9" it was hard for me to see over the lineman from a good pocket. This was not a good one. They knew we had to pass so the rush was coming hard. But in the midst of the chaos and confusion, Ivy dropped his block and slipped out to my right. I saw him out of the corner of my eye, and so as I felt myself being tugged down, I dropped the ball off to him. When I clawed out of the mass of bodies piled on me, I saw their safety and corner, drive Ivy out of bounds on their 48 yard line.

Coach called our last time out and I came to the sideline. This was the only time I loved Drucker. He never panicked in tight situations, and he usually had a plan. This was what he had for me: 'Call two plays in the huddle: 25 Iso Pass and have the receivers run a curl and a wheel (one went short, the other deep). And then run the exact same play again.' That was it, simple but effective. The first time we ran it, Jelly caught the pass for ten so now we were on their thirty eight but the clock was running down to fifty seconds.

The double play call saved us having to go into the huddle and gave us enough time to get the play off. This time they were all over Jelly but to my mind they had Ronnie covered, also. I managed to scramble outside the end with help of a great block by Ivy. How he got the end, I'll never know. So I turned as if to run out of bounds for one last desperation play and the defensive back paused for just a split second. He thought about coming up to keep me in bounds so the clock would run out. His brief hesitation was all I needed. I lofted the ball high and deep to the outside, enough so the safety could not get over to Ronnie. He made the catch diving almost out of the end zone but kept his feet in, touchdown: 31-28. The PAT was immaterial but our kicker made it.

The clock had run out as I had thrown that last pass, game over. Central High Hornets, the mighty green and gold, were 4-1 and I had played in every quarter of all the games but the first one, meaning, one more game and I'd letter again! I would earn that coveted senior jacket, and Mill could not call me little Johnny any more. Still I had one last issue to resolve, that other jacket which my friend, who was not my girlfriend, was wearing.

With that in mind I dressed quickly and headed out. Before I made it out the door, the Mill grabbed me and pulled me back in the locker room: 'I need to tell you something, JJ. You know my daddy raises hunting dogs, right? It's a funny thing. If you put a puppy behind a two foot fence, which is too high for him to jump, when he grows up, you don't have to make the fence higher. He just figures since he couldn't jump it then, he can't jump it now.

I've been your friend since you beat me up in fourth grade.' I interrupted him, 'I did not beat you up, Mill, I only hit you once.' He said, 'That attitude is what I'm talking about. You did beat me up, because I quit and you won. Dammit JJ, you need to quit acting like that puppy and letting your daddy be your fence.' It wasn't a perfect metaphor by any means, but I got his point.

He was on a roll now, so I thought I'd better let him finish. 'I knew you could whip Thad's ass, too. I just didn't think you knew. But now you do. And even though you still throw like a fucking girl, you get the ball where it needs to go. After tonight you ought to know that, too. You ain't ever gonna be big Johnny, that's a fact but you do pretty good as plain ol' JJ. Quit using him as your measuring stick and be yourself. You do that and we got a chance at state.

'Well, we got a chance if Jelly and Ivy keep playing for us, too, both of those things, JJ. But you matter a lot.' That was it. He was through, didn't wait for my response. The Mill didn't give a crap about my response. He turned and walked away but his words that night set me free to be me and that was enough. The Mill was a remarkable character, a great deal smarter than most people knew.

When I got out the door, Andi was standing there waiting on me. 'Do you have my jacket?' I asked. 'I'll take it on out to my car before we go inside.' She smiled, 'It's in my car. If I'm taking it home, to wear to school next week, I don't need it in the gym.' And like the Mill, she didn't wait for an answer, just took my hand and we headed for the dance. Maybe she and the Mill ought to be dating.

183

CHAPTER NINE

No matter how good the cook,
No one can make chicken salad out of chicken
shit.

Wallace Butts, University of Georgia

Saturday morning was feeling like a good day. The
Central Hornets were halfway through the regular season
with only one loss. I say regular season, because the
unspoken hope of everyone in town had now become
their belief. Central was going to the state playoffs this
season. For the first time in six years there would be more
than just a ten game regular season. This would not be a
6-4, 7-3, close but no cigar, season. Nobody was talking
about it out loud, yet. That's because everyone knew that
to do so at this point would jinx us.

Football players and them that follow their
exploits, are some of the most superstitious people in the
world. I'm pretty sure everybody in town had some ritual
they were performing before every game. As if one of our
many fan's failure to wear the same socks to the game
Friday would stifle Ivy's running ability that night.
Ridiculous to think that some pregame ritual could alter

the stars and usher in a defeat. All the same, I was hoping my old Hornets Tee shirt that I wore under my shoulder pads every game would make it through the season. Mom had already begun to wash it gently, by hand, as per instructions. The biggest superstition of all was that if you said out loud what you thought was going to happen, it wouldn't. So everybody was thinking playoffs but nobody dared say it yet.

When the Hero and I got to the school cafeteria that Saturday morning, the food service personnel had breakfast prepared and were setting it out in the buffet line. This Saturday shift was extra work for them but they were fine with it, because it was also extra pay. There would be no free breakfast in the Hero's cafeteria, well except the team. We ate free but everybody else shelled out a couple of bucks so the help could be paid.

We were the first two there, of course. The Hero was always first to arrive wherever he went. His normal routine was first in and last out. It never varied. Pretty soon Tree and the Mill arrived. Then Ronnie walked in with Jelly and Ivy. I was glad Jelly had talked Ivy into coming. I knew he had not wanted to be there but the reason we moved breakfast was for them to be able to attend and for the townspeople to put a face on numbers 81 and 34. I was afraid they might not come and that would have spoiled the reason for the move from Granddad's drug store to the school.

Some other players drifted in and with them about half the town, it seemed. Then some of our cheerleaders came in. I had not known them to stir before noon on Saturday. What were they doing up at this unholy football hour? Their presence meant it would be our first coed bull session. Wait a minute. That's an oxymoron, right? Dad, who had a gift for counting the house, later told me there were 200+ people eating that morning, twice the attendance of our Presbyterian church worship on any given Sunday! I was happy to see we had our priorities straight. Drucker was noticeable in absence. He would never condescend to a discussion of his football strategy with the uninitiated. Several of the assistant coaches were there, though. Drucker would not attend such a get together but he would want to know what was said and by whom.

First things first, everybody went through the line and ate. It was apparent that since so many people were there, drug store protocol would not work. An informal Q&A was not practical with this large of a crowd. Dad sent some of the staff to quickly get a podium and our portable sound system. My granddad suggested we gather all our players at one table and that we first introduce ourselves. Remember, most of the adults in the room only knew us as uniforms with numbers on back. Then the floor would be open for questions to individual players. Of course, everybody wanted to ask a lot of personal question of Ivy and Jelly but granddad again interposed himself: 'Let's keep the questions to the subject of the football game last night.'

A former player raised his hand and asked when we put in all the new plays, implying that a new offense must be the key to our success, or maybe it was better execution, or anything, heaven help us, but the new players on the team. I said, 'I can answer that one. We haven't added a play to the book since I was a freshman.' They knew that had to be true since I was the one calling them and setting them in motion. I needed to get the facts out so I went a bit further: 'The obvious difference between this season and the last few is personnel.

For example when we run the old 25 curl/arc with Ivy at tailback, the man covering the flats on defense has to get way out with Ivy, otherwise he will outrun them when he catches the pass. We have never had anyone as fast as him before. Speed is a game changer. But if they jump Ivy's arc route, Ronnie will be open on the curl every time. That's why he's going to end the season as our leading receiver in school history And when we run the boot/drag just like we have for ten years, we have a 230 pound tight end, who no linebacker can knock down, and who can outrun every safety we will face this year. When you have real chicken, you can make some pretty good chicken salad.'

Everybody in the room laughed because they all had heard that old joke before. And as for the plays, when I used all that esoteric terminology, it wasn't lost on the men in the room. They had run the same plays, numbered the same way. Someone asked Jelly his 100 yard dash time and he said, 'I think about 10.3' and you could hear an intake of breath around the room. It had never been imagined by anyone in the room that a body as large as that could move at such speeds.

But Jelly was not finished with his answer: 'Ivy is faster than me. Last year at the state meet he ran a 9.4 and still one boy beat him. That drew laughs of disbelief. Then somebody asked Ivy his first question. It was about the blocking up front. He stood up and said, 'It's pretty good.' The Mill jumped in, 'Shit, I mean shoot, sometimes we still miss 'em like we always have but with Ivy, it don't much matter. 'Sides, I never heard him gripe about our blocking and I sure 'preciate that. We all do.'

There were more questions but we had gotten to the heart of the matter early on. Our new guys were becoming more and more accepted, not only as great athletes, but as team players. Big TEAM, little me, remember? As for the rest of us, we all were winners now. Amazing what being able to play a silly game can do for your stock options.

The final question was the elephant in the living room. Everybody was seeing the possibility but it needed to be asked: 'Gonna make it to state this year?' And Granddad jumped in before we could say anything: 'Let's not go there quite yet. We have to wait a few games to see about that.'

As everyone was leaving Ivy pulled me aside: 'What you got going?' I said, 'Not much. Just going home and probably watch the game on TV.' He said, 'You got time to go somewhere with me? I'd like you to meet somebody.' I was flabbergasted. Ivy had never asked me to do anything with him. This was epic, groundbreaking stuff. So I said, as neutrally as possible, didn't want to spook him by appearing over anxious: 'Let me check with dad.' Dad told me he'd ride home with Granddad and I could have the car.

So after I dropped Jelly at his house, Ivy said, 'Jest head on out the highway toward Kerrville.' We drove until we were on the edge of our county and Ivy said, 'Turn right.' It was a dirt road again but this one was very well maintained. There were trees lining the way, obviously planted and well tended. We drove for two miles through some of the most beautiful piney woods I'd ever seen until we emerged into this big open valley, mostly fenced in, with a herd of horses scattered throughout.

On the far side of that valley I could see someone riding one of the horses, bare-backed, I thought. As he came closer I saw that it wasn't a he. It was a girl. I could tell because her hair in a pony tail was flying just above the horse's mane where she was leaning down on his neck. It would not be accurate to describe her as riding the horse. She was riding so fluidly, I could not tell where horse ended and girl began. It would be better to say that she and the horse were almost one. They were moving like the wind across that pasture. The closer she came the more mesmerized I became. Finally, she flew to a stop right in front of us and jumped from the horse in one motion.

She held out her hand and said, 'Hello John, my name is Ruth. I'm friends with Ivory.' She was the palest of chocolates, she had an aquiline nose and rather thin lips, but the most intriguing feature was her sea green eyes. I had seen pictures in National Geographic of women from the Arabian deserts, were they Berbers or Kurds, I can't remember which? She looked more like them than she looked African. As if African is any one look, I guess? And this vision before my eyes was Ivy's friend. I spent most of that day with them and I was never exactly sure what she meant by the two of them being friends. That remained a mystery for a long time but I did learn a lot of other interesting stuff.

Ruth lived on this farm part of the year with her mother and father. She had no brothers or sisters. She was an only child. She did not go to school here. She was just home for the weekend. She attended a boarding school in Philadelphia. But next year she planned to enroll at Spelmen Women's College in Atlanta.

When I got home that day, I looked up Spelmen in Britannica. This is what I found: 'A four year women's liberal arts college in Atlanta. Founded in 1881 as Atlanta Baptist Female Seminary. The school received its academic charter in 1921, the fourth historic black female institution to receive that distinction. It is considered by academic authorities to be one of the top ten women's colleges in the United States.' That last bit did not say Negro colleges. It said, women's colleges, period. Wow, this young woman was educated, cultured and had obviously seen much more of the world than I had. I did not need to be a rocket scientist to know that I was neck high in tall cotton that day. This young woman was way out of my league or anyone else I knew. I was just becoming acquainted with the word cosmopolitan. I thought that she might be it.

What else I learned that day from Ruth was that her forebears had been among the first 'free Negros' in this country. They had lived for generations in and around Philadelphia. She still had relatives there but her immediate family had moved to the Atlanta area at the turn of the century. Her grandfather had bought this land for the purpose of breeding horses, thoroughbreds, I gathered. I did not really know much about horses but the ones in this pasture looked special to me. Her parents lived here part of the year and part of the year in Atlanta.

The authorities of our county were aware, of course, of this farm and the owners. However, her family's connections ran well past the jurisdiction of our local authorities. Ruth's family had powerful friends. In other words, they remained anonymous and safe in Atlanta and also in this remote part of our state. Some of this Ruth told me that day. Most of it I found out much later in life. Today, as I write this story, the farm is still in operation and Ruth still manages it. That day in 1966, however, was school for me.

There were many things about my world, I assumed I understood but I was moving into new areas of awareness. Long story short, Ruth became connected to Ivy years ago. First, Ivy's grandfather had worked for her grandfather. When Ivy's family had run into trouble with the local ignoramuses of our back water county, Ruth's family intervened. After the unpleasantness Yorky had become an unofficial ward of Ruth's father. When Ivy was born, he inherited that position from his granddad. I was here today because Ruth wanted to meet me. It turns out it had been her idea for this little road trip, not Ivy's after all.

After she introduced herself, Ruth told Ivy that her dad needed to talk with him. He left us to go inside to talk with Ruth's father and she invited me to ride horses with her. That's when I heard her story. As for horses, I knew how to ride, but not all that well, so I was provided with saddle. Ruth continued to ride bare back. We certainly did not gallop in the manner I had seen her coming across the meadow originally. We could not have talked at that speed and I could not have stayed upright. We did what I think is called trail riding and there were plenty of them to choose.

Ruth did most of the talking at first. She told me some more of Ivy's history: 'Ivory's father was killed in Korea. I think you know that? Ten years before that Ivory's uncle had been killed, also, It was in some local trouble. After his dad was killed, Ivory's mother left for New York City where she had friends. She refused to take him. As he had nowhere else to go, his grandfather brought him to the farm. I think you have seen the place? He was four years old when he moved to the farm. Ivory's grandfather had worked for my family and was a friend as well as diligent employee.

My grandfather decided that we would help his friend raise his grandson Ivory. My father has kept that arrangement, mainly working in the background of Ivory's life, to make sure he stays in school and out of trouble. I can tell you that his future is secure even though he is not aware of that yet. I would appreciate it if you did not mention that to Ivory. My father is also a friend of your father and they talk from time to time.' This was news to me. I could not think of anything to say to Ruth in response to that new information. I knew I would not be able to ask the Hero about it because he wouldn't tell me anything, anyway.

191

Ruth continued, 'I appreciate what you have tried to do for Ivory and he appreciates it, too, though I'm sure he has not told you.' I said, 'No, he doesn't say much about his life, although I was pleased Jelly took me out to the farm. He's not very comfortable saying thanks for things, either, but most guys aren't.' She laughed and changed the subject: 'Bertrand has always been a loyal friend to Ivory.'

I was intrigued that Ruth always said Ivory and Bertrand, never Jelly and Ivy. I asked her about that seeming formality. She explained herself: 'You may be figuring out by now, I consider most black nicknames pejorative, even if they give those names to themselves. With our people, those funny names are a type of self-loathing. We need desperately to get past that phase of our existence. We need to overcome those nicknames, as we need to overcome other things.'

I said, 'You understand, that if I don't use their nicknames around teammates, it would seem odd to the others because we all have nicknames?' She said, 'I understand that, but with us for now, let it be their Christian names.' I agreed but added, 'You can call me JJ, I like my nickname,' to which she replied, 'I'd prefer to call you John.' So I said, 'Okay, that will be fine. So Ruth, tell me what you think about Bertrand and Ivory playing football and going to Central?'

She said, 'We agreed last year that it would be the best thing for both of them.' And I wondered, 'Who is we?' But didn't ask her. So I asked the important question, 'Why didn't you, whoever you is, do anything about it, then? They'd probably never have gotten to Central if I hadn't met them this summer.' She smiled enigmatically, 'I think you are right about that, John. I'm so glad it worked out the way it did, your accidentally meeting them. What a wonderful coincidence you ended up working with them this past summer.' I smiled, 'Coincidence? No, you can thank everybody's 'Hero, I mean my dad. He got me my summer job. Sorry. I know, no nicknames. You can thank my dad for me meeting Ivory and Bertrand. Meeting them was coincidence, the job was entirely his idea.'

She changed the subject: 'I really appreciate the fact that you put your high school athletic career on the line for two boys you hardly knew. But before you start congratulating yourself, remember that you had an ulterior motive.' I turned red, because I knew what she meant and that it was true. But trying to defend myself, I said, 'Well yeah, but I liked them, too. It wasn't all about the fact they were good football players.' She went on, 'But had they not been outstanding football players who could help you get to the playoffs this year, your senior year, would you have helped them? If they had just been outstanding students, which they actually are, but not football players, would you have invited them to enroll at Central?'

I said, 'No, I guess not.' 'John,' she said, 'All of us have a long way to go, the white race and also the Negro race. Racism runs deep in us all.' I countered, 'I don't think I'm racist. I have never said anything demeaning about Negros and I have never done anything to hurt anybody of your race.' She said, 'That's not racism, John, not the deeper racism to which I am referring. Racism is not what you do or say, it's what you think. When you were teaching Bertrand to swim, didn't you think, 'Well, none of them can swim much, because they are afraid of the water? And tell the truth. Don't you think we can dance better than you, that we have natural rhythm?' I said, 'Ivory and Bertrand can dance better than I can.' She laughed, 'And they can dance better than I can as well.

193

Would you believe I'm not a good dancer? Probably not, John. Are you starting to understand me?'

Going on she said, 'And don't you think we like certain foods: watermelon, fried chicken, grits? John don't get upset. I'm not attacking you. I'm racist, too. I'm prejudiced against your race. I have a difficult time not believing that an innate streak of sadistic cruelty runs through you all.' I said, 'I understand, but why are you telling me this?' She said, 'I'm telling you all this for your sake, John. I think you have a good heart, like your father, and I think you can be an agent of change. As the year goes on, try not to think of Ivory and Bertrand just as football players. Get to know them better and let them get to know you. It's important, John. One day there won't be any football left for you, Ivory and Bertrand. I want you to still be friends then. I want us all to be friends then.'

At that time we rode up to the front of house, which I had not yet seen. We had left the car at the opening to the valley and the house wasn't visible from there. When I met Ruth, I guess I forgot about the car. The house was impressive. I felt like I was on the set of Gone With the Wind, not Tara, Seven Oaks, the bigger plantation. It was a plantation house if I'd ever seen one, white painted brick, eight columns, large front porch. Talk about the shoe on the other foot. There was my car. Someone had brought it from the edge of the valley to the gravel drive that circled in front of the house. We dropped our horses reins and dismounted.

Ivy was there, sitting half way up the circular front steps, waiting. That was it. I never knew if Ruth's parents were in the house that day or not. They probably were but they did not come out to introduce themselves. Ruth kissed our cheeks, mine and Ivy's, and we got in the car. She said, 'John, I may not see you for quite a while, but if you have occasion to be in Philadelphia this fall, or

194

Atlanta over Christmas, Ivory knows how to reach me. I'd enjoy seeing you again. I'm sure I'll see you before too long but for now, goodbye.' As we drove down the gravel drive toward the dirt road, she stood holding the horses' reins and watching.

Driving home, I tried to quiz Ivy about Ruth and her family but he knew little more than what she had told me. Or if he did, he was not telling more. His granddad and hers had been friends. His granddad did some work for them. After his dad was killed, Ruth's parents helped out by taking care of him. Ivy had gotten in trouble with the law once. It should have been a minor thing. It would have been for a white boy like me. Life was not the same for colored boys, however. In the case of young colored men, minor infractions can wind up with jail time.

While he waited in a holding cell at the county jail, a lawyer from Atlanta showed up, a white lawyer, and he was out of jail in no time flat. He never heard anything more about the situation, no trial, his arrest just went away. He received a letter from Ruth's dad, admonishing him to be more responsible in the future, and he had been. He had never needed much help after that, at least on legal grounds, but he felt that had he needed anything, it would have been provided. He didn't know why, just believed it.

I was sure I'd not get to the bottom of all the history beneath the events of this day any time soon. Even so, it was exciting to feel myself part of an ongoing mystery, affecting the lives of people more important than me. It was like being added to the cast in a mystery story. I'd do my best to fulfill my small role.

When I picked up Andi that night, I told her all about my day. She seemed a little jealous so I told her to relax. It wasn't like that. Ruth lived in a completely different world than we ever would. I was sure I'd see her again one day, probably on the cover of a magazine or in a major news story. But for now, we'd just go on being us. Ruth could be part of our lives later, or not.

Right now, we were going to a party at Tree's house. His birthday was Monday so Beefy and his wife wanted to celebrate on Saturday. It was great because they had invited Ivy and Jelly to come and bring dates. In the south some rules trumped others. Racism was a foregone conclusion but there was a rule above that one. The southerner's home was sacred and the homeowner made the rules there. Thus, Beefy could invite anyone to his house he chose. But my mom showed up with the Hero and the Driscolls and the DeLoaches also came that night. It was as if they were endorsing the Sizemore's decision to host a bi-racial event. There is great strength in numbers as you must know.

The adults went in the living room and left us alone in the family room. Jelly showed up with Ivy. He brought a cute girl I'd never seen before, obviously a student at Birney. Ivy didn't bring a date. But guess who did? The Mill, the Mill brought a date! By my recollection the Mill had had two dates in his entire life and one was with his sister!

But here he was with Julia Sims, the absolute brainiest girl in school, talk about opposites. I had no idea those two even knew each other. I was sure they'd never been in a class together. Julia didn't take automotive shop and the Mill was no friend of Physics. I was not sure she went to football games, either. I wasn't even sure they spoke the same language. I mean the Mill spoke pure redneck, but here they were. And they looked happy to be here and comfortable with each other. Normally the guy in this situation, new girl and all, took some ribbing from his friends. I had taken a ton of crap over Andi and Mill was the worst offender in the jokes that were on me.

Payback time, you're thinking? Right, this was the Mill, for goodness sake. Who was going to kid him? Tree maybe, Jelly, but it certainly would not be me.

We watched the night college game for a while but it was a walkover so we played a few parlor games, the non alcohol variety, of course. Then the Sizemore's came into the family room with a 16mm projector and the fun was on. We watched about an hour of home movies from the time Tree and, of course, the rest of us were in fourth grade. It was hilarious to see ourselves when we were ten. There was Andi with braces and big horn rim glasses in an ill-fitting cheerleader costume from Halloween. We whooped and hollered. She was not amused. Of course the teeth are perfect now and she's worn contacts for years. There was one shot of boys only at the lake skinny dipping and Beefy did not edit the film. You should have seen everybody trying to figure out who was who. Of course, the Mill was easy. He'd always been the fattest kid in the group.

I glanced over at Julia to see how she was taking it but she was laughing with the rest of us. I had always liked her. I hoped she would hang around with us more. She could only improve the Mill. Jelly and Ivy were the life of the party when they did an impression of Drucker talking to me on the sideline. Jelly did a perfect Drucker and Ivy was no slouch portraying me. Now it was Andi's turn to laugh. Their skit was about me having to go to the bathroom to take a leak during the heat of a game. It ended with Drucker saying, 'Just tie a knot in it, dumb ass, and get back out there.'

When we left that night, Andi suggested a side trip over to the lake. I was shocked. That was the favorite parking spot of steady couples. The cops came out and rousted kids from time to time but they knew the players' cars and left us alone. When she said it, I almost swallowed my chewing gum. Well, it was her idea, I promise. We went as she suggested but I'm not telling about that, not even twenty years later. I couldn't talk about it then and still can't. Even at forty, I still blush when I try to write about stuff like that. I will say that the next time she suggested it, and the next, I was ready and willing. And the next, and the next! If you have ever parked out by the lake on a cool southern fall night, you probably remember a sky filled with stars and you might remember other stuff. Use your imagination. I'm not talking.

Ronnie won the pool on Sunday. He guessed that Drucker would completely ignore the success we had passing and stress the good execution on running plays. He was absolutely dead on, right. Drucker seemed to be on a mission to table our burgeoning passing attack and get back to what he knew and liked best. He didn't mention our passes at all, except to criticize routes and point out my lack of accuracy and distance, never mind that I threw three touchdowns, a record for our school.

The Mill leaned over and whispered, 'Don't worry. We'll miss a few blocks on purpose this week so we get ourselves in a situation where only your raggedy ass arm can get us out.' I mumbled back, 'You don't have to try all that hard, fatso, you miss plenty of blocks with no effort at all.' The younger kids, who by now had gravitated to our spot in the field house, were cracking up, holding their mouths to keep from laughing out loud. Our asides to Drucker's commentary every Sunday had become very popular among the underclassmen. Drucker shouted, 'Cut out the snickering over there and pay attention to this beautifully executed running play, 25 Iso.

On Monday when Andi walked in the breezeway door to school wearing my letterman's jacket, the Mill punched me in the arm. Dang it hurt. He laughed, 'She must have won that from you in a passing contest.' Everybody in our group of ball players started to laugh, except Ronnie. At least he appreciated my passing skills. Andi stood there waiting, and ever quick on the uptake, I took the hint and walked her to her locker. This time it didn't only feel to me like every eye in the high school was on us. It was a fact that every eye in the school was on us, without doubt. I put a good face on it and acted as if it were the most natural thing in the world for the prettiest girl in school to be wearing my jacket. Who wouldn't want to be wearing the QB's jacket? Right?

That afternoon I knew practice would be easy. In fact, it would be an easy week of practice. We always played Driscol at this time and Drucker used the week to rest us and heal injuries. Driscol was the weakest city team in our league. They had not had a winning season in many years. I was pretty sure we could beat them without throwing a pass and predicted that would be what would happen. Ronnie and I were pretty bummed about that but we could see smash mouth football written all over Drucker's face.

Anyway it was a great week to have a genuinely easy opponent because it was FAIR week in Central. The southern country fair in our small town ranked right up there with Halloween, Thanksgiving and Christmas as fall highlights. At lunch on Monday we were talking about all the fun things there were to do at the fair, the rides, the games. The Mill casually asked Jelly if he were going. Jelly said, 'Yeah, on Thursday.' Tree asked, 'Why don't you go with us on Wednesday?' Jelly said, 'Thursday is colored day,' and that was true. Wednesday was free admission for white school kids, and half priced rides. Thursday was for colored kids. It was a hard and fast rule. Andi said, 'Well, if you can't come with us on Wednesday, then we are going with you on Thursday instead.' I loved that girl, she was a natural disaster waiting to happen, she had no fear.

So we talked it over with our parents and they didn't see any reason for us to not go with our new colored friends on Thursday since Jelly and Ivy could not go with us on Wednesday. After shorts practice that afternoon, we headed on out to the fair. It was set up in a big pasture just on the south edge of town. The group going were Tree, the Mill, Ronnie, me and Andi, and, of course Jelly and Ivy. The fair grounds, as I said, were just a big flat field with a set of grand stands in the middle. They had cattle auctions there at other times of the year.

The county fair is a southern tradition. It is the time when the farmers show off their prize animals. There are cooking contests and sewing contests and even flower arranging. But for us the attraction was the midway, all the rides and games, and the freak shows. That's when we found out that the Mill wasn't the only one scared of the Wild Mouse. The Wild Mouse was a compact, gut wrenching mini coaster. It was about three stories tall with tight curves and stomach turning drops. As the little cars rolled around the course, the entire edifice shook and swayed. Truthfully, had we gone out on Sunday when the rides were put together and watched the construction, probably we'd all have been terrified.

But the Mill was really scared. He had reason to be. He was too big to have anyone ride with him. Andi and I could fit in one of the cars together but the Mill filled that little car to the brim. He began to sweat as soon as we got in line. We were all laughing at Mill but then I looked at Jelly and that boy was positively white, not even possible, was it? So we made them ride in the first two cars. That way the rest of us could watch from behind. It turned out to be the best show at the fair that night. When everyone heard the screams coming from the rails of the Wild

Mouse, a huge crowd gathered to watch. I'm sure the two of them exceeded any weight limit the health inspector might have put on the individual cars on that coaster. How those tiny cars stayed on the track was anybody's guess. They screamed like girls the whole time. Well, not all girls. Andi didn't scream at all.

When they got off, the ride the Mill puked. 'Way to go, fatso,' I laughed, 'That sure makes me hungry. Why don't we go eat now.' And that thought made Jelly puke, too. So we did go eat. The local Lions Club made the best barbeque sandwiches you've ever tasted and after those we had funnel cakes and cotton candy. But we weren't alone by then.

I realized we had attracted quite a crowd, and not just to watch Mill and Jelly throw up. Little colored kids were gathered all around us, like we were the fair's main attraction. That's when I began to understand what great heroes Ivy and Jelly were in their community. Those kids danced around them and shouted to get their attention. Ivy and Jelly acted as if they could not see them. But the kids weren't the only ones.

As we walked the midway adults would say things like, 'You show dem white boys how to play football.' We met some of their old teammates and even they were nice. You'd think they'd be bitter at losing the best players on their team but they were more proud to have two of their own starring for the local white team. What Jelly and Ivy were doing for their community was something you could see in the faces of kids and adults alike. I felt I was walking around with the Legion of Superheroes!

After riding the Scrambler, the Ferris wheel, killing each other in bumper cars, we decided to try a few games. There was the one with the tires, which you threw footballs through. I had a weak arm, but I was accurate. After I won six teddy bears, the barker made me quit. I gave one to Andi and the rest to the kids who were still following us. We almost had a riot but I made sure all the little girls got a bear. One little girl, who didn't get one, started to cry, so Andi gave her the one she had.

Ronnie, who was our ace pitcher on Central's baseball team, knocked the milk bottles over three times and they made him quit, too. We were breaking the bank. We all had a try at the basketball toss, a rigged game because the rims are smaller than standard. But Ivy hit about eight straight shots and they ran us off again. I had forgotten that he was a really good basketball player. Some said better at that than football. I did not think that was possible.

We were about out of money and time when the Mill started chanting, 'Hootchie Kootchie, Hootchie Kootchie.' That phrase is southernese, male southernese, for the strip tease show. Back then every fair had one. It was behind the midway, sort of out of sight. According to the local constabulary you had to be eighteen to get in, which was a joke. I went to the show with some older boys when I was about thirteen. The Mill said, 'Andi, you wait for us out here.' She said, 'No dice, Mill. I'm coming, too, or I'm gonna tell that cop there how old you all are.' We could not stop her, didn't try, because we figured the cop would do it for us. Girls, no matter their age, were simply not allowed inside that tent.

But she had on blue jeans like the rest of us, so she pulled her hair up and put on Ronnie's baseball cap. She already had on my jacket, so we put her in the middle of the group and she sneaked in. Natural disaster, that girl, I already told you that. I was so embarrassed, I made the Mill sit beside her. Usually, there was a policeman outside the tent to cull the crowd and one inside the to keep the show semi-decent. The inside fuzz must have been getting a funnel cake himself or riding the mouse, or something.

So the three women bared all to the hoots and whistles of everyone in the tent. As I think back I wonder that we would ever do anything as raunchy and chauvinistic as that but there we were. It was 1966, we were seventeen, and really stupid. And besides, everyone else did it. Lot's of lame excuses, sorry. When we came out, Andi said, 'Okay, been there now, done that. I'll mark it off my bucket list. Never again.' She wasn't laughing either.

The next night's game was in the city as Driscol was a city team and there's not much to tell. It was 28-0 at half and coach took Ivy out after he scored for the fourth time. He didn't even let the starters play in the second half. We won 49-0. Coach was so relaxed he let the cheerleaders, not only eat the post game meal with us, but also ride back on the bus. Of course, they had to sit in the front and not with boys next to them. Since we were in the city, we easily found a restaurant that would take the entire team. All in all, it was a great game and now we had our winning season: 6-1. On Monday the first state rankings would be coming out. I was pretty sure we would make the top ten.

CHAPTER TEN

Son, you will never be able to play this game
until you understand the difference between pain and injury.

Any head coach who ever lived!

When I woke up Saturday morning, my ankle was so stiff I could barely get out of bed to hobble to the bathroom. I remember the pain to this day. Worse than the pain was the sickening realization that I might not be able to play in the next game. I sprained my ankle on the last play of the half, the last play in which I participated Friday night. We ran a quarterback sneak to bleed off the remaining seconds on the clock. There was a pile of bodies as there always is on a play like that and someone fell on my ankle in the pile and I felt a sharp tweak. Ironically, it could as easily have been one of my teammates as our opponents who fell on me.

At the time it hurt but the adrenaline that runs through a player's body during a game is also an effective pain suppressant so I thought little of it at the time. It had not bothered me much on the bus ride home. Had I felt it more that night, I'd have wrapped it in an Ace bandage and probably put some ice on it to avoid swelling. It was too late on Saturday for any of those preventive measures.

When I crawled out of bed that morning, it was twice it's usual size and I could see a bluish tinge on the outside of the ankle streaking down toward my toes. I had rolled the top of my foot outward and the ankle went down underneath. There are several ways to turn and ankle but a pronated sprain like mine was the worst kind.

When I showed it to the Hero that morning, he took one good look and said, 'Go see Doc Meadows, now.' Doc did not work on Saturdays except during football season. Then he held a private clinic for the football team. Anybody hurt in the game was supposed to report to him between seven and nine o'clock. If you came to films with a visible injury on Sunday and did not have a note from Doc that you were in clinic with him Saturday morning, you'd be in serious trouble with Drucker. If you did not have your injuries checked immediately and lost practice time, he'd let Doc nurse you back to health so he could kill you afterward.

When I got to the clinic, Tree was already there, having his knee drained. There were a couple of other players icing various body parts. When I came in Doc took one look at my ankle and said, 'We're going to drain it, right now. 'No Doc,' I thought, 'Not we, you are going to drain it. I'm going to watch and try to remain conscious so I can experience the intense pain.'

He left me on his examination table for a few minutes with only my keen imagination for company. When he came back he had a very large syringe with a four-inch needle attached. First, he gave me shot of novocaine (actually xylocaine by 1966). That process was frightening as I could feel the needle probing between my ankle bones, scraping off this one and into that one. Every now and then he'd shoot a little juice and then move on. I stopped complaining in my head (never did you complain out loud) when the pain killer took effect.

When he unscrewed the first syringe from the needle, he attached a larger one and he put the needle in even more deeply. Even with the xylocaine, I could feel a twinge as he probed. Suddenly, the syringe began to fill on its on with a milky red substance. When it began to fill up, Doc helped by drawing back the plunger further. He filled the first syringe and unscrewed it from the needle. He left the room to get replacement syringes, apparently there was more liquid to be extracted. It's more than a little disconcerting to see an open needle protruding from your ankle, especially since it was oozing bodily fluids onto me and the examining table.

He ended up drawing out three syringes of fluid. I admit that it felt much looser already. Of course, I couldn't tell about the pain because the xylocaine was still working its magic. Next he inserted a small syringe of dark viscous fluid. He told me it was cortisone. Even with the pain killer, it burned my ankle like fire. After that he sent me out into the clinic to soak my ankle in ice cold water. After about an hour of soaking, the xylocaine began to wear off. It hurt but with the swelling reduced and all the go-go juice in there, it felt much better. I asked should I stay off of it, expecting crutches. He told me to walk on it as much as possible. No dancing, however. No problem there, Doc.

I missed the Breakfast Club that day, of course, but the Mill filled me in. Ivy was asked a ton of questions, whether he thought he'd break our school's rushing yards and touchdown records, all held by the Hero, by the way. It was a loaded question since the Hero was right there in the room. The Mill told me that he handled it very well and hardly boasted at all. When he was asked if he'd heard from any colleges, he replied that he had gotten some letters, mostly from schools up north and one from Southern Cal actually signed by John McKay himself.

To myself, I thought, 'Typical.' I didn't figure he'd get anything from our instate schools or the close schools in other southern states. The rumor was that Bear Bryant was going to break the color barrier at Alabama next season, or the one after. Maybe that would spur our schools to action but I expected Ivy was a year or two early to get to play anywhere near home. I doubted he wanted to play for any of them anyway.

Tree, who had left clinic with me, asked if I thought I'd be able to play next week, such a thoughtful guy. Worried about my health, or maybe worried that my backup who was a ninth grade kid, who'd not taken a snap until last night, might have to start this coming week. I said, 'Sure. I going to play.' What else could I say?

The Mill said, "You'd better have your sorry ass ready. Kerrville is always trouble and if we have to rely on our ground game alone, we're gonna have a fight on our hands. That freshman will be good in some other life time but not ours. You better get your sorry ass ready, JJ, or I'll kill you myself.' So the Mill was concerned for my health, also. His threat was almost a compliment coming from the Mill.

The next game was Kerrville, as I said. It was also homecoming. In our small town homecoming was about the biggest social event outside of Christmas. The whole town was involved in the festivities. There was a dance after the game with a live band and in the middle of the dance the homecoming queen was crowned. The festivities began on Thursday with a parade down Main Street. There were floats from each class in school, some of our clubs, as well as various civic organizations. The homecoming court rode in fancy convertibles, the VFW band led it out, and the team brought up the rear, all of us perched on the big hook and ladder from the fire department.

Sometimes the game itself got lost in the hoopla but I knew it had better not this year. We had a tough opponent. Usually, the homecoming date was chosen to correspond with a game against a patsy, There was nothing worse then losing your homecoming game. But Kerrville was never easy. They always gave us a good run and we had lost to them last year at their place. I promised myself that even with all the hoopla of the coming week, I would not let the team lose its focus. Oh, and I'd get well, too. According to the Mill, my long term health depended on my getting well soon.

That afternoon we went to Tree's house to work on our class float. We built it there every year, because he had a fenced in back yard and the other classes couldn't spy on us and steal any ideas, as if we had any. Also, his drive way went to the back of his house, so we could hitch the Mill's truck to the trailer and pull it out to the street.

That Saturday there were about thirty of us seniors, including the usual suspects: me, Tree, the Mill, Ronnie, all the senior cheerleaders. Only this time Jelly and Ivy showed along with Julia Sims, who to my recollection had never been to our floating chaos before. I gave our construction project the name floating chaos because it was.

Every year since ninth grade the girls took this job very seriously and worked diligently on the float. While they did this, we watched football in Tree's den. Then the girls would come in and plead and cajole until we came out to help. But we weren't much help. Inevitably, horse play would break out among the boys and all or parts of the float would be destroyed. At that point the girls either sent us home or banished us to Tree's den for the remainder of the construction.

This year, as always, we went in to watch the game, all except Jelly and Ivy who stayed in the backyard to help the girls. They actually thought we were there to help. I had begun to notice that those two were much more relaxed around the girls in our class than around us. I don't think it was in any way sexual. As I think about it now from the perspective of many more years, I have a theory that they, both women and negros, resented being under the thumb of the southern white male. So they made common cause at least, maybe a little, or maybe I'm just reading too much into it. Preachers do that, you know?

That day the game on TV was boring so I went out to join them and help, no really! Our job was build the float, not to design it. The girls had a plan and they gave the orders. We nailed wood together, attached chicken wire, and stuffed green and gold crepe streamers where we were told. But I remember the girls being stumped once, something about the design, and they asked Jelly's opinion. He gave advice and they followed it and it worked. I had to find out his secret. Maybe he was good with design like his dad and the girls grasped intuitively that he had that ability.

At any rate, they kept asking Jelly questions and ignoring me and Ivy and the rest, oh well. Eventually, we broke for dinner and everybody went to the Rib Shack. We brought back take out food for Ivy and Jelly. The night was spent, girls working like crazy and boys working halfheartedly, on the float, but at least no major destruction was done. And we all parted friends, for once.

On Sunday Jelly won the pool. He told us that Drucker would be harping on mental attitude. He would tell us that we would need to be a great deal more disciplined and focused for the remainder of this year. It was the only way we could hope to be history makers. To underscore his comments, Coach would trash us in films that day. This was the Jelly man's opinion.

As we watched the film, Drucker's snide comments seemed to be about a different game than the one I thought we were watching. I leaned in and whispered to the Mill, 'Is he watching the same film as us? We are killing these guys. In the film he is watching we must be losing.' The Mill whispered back, 'We always lose in his film. We shouldn't even watch. Every mother fucker dies in the end of his version.' The freshmen and sophomores were sniggering. By the time we tuned Drucker back in, he was rolling but on a tangent having nothing to do with the current movie. He was ranting about mental toughness, particularly the ability to distinguish between pain and injury.

Why did he keep looking my way? This discussion was getting too painfully close to home. I muttered to the Mill, 'I know the difference and the similarity between pain and injury. I'm injured and it's very painful.' The Mill whispered, 'I don't care if your fucking foot gets ampertated. Your ass had better be on the damn field Friday night, even if it's attached to a wheelchair.' I said, 'No problem, Dr. Butt hole. With you and Drucker treating my mental condition and Doc Meadows treating my physical one, I'm practically well already.'

That drew some snickers from the underclassmen who always gathered around the two of us at films to witness our comedy routine. Drucker shouted, 'Why don't you two come up here and run the projector, since you seem to know so much. The Mill was standing up as if to accept the invitation when coach said, 'Sit your ass down and shut up. Any more from the peanut gallery and it will be a ton of up/downs tomorrow.' The Mill could not resist; he whispered, 'That ought to help your ankle, pussy.'

Monday was our initial feedback as to what the rest of the state thought about the Central Hornets football team. We were apparently well thought of, ranked #7 in our state classification. My freshman year we finished #10 and that was the highest rank we had been given since then. Now, the first week of rankings we were up at #7. I was not sure who at the big newspaper had heard about us or how but I was betting someone down there had found out that we had some new players on our team.

The state rankings came from the newspaper in the capitol so news was beginning to seep down that way, apparently. But there was another ranking coming out that Monday, an individual one for every student in our school. It was first nine weeks report card day. This was when the senior sheep were separated from the senior goats. If you made all A's and B's on your report card, and had on your person that all important note from your parents, you were excused to go out to lunch for the rest of the year. That meant, the slop house would see a decline in attendance and business would pick up at McDonalds, Hardees, and the Rib Shack.

But it also meant we wouldn't be eating with the Mill anymore. He had not made all B's since first or second grade, when everybody got all A's and B's. Ivy walked up and said, 'Look at my report card. I can go out to lunch, except there ain't any place that will let me in. Jelly, can't go out, because he made too good grades, all A's.' That was an understatement of Jelly's performance. The rumor going around was that Jelly had made 100's on several final exams and that he might give Julia a run for valedictorian of our class.

The Mill walked up and said expansively, 'Where we all going to lunch today?' He showed me his report card and he had one A and 5 B's. I was pretty sure it was a forged document. Then I remembered Julia. She was either a good influence on the Mill or she was doing his homework, or both. Andi, of course, made the lunch-bunch. She had only made one B in her entire high school career. I made about half A's and half B's as usual so I made the travel squad as well. To celebrate at lunch that day we all loaded into Andi's Impala for our first lunch out. We got to the parking lot entrance and she stopped: 'This isn't right.'

She doubled back toward the field house where lots of the underclass football guys were hanging out for lunch. There were Jelly and Ivy. 'Get in,' she commanded. We had to rearrange but with the Mill and Jelly in front and me, Tree and Ivy in the back, we just fit. Remember, a '62 Impala was as big as a small motor home! It was still warm, so we put her top down and the three of us in the back sat on the trunk with feet on the seat waving to the underclass folk in the parking lot, like the homecoming court. Ronnie followed right behind us in his car with six other boys and girls.

In those days, McDonald's sold hamburgers for 25 cents and they still had a banner saying how many millions they had sold. Two burgers, fries and coke were about a dollar. So we were able to scrape enough together to get food for everybody. We left the take out window and drove to a public picnic table a few blocks away. While we were eating, one of our three police cars stopped and the officer came to the table. 'Oh,' he said, 'I didn't recognize you guys from a distance. Have a nice lunch. How's the ankle, JJ? How many you gonna score this week, boy?' Ivy swallowed his urge to say what he actually thought and said, 'As many as I can, officer.' The policeman turned to walk away: 'You all have a nice lunch and beat Kerrville.' Right about then I was thinking to myself how good it was to be a ball player in a town where everyone wants you to go to state.

That afternoon I wore a gold jersey while the rest of the team wore the usual green. That gold jersey was gold to me! It meant they couldn't hit me in the scrimmage. The Mill said, 'Oh boy, coaches got you in gold. Must be 'smear the queer' day and they wanted us to have a target.' As he was walking away he said, 'It's probably more like, leave the pussy alone day.'

My ankle was strapped so tight with tape my toes were about to pop off but I thought about taking a running jump and kicking him square in the butt. That afternoon with a little work, I found I could push off my plant foot (the injured one) and throw the ball. That was a good start, because a cripple could handle our running plays but only a semi-cripple would be able to pass the ball. By now almost every running play consisted of handing the ball to Ivy and getting out of the way and watching him run. As for my own running, it was very limited but I felt better than I had on the weekend. Monday night it was back to the clinic for a regimen of drain and pain: take the fluid out and stick in the cortisone.

Thursday was the biggest day of the year for football in Central not counting the actual games, of course. We had our school pep rally after lunch and then the entire school was let out for the parade. The local VFW band led off, followed by all the vets: we had WW I, WW II, Korea, and we still had two guys who had fought in the Spanish-American War, but they were in wheel chairs.

Next in the line came our girls' drill corps, followed by the ROTC unit. Then interspersed among class floats were all the girl-vertables: Corvettes, Thunder-Birds, Impalas, with tops down. There was one girl from each class in school on the home coming court and then the three seniors who were in the running for queen, six girls in all. We would not know the homecoming queen until after the game tomorrow night at the dance.

213

The team came at the end of the parade on the fire department's hook and ladder truck. This always scared Drucker because we tended to balance in precarious ways, as dangerously as possible for crowd effect and photo ops. He told us every year without fail that if any of us fell off and got hurt, we might as well roll on under a tire of the big truck because he would kill us anyway. And still we performed stupid balancing acts!

The parade ended at the school baseball field where there was a huge bonfire. There we had a second pep rally and Drucker introduced the coaches and the players to everyone, officially for the first time all year. Of course, as the policeman demonstrated earlier in the week, no introductions were really necessary. Everyone in town already knew who most of us were. It was fun for the younger guys because they had never been introduced before. It was a yawner for the seniors, of course. Then we lit the fire and stood around singing school songs. After all that, we went home and tried to come down off the high in order to get some sleep.

After lunch Friday all the classes were turned out for final decoration of the gym for the dance. It was just as well. Classes in the morning were a waste of time. Nobody was doing any learning. At about three, we left for the cafeteria and our pregame meal. For homecoming we had prime rib, mashed potatoes, rolls and salad.

Today's athletes just eat a pasta dish and drink plenty of liquids. In our day coaches thought we needed a pound or two of red meat to be ready to play. What did they know? Those days coaches still handed out salt tablets to prevent cramping. I'm surprised they didn't use leeches on us! Well, the doc still leeches. Only he used a new fangled thing, a syringe.

From dinner it was meet, wrap ankles and try to relax before the warm up. When the team went out for our warm up, Tree and I stayed behind with an assistant coach and Doc Meadows. This cloak and dagger stuff was because we were getting pain killers. These xylocaine shots, of course, were illegal and so we were supposed to get the shots without anyone seeing. As if everybody on the team didn't know what was going on back in the locker room when they left.

The only ones who didn't know were our mothers. There is no way I'd tell my mom I was doing anything so dangerous as taking pain killers to play a game. Of course, the Hero knew but it was a secret he took to the grave and my mom still doesn't know, because I wouldn't dare tell her about the shots, even now. So then after the shots, the coach wrapped my ankle and Tree's knee and we rejoined the team.

We easily won the game: 28-14. I'm not going into all the details of this one. Probably, you are weary of hearing the technical stuff anyhow. It was a good game, always was with Kerrville. For some reason, year in and year out, they were the biggest team we played. They outweighed our line by ten pounds a man, at least. We had a difficult time running over them. But they were always slow so we were able to run around them, Ivy was able, that is. And we passed over them. I threw two TD's, one to Jelly and one to Ronnie. We got out two TD's ahead 'from the git go' and led most of the game by that same margin.

There was an interesting series of incidents in the game, however. Fans don't see all the ins an outs of the game but there is sometimes personal stuff going on. Tonight it got really personal between one of their linebackers and me. Somehow they had gotten word of my ankle injury. It is difficult to keep the lid on injuries to key personnel like quarterbacks and running backs. And even though it is not ethical, their coach might have

215

mentioned that they ought to rush me hard and see if they could intimidate me into making a mistake, maybe even hit me after I had handed the ball off to try to get in my head. Yes, stuff like that goes on, not rule breaking exactly, but rule stretching for sure.

This game Drucker had decided I needed to stay in the pocket to pass. He thought that since my mobility was limited, I'd be better protected that way. Because I am short, I really didn't like pocket passing. I can't see over the linemen. And protecting a pocket is the most difficult blocking for high school linemen. I would have preferred us to use a moving pocket or do some bootleg passing. I really like passing from out in the open. But here I was in the pocket and this LB kept blitzing. I mentioned that our guards were young and this guy was beating them off the snap pretty good.

I never was sacked but as I got the pass off, he'd hit me. A couple of times the contact was pretty late, border lining on unnecessary roughness. And as he walked back to his huddle, he always had a comment about my toughness, or rather, lack thereof. I kept my mouth shut. You can never let an opponent know he is getting to you, that only makes things worse. But I guess Tree and Ivy overheard him make a comment after a particularly late hit.

The next pass, Tree shoved his man way to the outside and that freed him to come over from the left and blind side this guy right in the ribs. He had his arms up in pass rush and was vulnerable anyway. Tree's hit lifted him up in the air off his feet. As he was in that very vulnerable position, Ivy had broken his flare route and doubled back. He hit this guy from the other side in the knees and between them they scissored him completely upside down. He landed on his head with both of them on top of him.

And he stayed on the ground. He had to be helped off the field, toes barely touching the turf. This was near the end of the first half. He didn't come back in the second half and my passing improved dramatically. It was after he left the game that I got my two TD passes. These kinds of individual battles happen all the time in football. And so when you play QB and have to stand in the pocket, it is good to have a posse around like I had.

And the game was over and on to the real game that night, crowning the Homecoming Queen. The homecoming court was always one freshman, one sophomore, one junior, and three seniors. I think I told you that already. The underclass girls were not eligible to win Miss Homecoming, but it was a great honor to be on the court. The senior girls that year were: Andi, Sally Jamison, and Rhonda Hadley. The entire school voted on the queen. There was no politics involved. No one gave a speech. It was purely and simply a popularity contest. The girl her classmates most liked was generally the winner, but there had been a few surprise winners in the past, so you never knew.

Most people were telling me that Andi was sure to win, of course, that was my friends talking. Lots of schools had begun to announce the queen at the half of the game. We crowned the queen the old fashioned way, at the dance after the game. All six girls stood together on the portable stage and the Master of Ceremonies announced the underclass girls first. Then he announced the queen in last to first order: 'Our homecoming queen 'runnerup is Rhonda Hadley. Our first runnerup this year is Sally Jamison. And the winner of Central High school's Homecoming Queen for 1966 is Andi DeLoach. So everybody on the stage cried and hugged. And since they really were good friends, they were all happy to be there together and I was glad it was over.

The job of the homecoming court's dates was to escort them down the center of the gym, help them up the steps to the stage and then stand there and try to not look too self conscious. We were required to wear tails. The rest of our football team wore rented tuxedos and regular male students wore coat and tie. It was a tradition at Central.

I was probably the shortest homecoming escort ever, probably looked more like a penguin in those tails than an escort. If the girls didn't have a boyfriend, they always chose the tallest, most handsome boys in their class to escort them. I lost by both counts. Tree escorted Sally. Rhonda was escorted by Ronnie (they were dating, but he was tall anyway). And Andi got the runt with the weak arm. It was a great party. We had a winning season, and my ankle was feeling better. I'm pretty sure the best looking guy at the dance that night was not one of the homecoming escorts, however. In my estimation it was Ivory York, hands down.

CHAPTER ELEVEN

I want my players to be agile, mobile, and hostile.

Jake Gaither, Florida A&M

That Saturday morning I felt like I woke up in new world. The pain in my ankle was almost gone and that meant no more trips to the doctor. From my perspective, twenty-five years later, I am still amazed at the resilience of my youthful body. That ability to recover, of course, fades away with age. It's probably why very few football players stay in the game after thirty.

The Breakfast Club at the school cafeteria was packed today. Not one, but all of our assistant coaches had come. Of course, Drucker was a no show. He had sent his minions to scope the scene as usual, this time with reinforcements, to make sure his players were conducting themselves according to his strict standards. Like most head coaches, Drucker was a control freak. He didn't want us talking about the team in public but if we were allowed to do so, he wanted some constraints. He was probably right about that. Seeing our coaches out in the crowd, no doubt, kept us at least a tiny bit circumspect.

We said all the proper things like, 'We are just playing to the best of our ability.' We used the tried and true, 'giving 110%,' and all the rest of the football humble speak. Our backs must have said, 'I owe it all to my lineman,' a hundred times. The Mill and Ivy wisely stayed silent on questions about how they thought they had played because neither of them believed that they owed anything to their teammates. I'm kidding, well kinda, sorta kidding. But they did say, 'Our coaches are doing a great job getting us prepared each week,' true but a bit corny. And the Mill added, 'We just have to keep our focus and play as best we can and let the playoffs take care of themselves.'

We said it that way, you know, the part about the playoffs taking care of themselves but every player in the room believed we were going to state this year. We didn't say it but we believed it. We only had to win two out of three of the games left on the schedule since one of the three was Howard Banks, a different classification team, who did not count toward our region schedule. So it went that morning. Instead of eggs everybody in the room was getting a large serving of humble pie.

FYI, As to how the playoffs worked. In those ancient days 32 teams didn't make the playoffs in each classification as they do today. Back then there weren't but a few more than 32 teams in any of the three different divisions. In 1966 the state's public schools were divided by student population: the largest division was AAA, in the middle was AA, and the small schools were class A. We were AA, in the middle, and our classification had eight Regions around the state, maybe 50 schools all told.

The winner of each of the eight Regions advanced to the playoffs.

From there it was win, or go home. Even now I find it interesting that seven out of eight of the best teams in the state were destined to end the year a loser with a bitter taste in their mouth. There is nothing worse than to lose the last game of your season and that happened to all but one team in the playoffs every year. Win all year only to lose in the end, what a terrible fate. Enough of this looking ahead stuff. No good team looks ahead. Play 'em one game at a time. I'm worried. I'm starting to think and talk like my coach.

Anyway, here's what lay ahead for us. Forget Howard Banks. We had to win both of our last two region games: Parnassus and Royal. The reason we had to win both was we had that one Region loss, our only blemish. Remember, it came in that first game when eight of us did not play. Camden had beaten us that night but Camden had lost three games since then so they were out. Parnassus, who we played this week, was a walk-over but we could not overlook them. We had to have that win, because Royal, our big rival, was undefeated in the region. We had to get to that game with only the one loss.

Then if we could beat Royal, even though our records would be identical, we'd be region champs because we would have beaten then in our head to head contest. Yeah, I know, it's complicated but our team and everyone in the town of Central understood the math. We had to win.

Even though the playoffs were still weeks away, we were already in the win or go home mode. Any loss other than HB from here on would be the end of our dream. But if we won this week, next week, and forever more, then we'd win it all. Our path to state, though not a cake walk, was crystal clear. We knew what we had to do to win it all. The destiny of our team was in our hands.

But I have digressed yet again. I intended to introduce you to our assistant coaches and got off on the playoffs. That's okay, because you need to know how the playoffs worked in those days. Now for the coaches: Drucker was our head coach. What can I tell you about him that I haven't already? The four assistants were teachers at our school, actually one taught PE at the junior high. Remember Drucker's OCD? We had exactly 66 boys who dressed on our varsity and junior varsity, 33 on each team (only this year the varsity had one more as Ivy was a late addition #34). The jersey numbers each team wore were exactly the same, because the JV wore last year's varsity jerseys.

There were ten members of the JV team who were juniors in school and they practiced with us everyday, which meant varsity practice had 34 players plus ten warm bodies, Drucker's terminology, not mine. The rest of the JV practiced on the other end of the field. Occasionally Drucker would call them over to be cannon fodder and run plays against us but not often. Usually, the 44 of us were all we had for practice. We were coached by the four assistants while Drucker wandered from drill to drill, making a nuisance of himself. When the scrimmaging began, however, Drucker took charge.

Since most of us played on both sides of the ball, at least from time to time we did, there were not offensive and defensive coaches as there are today. Coaches coached both offense and defense. Tad Simpson was our running backs/linebackers coach. He had played junior college ball at the nearby school, but finished at the big school my dad attended although he didn't play football there. Jeff Bridger was our line coach on both sides of the ball. He had played for Drucker in high school and then went to a small college and played four years. Mike Patton coached wide receivers and defensive backs and he had played high school ball for Drucker, too, but did not play in college. John Oakes was my coach. He coached QB's on offense and safeties on defense. He had played at the university where my dad had played earlier. He lettered there but had never started.

All of our assistant coaches were young and, for the most part, ambitious. I don't think any of them wanted to spend their entire career slaving under Drucker. But they were willing to pay their dues for the time being and they would need Drucker's recommendation to advance and become head coaches one day. Thus, they could be counted on to toe the party line. In other words, they belonged to Drucker, body and soul. The big man was the coordinator on both sides of the ball. He called every offensive play, using hand signals and though he let Tad Simpson call the defense he had the right to override every call Tad made if he chose to.

Of course no player had ever witnessed a coaches' meeting, but the word was that things were done democratically. Every coach got one vote and Drucker got five. Coach Oakes, my mentor, was not going to vary one iota from the course set by Drucker but he and I were able to talk about things and he was pretty good at listening and, at least, sharing my ideas with Drucker. I never went to Drucker with an idea. Drucker never heard a word from me unless asked but I could go to Coach Oakes without being asked.

The assistants were often our buffer to deflect the raging insanity we sometimes faced from the top. I said that our assistant coaches were young. They were all just out of college themselves, all in their twenties. All of them were bigger stronger and faster than most of us because they had just finished their college careers. Drucker could have dressed them out and played them along with our scrubs and they'd have given the varsity starters a good game. Probably they would have beaten us.

Drucker threatened to do just that more than once when practice became lackadaisical. But he never went that far. In the hierarchy our assistants were below the head coach and definitely somewhere above us. But since Drucker tended to dominate them, like he did us, we could at least count on their sympathy if nothing else. They were like big brothers to us and we were able to come to them with problems of all kinds that we would never have told to Drucker. It was good to have them also as a sort of release valve for all the steam Drucker could boil up in us.

There was more than one player who had quit in his mind but came back because of a sympathetic assistant. If it weren't for Jeff Bridger, the Mill would have been gone shortly after Drucker abused him in films that day long ago and gave him the horrible nickname which we all loved to call him by. The Mill eventually became inured to the nickname, I think he even liked it. But he never came to terms with Drucker and his methods.

Anyway, the day it happened, Mill came to coach Bridger in tears with his uniform in hand. He was halfway out the door and Bridger told him a story about how a coach had abused him one time. Instead of quitting, he decided he would stick it out and make Coach eat his words. I cannot tell you how many times Drucker has benefited from the Mill's decision to do as his assistant coach had done. Sometimes I think that if it weren't for assistant coaches there would be no players to play the game. Drucker was the only officer in our army so thank God for the sergeants.

Having said all those nice things about them, I need to tell you that none of our assistants went to bat for the fated eight nor did they put in a good word for Jelly or Ivy during preseason. They really wanted them on the team after they watched them in summer practice. But they couldn't have said anything to Drucker. They would have been wasting their breath. Once the dust had settled and both of them were on the team, the assistant coaches encouraged Jelly and Ivy every chance they could. And they also made sure that the potentially disgruntled red neck white players put the team before their personal feelings. They made sure that the potential bigots kept their opinions to themselves.

Our team, for the most part was unified but it was more than just our very good assistant coaches who made that possible. It was also due to Ronnie's unselfishness, Tree's steady support, and the Mill's complete change of heart. I did what I could too. But without our assistant coaches' wholehearted support, I think we'd have had more problems in 1966 than we ever did. We were grateful for all our assistants did to make life easier on our football team.

Of course, the most important thing for a smoothly running team is victories on the field. When a team is winning, everybody is happy from the top down. How does that old coaching aphorism go? 'When you're losing, you don't have any friends and when you're winning, you don't need any.' And football-wise we were kicking tail and taking names. So far, so good. Still we had two region games left to play. They would tell the tale. After that we would see how united this team was.

There had been a tradition for years in our small, football crazy town that the girls would have a ladies only night out together the Saturday night after the homecoming game. I'm not sure what they did when they went out on the town. After all, in Central there was not much out in our town to go out on. Central, so far as entertainment went, had a limited repertoire for all of us, boys and girls. But as far as ladies night went, I had never heard a single boy complain about it.

In a town as small as ours, one ran out of dating options pretty quickly and the boys needed a break from all that difficult planning. Also, boys paid for everything in those days (or boys' parents) so a low expense night was a good thing, too. All in all, it was win/win. The girls had their night and we had a break. So we got together at my house to think about our night of freedom. It was Ronnie, the Mill, Tree, and me. Then out of the blue, Jelly and Ivy walked in with an offer we were afraid to refuse.

Ivy said, 'We want you cracker white, whities to come with us tonight. We gonna show you how to really have some fun. You be too whitie tightie. You needs to find out how to be loose and we gone show you.' Ivy, talking 'street' meant he and Jelly had interesting plans for us. Ronnie asked, 'Where are we going?' Jelly said, 'Don't worry about it. We'll take care of you, unless you are scared.' Of course, Jelly knew when he said that, there was no way we would dare say, 'No.' So I asked, 'Where do we meet?' Jelly said, 'Come to my house at 7:00 and don't eat before you come.'

When we got to Jelly's, he and Ivy were on the front porch. They had Jelly's stereo out there and it was blaring Temptations' songs. We sat around talking and listening to music until Jelly's dad came out and said, 'Let's go.' We pilled into his car and his wife's and drove about a mile further on some of the narrowest dirt roads I'd seen until we came to this house in the middle of the woods.

There were about 100 people out in the yard and on the porch. More soul music was blaring. It didn't require further counting for me to see that of the hundred people in attendance that night, there were four white guys. That would be us. When they saw the four of us, no one seemed the least surprised by the salt in their pepper. I had a feeling everyone there had known we were coming. There were rounds of welcome and people began to congratulate us on our successful season.

I realized then I had seen lots of these folks down in the end zone section of our field. There were old stands down there, sort of like the balcony in the picture show. So they hadn't just heard about our team. Some of them had been to our games. I asked Jelly where we were and he said, 'We just call it Joe's Place. It's a cafe and bar but it ain't registered with the city health inspector so don't tell your white friends about it. That's Joe over there.' And he pointed out the biggest man at the party.

Joe was bigger than Jelly. In fact, he was bigger than anybody I'd ever seen. I'd guess he was 6' 6", maybe 300 pounds. Remember, this was 1966. Nobody around was that big then. He was turning whole hogs over an open fire by himself. Further along the food line there were shrimp boiling in two 40 gallon oil drums. A bit farther a man was shoveling oysters on a hot iron slab with a fire underneath, while another kept a hose gently streaming on the iron to create steam. Jelly said, 'Everybody paid ten dollars to be here, including food, music, and drinks. You four are our guests.' I asked where the fresh seafood came from, and he said, 'Joe went down to the coast yesterday and brought it back in his truck.'

There were several firsts for me that night. After dinner of pig, oysters, and shrimp, Ivy said, 'Let me get you boys something to drink.' We said, 'Sure,' and he came back with Pabst Blue Ribbon. I hesitated, 'I er, never had a beer, Ivy.' He said, 'Stop bragging, choir boy, these things go real good with what you just ate.' If we had been anywhere else but there, I'm pretty sure I'd have said no but he timed it perfectly.'

I had always heard guys talk about how much they enjoyed a cold one after a hard days work. So why not? I have to say my first beer was about the worst thing I had ever tasted. But everybody was acting like they were enjoying theirs and watching me so I finished it. A little later, Jelly handed me a Colt 45 Malt Liquor and said, 'Try this, JJ. It's better.' I have to admit it was easier to drink than the Pabst and when I finished this one, I thought could hear a little buzzing noise in my head, like static on an AM radio when your car gets a little too far from the station. After one more, the static went away and the happiest feeling just sort of overcame me.

Then the biggest woman I'd ever seen, I think, came and grabbed me and said, 'You need to dance, sugah. Come on.' For some reason, I didn't resist and before I knew it I was in the middle of that crowd of jumping, stomping people and for the first time I was not the least self conscious of my dancing skills. When the dance was over and I came back to the fire where the guys were sitting, Ronnie said, 'Grab a beer out of that barrel over there.' Everyone else had one so I just went over and helped myself.

So went the night. After a while things got a little blurry but it felt fuzzy in a nice way. Toward the end of the evening Big Joe came over to talk about football. It turned out he had played for Jake Gaither at Florida A&M and he was from our town. He had played for Birney at about the same time the hero played for Central yet I'd never even heard of him. After playing for A&M, he signed as a free agent with the Pittsburgh Steelers and would have made the team had he not injured his knee the last week of preseason. He had done all of this and was from Central and none of us except Ivy and Jelly had heard of him.

No one in our town ever talked about him when the conversation turned on great football players from Central. In the middle of the talking he said, 'You boys try some of this in the jar, made it myself. Just take a sip and chase it on down with your beer.' Everyone else tried it so I did, too. Even after four beers it felt like my throat was on fire. I took a big swig of beer and asked Jelly, 'What is that stuff?' Jelly said, 'Folks call it 'Mus-I-Clown'? It's what you call white lightning, mostly it's alcohol, made in the back yard in an old tub.'

The mason jar came around one more time and again and again. At some point I think I fell asleep. I woke up when the Mill punched me and said, 'JJ, you little pussy, wake yourself up and tell everybody goodnight. We gotta go.' On the way back I told Jelly I wasn't feeling too good. When we got to his house, he took me out back and said, 'Bend over and stick your finger as far as you can down your throat.' When I did that, I threw up about ten times: barbeque, oysters, shrimp and all the alcohol I had drunk that night. Even after that my head was still buzzing but I was a whole bunch clearer than I had been. I probably wasn't going to get a plate of spaghetti on the way home but my stomach recovered some of its poise.

When he saw me, Ivy said, 'Now after all that chuckin', you a real white boy. You the whitest, white boy I ever did see. Now you ghost white.' So we laughed, said good night, and told them thanks. I should have said, 'Thanks for nothing,' because I had less in my system when we left than when we came.' Anyhow I made it up to my room without waking anybody and slept like a baby until they woke me for breakfast and church.

Coming home from church that day, the hero asked me about my night. I told him the minimum and he

229

asked, 'While you were there did you happen to meet Big Joe Driggers?' I told him that I had and he said, 'He's the best football player ever to come out of this town, son.' Coming from the Hero, who everybody else said was the best, that was quite a testament.

When I got home from films that Sunday afternoon, the biggest blackest Cadillac I'd ever seen was parked in the driveway. Andi could have put her Impala in the trunk of that beast. When I went in the house, there was Big Joe Driggers filling up our couch in the den from just about end to end. He was in close conversation with the hero. As I was passing, trying not to overhear, Dad said, 'I think you met Joe last night,' and I think that I thought, 'Oh crap. I guess I'm in for it.' But 'Big Joe' wasn't there to talk to the Hero about my drinking prowess or lack thereof.

It seemed that Ivy's granddad had a stroke while we were at the party and was being sent by ambulance to Grady Hospital in Atlanta. There had been some trouble out at the farm, a fire or something. The Hero said, 'I have agreed to let Ivy stay here with us until the situation with his grandfather is resolved.' That was all the explanation I received. I had the presence of mind not to ask for more details and responded with the southern coverall, 'Yes sir.' Dad wanted me to ride with him over to 'Big Joe's' to pick up Ivy. Then we'd go out to the farm to get Ivy's belongings. Ivy had stayed with Jelly after the party and gone with him to films that day. When Ivy and Jelly had gotten home from films, Ivy had gone over to Joe's to help clean up from the party so he had not been back to the farm yet.

By the time we got there, order had been restored to Big Joe's, for the most part. There were still mounds of beer cans and trash cans filled with the debris of the party. Dad asked cryptically, 'You and your friends came here last night? Good thing you don't drink, son, because you are in training.' I glanced sidelong at Big Joe and said, 'Yes sir, that's right. The food sure was good, though.' Joe laughed. He had a laugh that rumbled up like it came from the bottom of a volcano, 'Glad you enjoyed it JJ.'

Since we were there, dad didn't see any reason for me to not help with the clean up. He went inside to talk with Big Joe and I joined Jelly and Ivy, loading trash cans into a pickup truck. After about an hour and many cans later, the Hero came out of the house, 'Ivy, Johnny, come on and get in the car. We need to go get Ivy's things.' We drove out the highway and even from a few miles distance you could see smoke was still rising in the sky. When we got to the house, I could see a sheriff's car parked in the drive.

The same officer who accosted us at our impromptu picnic the other day came out of the house: 'Hello Big John, everything seems okay. Want me to hang around while you pack up Ivy?' The hero said, 'No, but if you'll wait out by the gate and then if you would, follow us to town.' All this time Ivy hadn't said a word. When we went to his room, the hero said, 'Ivy, your grandfather is doing very well. He should be fine in a week or two but he will be staying with the Carvers in Atlanta. He's going to go through a process of physical therapy and rehab, and when he is 100%, he will come back. Until then, you are most welcome to stay in our home. Probably, that will be until Christmas, at least.'

The Hero said it politely, as if it were an invitation. I could tell by his tone that Ivy would not be expected to say, 'No.' He didn't. 'Yes sir,' he said. In those days, colored or white, kids said, 'Yes sir,' to most white adults. Again, on the way to our house, Ivy was silent as the grave and, of course, the hero never talked in the car. So it was real quiet in that Buick. I wasn't about to open my mouth. The sheriff's patrol car followed ours back into town, not too close, but close enough to be visible to anybody who might be interested in what was going on.

When we got home, we took Ivy to the guest bedroom which mom had been simplifying, read here, making less feminine, while we were gone. I noticed even the pictures on the walls had been changed. This bedroom had its own bathroom, whereas my sister and I shared one. The guest bedroom and our rooms were upstairs. The Hero and mom had a bedroom downstairs. So now, we had the equivalent of a coed dorm upstairs and this in 1966 so it was the first one I'd heard of.

There would be no worries on that account. My sister was fifteen and Ivy was a gentleman. He would have more worries from her than she would have from him. I was of the opinion ninth graders should be housed in a separate building from actual high school students but that was my opinion. I was also of the opinion ninth graders would be better off on a separate planet. That, too, was my opinion. After he had put his things away, Ivy came to my room. 'What's up?' I asked, knowing from his demeanor he wanted to tell me about last night.

Ivy said, 'While we were at the party, some men came to the house looking for me. They beat up my granddad and burned down our barn. I don't know who they were but they wanted me because of what happened the night you got in the fight with Thad.' I said, 'What happened?' He said, 'Remember, when I grabbed his friend to get him off you? Those men claimed I beat up a white boy but I never hit him, even once. I wanted to but I knew better. White folks don't care if I knock the piss out of a white boy in a football game. But I damn sure better not do that anywhere else.'

232

I thought about the linebacker from Parnassus he had clocked the other night. Nobody worried about him hitting that white boy. He went on, 'I wanted to quit the team and go with Granddad to Atlanta, but Big Joe wouldn't let me. He told me I'd be staying with you for a while.' I had to ask, 'Who is Big Joe really, Ivy? I mean what's he do?' He laughed sardonically, 'In my town, you know, colored town, Big Joe is the sheriff and the mayor and the judge. If you want to get along in my town, best follow Big Joe's advice. He's a lot like your dad, JJ.'

I didn't really have a clue what Ivy meant. My dad was a school principal and as such he put the fear of God in lots of kids but what influence other than being the object of hero worship did he have over any of the adults in town? When he read my look of incomprehension, Ivy laughed and said, 'You don't get it, do you?

In this town most of the adults either watched your dad play ball, or played with him, or they played on a team he coached, or they were students in his school. Do you know what that means about your daddy?' Well, I had not seen it clearly before but from Ivy's point of view, the haze was beginning to lift. And it scared me to think that others might think about him in the same way that I did. Could he actually have that kind of influence in Central?

So now after the drama, of the previous night, back to the game. Parnassus, as I already told you, was an easy A, probably the last one of our season, however long we lasted. There was no way Drucker would ever convince us otherwise. Practice that week was gentle by Drucker standards. We did not have one full speed scrimmage. Almost everything was timing and finesse. At one point, it seemed to me almost as if Drucker were already preparing for Howard Banks, next week's opponent and last year's state champion in AAA, the division above ours. The weather was cool and practices were short.

When we finished there was time to sit around and watch the basketball team as they began their year with preseason practice. Of course, it was not like watching the full team as Ronnie, Jelly, Ivy and I could not yet practice with the team. Still, it was nice to sit in the stands and see other people sweating and to hear coaches yelling at someone else. I was tempted to heft a ball and arc it toward the hoop. Ivy even dared pick one up but Ronnie and I stopped him. If Drucker were to come out of his office and see a football player holding a basketball at this point in the season, the explosion would have flattened the gym. I warned him, 'Stick to your knitting, my friend. Dance with the one what brung you, all that crap. But please don't handle that round ball. Basketball will come in due season. For now we have other things to do.' For once Ivy did not have anything to say about the stupidity of white man's rules.

With the weather and the easy practices and the consequent increase in energy it was inevitable that someone would call for the yearly Road Trip. What road trip meant was a select group of seniors with enough fortitude would slip out the windows of their bedrooms and meet at the designated spot and head down to the river. Cars would roll out of driveways in neutral and not be cranked until out of earshot. Always it was the senior football players, the senior cheerleaders and drill corps and their dates, about forty or fifty of us, all upper classmen, no juniors please. And the stealth was just a sham. Every parent knew we were doing it and every child knew they were known. But the rule was, 'don't ask, don't tell'. If there were a few parents, hanging out within earshot of the river's shoals, and if an occasional police car trolled by, well who knew or cared?

The shoals were a bend in the local river where sand and rock deposited on our town's side, making a nice beach for a picnic or in this case a bonfire. Drucker's only issued three 'no's' to his senior players concerning the road trip: no drinking, no swimming, and not on a Thursday (the day before the game). He had to know the night so someone would slip a note under his door with one word, Tonight.

For our road trip Jelly would be coming with a date, the girl from Birney, and Ivy would be coming with me and Andi, no girl for Ivy, though. So I dropped my teeth when Jelly turned up with his date and there with him was Ivy with Ruth, as well. She was home for fall break and her parents had come over to the farm from Atlanta. She was like a vision from the Arabian Nights.

It was interesting to watch when she met Andi. It was as if there was an unspoken question between them: Who would be homecoming queen for tonight's road trip? But it was apparent to me that a bond formed almost immediately, so strong, that there need be no pecking order established.

They spent the first hour talking together so closely that I became annoyed and said, 'Ivy, why don't you go get Ruth.' He asked, 'Why don't you go get Andi? You're the QB.' I said, 'Both us,' so we did. And I guess they'd talked enough. I'm sure they would not have come with us willingly, if they had not finished their business. I wonder to this day exactly what they talked about but have never asked. Neither of those two were to be managed.

When we were alone, Andi said, 'You didn't tell me how nice she was.' I said, 'I did too tell you how nice she was.' She said, 'Well, you just didn't make it clear.' I wanted to say, 'No matter how clearly I tried to explain about her, you were going to take it how you wanted to.' What I actually said was, 'Sorry, I should have explained myself better.' At the time I thought, 'I'm going to make some girl a great husband one day! The Mill is right; I am a wussy.'

The rest of my night was spent holding hands and making out on a sandy blanket. When it was time to leave, Ruth said, 'I'll drive you two home,' meaning Ivy and me. Andi did not protest. I'm sure this must have been part of the interminable parlay at the outset of our road trip night.

In the car Ruth said, 'Ivy's grandfather is doing really well but he may be staying with us in Atlanta for a while, even longer than Christmas.' I told her, 'Ivy filled me in on what happened.' He nodded. She said, 'Then I'm sure you know there is no good reason for him to come back here, now. He knows Ivy will be alright and he will be much safer with us. My father is selling the farm for him, so he will have enough money to live out his life comfortably. We have found a nice house in a good neighborhood in Atlanta. It will be difficult for him at first since he is accustomed to farm life but he will adapt.'

I wondered if her dad might not be the buyer of Yorky's farm, I but didn't ask. When we got to my house, Ruth's father came out with the Hero. He nodded to us and got in Ruth's car and they drove away. If I live to be hundred, I'll never figure all that out.

There was not much to tell about the Parnassus' game except it was a long bus ride. They were on the far side of the region so it was a two hour drive, even by gray hound. We stopped in Midlands on the way over and back to eat our pre and post game meals. We beat them 56-0. I threw three touchdown passes, two to Ronnie and one to Jelly. Ivy had 239 rushing yards in the first half.

And the Mill scored a touchdown. Here's how it happened. In the third quarter we were so far ahead none of the starters were in the game. Coach yelled, 'Mill, go in at tailback and tell them to run 25 Iso. That's where the fullback leads the tailback into the off tackle hole. The Mill jumped up and ran into the game. We were on the three yard line when they gave him the ball. He looked like a bear at the circus, lumbering into the hole. Three different guys on the other team had him by the legs and he still dragged them across the goal line.

It was his first touchdown in seven years of football. He came to the sidelines, still holding the ball. The referee had to come over: 'Son, if you don't mind, we need that thing for the extra point.' As the ref left, Drucker said, 'Don't worry, son, you can have the ball when the game's over. Just promise not to eat it.' The Mill still has that ball on his mantel at home. It did not erase years of hatred, but it was a nice gesture by Drucker.

CHAPTER TWELVE

When the Great Scorer comes to mark against your name,
He'll write not whether you won or lost,
but how you played the game.

Grantland Rice

On Saturday when we got up, the hero was sitting in the kitchen, waiting to give us a ride to the breakfast club. On the way he started to talk, which was uncharacteristic. He seldom spoke at all and never while he drove: 'Boys, there is going to be great enthusiasm and energy in the room this morning. People are going to be excited and they are going to ask you about the game this week against Howard Banks. What they want you to say is that you are confident that you can win Friday night. They want platitudes like the Banks Boys put their pants on one leg at a time, just like you, things like that.

    'My advice is don't give them those platitudes. Be less confident in your answers. Don't talk to them about what you are going to do Friday night. Don't talk about yourselves at all. Just talk about Howard Banks and focus any platitudes on them. Talk about what an honor it is to play a great team who have built so much pride and tradition. Lay it on thick. Ivy, I know what you are thinking already, 'Here is that white man's awe shucks, attitude, again and it is. That is exactly what it is, just an attitude, a pose if you will. It's not what you believe, but it's what you ought to say. Not just because it will sound good to a white audience either. There are good reasons to take that tack at breakfast this morning. You guys are breaking ground. You are entering into head game territory now. You've never been there but Howard Banks lives there.

'This week, did you realize, there will be articles in the state paper about this game. People here and there will be asking you questions that can easily get posted on the Banks Boys' bulletin board. Until now you were a local phenomenon, only. If you want to play with the big boys, then the game does not kickoff on Friday night. The game begins this morning. And the game I'm speaking of is the hype game. You cannot let Howard Banks get into your heads. You ought to try your best to get into theirs. Anything you say from here on will be in some newspaper so aim your words at making Howard Banks overconfident.'

We listened because he'd been the big college player. He knew how to play the bigger game. He parked the car and got out and went in the cafeteria, leaving us to sort through his words. I said, 'What have we got to lose, Ivy? If he's right, it will help us win. If he's wrong, it can't hurt us.' Ivy said, 'It's not what I want to say this morning but I trust yo daddy. Let's do it like he says.'

That morning there was not an empty seat in the cafeteria and they had even brought in extra tables and chairs from the Home Economics department. The entire team was sitting at the head table with our assistant coaches and there were three hundred people besides us in attendance.

Even though this was a game that would not affect us one way or the other in our quest for the playoffs, it was obvious it meant a great deal to the citizens of our town. This week there was the usual microphone in the center of the room but now there also was one at the table where Ivy and I were seated. Tree, the Mill, Jelly, and Ronnie were around us. We were the seniors so we would be addressing the gathering.

The first question was, 'How do you compare yourself to the '48 team?' I took that one: 'First of all, since I wasn't around to see them play (laughs all around), I'm not sure. But I can definitely say that they won the state championship and we have not yet even won our region. It's difficult for any of us to see ourselves in their class.' 'Hey Mill,' someone asked, 'How will you do against double sevens?' The player to whom the questioner referred wore jersey number 77 for Howard Banks. He was their third year in a row all-state tackle, who was probably headed to Georgia on scholarship.

The Mill said, 'This is the third year I've faced him. I figure I'll finally block him at least once in this game,' which drew loud laughter all around. 'I don't know what it will be like this year,' the Mill said, 'But it will be fun to play against him. He is a great yard stick for any opponent to measure himself by.' He sat and looked at me as if to ask, 'How was that?' And I was thinking, 'If Julia did not write that, she should have.'

They asked if we had anything special planned for the Banks Boys? And Coach Oakes said, 'No, we just hope to be able to execute what we have been doing all year. We aren't going to rewrite the playbook for this game. In fact, we don't plan to change anything this week, just try to improve on what we've done. Against a great team like this one, trickery is not of much use.'

Someone asked, 'Any predictions on the outcome?' Jelly said, 'I'm pretty sure they are going to show up at our field so we will definitely have a game. That's the only thing I know for sure. I hope we play our best and make you proud of us.'

Cheers and applause came from everywhere in the cafeteria. There were other questions but one thing for sure. If Howard Banks wanted quote clippings from our local paper, the ones offered this morning would not be much use on their bulletin board. By the way, the editor of our local paper was there that morning and there was another reporter-looking type sitting with him, a man whom I did not recognize. He definitely was not local.

When we got home, the hero sat us down: 'You handled yourselves well this morning. Did you notice a stranger in the back right corner of the room?' I said, 'Yes sir, I wondered who he might have been.' The hero said, 'That was Jack Sanders, assistant sports editor of the state paper. There will be an article in Sunday's paper about both teams. I was told by Jack this morning that You are moving up to #1 in the state rankings this week and Howard Banks is already #1 in AAA. It will be the first time two #1's have squared off in the history of the state.

'It seems to me the state paper has jumped you several places this week over some good teams. They must have done it because they want to make this game historical but also they want to make some headlines for themselves. Don't get me wrong. I think you are deserving of a #1 ranking but you had better reach deeply this week. Howard Banks is definitely a #1 team whether you are yet or not. As far as the hype, you are going to have an interesting week. Jack Sanders will be here all week writing on the scene stories about the town, the school, and the team. The state sports editor will be with Howard Banks. It's a bit over the top for high school football, if you ask me. You don't need any more pressure than you have, but this is the price of success. It is what it is.'

When he left, I told Ivy, 'We need to get the team together at Tree's house this afternoon.' He agreed, so the phone calls were made and all 34 of us, plus our 10 scrubs had assembled at the Sizemore's house at 3:00. In my opinion, we were all part of the Central team whether Drucker acknowledged the scrubs or not.

I started the team meeting, our second illicit team meeting, by telling them what the hero had related to Ivy and me after breakfast about Jack Sanders. There was a chorus of breaths taken in around the room. We were small town boys who loved to play football but had never experienced much limelight before. Most of us played because we loved the game, never expecting anything more.

Jelly said 'This is a great opportunity for us to show the state that we are a good football team, but I hope we do it by the way we play and not by anything we say, before of after the game.' The Mill said, 'I'm playing the toughest bastard in the whole state this week and I expect some help from those of you who play around me. We have got to be a team, beginning to end.' The Tree said, 'We have got to have the best practices of the year.' Ivy said, 'No bragging, and that starts with me.' Ronnie said, 'If anybody tells Drucker we had this meeting, the Mill will kick your ass.' That was it. The seniors all had spoken their piece so we adjourned.

That night the seniors and their dates came to my house. The hero of '48 grilled hamburgers and we tried to relax, watching the USC-Notre Dame game. It was a huge game as both teams were highly ranked and since Notre Dame in 1966 had not begun to play in bowl games yet, it was like a bowl for them. Ironically, the stars for both teams were negro players, and they played well. The Mill said, 'Ivy, you should go to Notre Dame. You'd look good in puke' green. Ivy said, 'It's Kelly green, Mill,' which floored us all. How did Ivy know what shade of green the Irish wore? He told us how, 'I talked to their coach the other day and he's coming to the game Friday.' I could have gone all night without news like that.

The Hero, who had drifted in, added, 'Boys, don't want to make you nervous but there will be a coach from USC, that's the one in California, and Ohio State here, too. And there will be three or four ACC and SEC coaches as well. I heard a couple of head coaches, maybe. Don't worry though. They will mostly be looking at a couple of the Banks Boys.'

I knew he was teasing and challenging one boy in particular who happened to be in the room. Every coach there Friday would have their eyes on Ivy. The southern coaches would be Kelly green with envy because they would not be able to recruit him. Also, every small school in the northern part of the state would be represented. I wondered if I would sleep at all this week, not because anyone would be interested in me as a player, but if you're even at the dance, it would feel as if they were watching you: 'Lord, help my raggedy arm.'

At Sunday films Drucker was at his OCD best. He had us sit by position so the Mill, who usually sat beside me, was across the room. His acerbic side comments were the only thing that made the sessions bearable. I was pretty sure this might be the only sleep I'd get all week. A good athlete takes advantage of opportunities when they present themselves so I did. I woke up with a start to Drucker yelling even more loudly than usual about keeping our mouths shut this week.

He laid down the law. No one would speak to a reporter unless he was within earshot. In an hour he covered all the things the seniors covered in a fifteen minute meeting, which thankfully, he'd never know about. After the rant session Coach Oakes asked me, 'Did Drucker cover anything you guys missed in your meeting yesterday?' I asked innocently, 'What meeting?' He laughed, 'Don't worry, your secret is safe. Besides, it was a good thing to do.'

I almost swallowed my gum. His admission was borderline treason. He could be summarily court martialed and then probably keel hauled for such comments. Fortunately, for him players never talk to the head coach about teammates or assistant coaches. Fortunately, for me that disclosure system was a two way street. What coach Oakes knew would go no further up the food chain.

This week at school was traditionally Trick or Treat week. Halloween fell on Friday this year and coincidentally it was this particular Friday that we played the Banks Boys. Talk about perfect timing. Friday was Halloween and monsters were coming to our town looking for us.

As Ivy and I walked up to the main entrance from the breezeway on Monday, there was a huge sign hung up over the doors, painted in the school colors of Howard Banks: 'Watch Out Central Weenies, the Monsters Will Be At Your House Friday Night.' Our custodian had put up a ladder and a couple of JV players were up at the top, trying to pull down the sign. When it finally fell, the entire student body had gathered to watch and they let out a roar of approval as it fluttered to the ground.

We were country bumpkins for sure, compared to Howard Banks, but none of us had fallen off the turnip truck yesterday. We, at least the ball players, were pretty darn sure somebody from our side had put up that sign to fire us up. But as my English teacher had pointed out numerous times in his class, there could be no good fictive work without a willing suspension of disbelief. We had that willingness flowing through our student body's veins that week, and so we were all getting ready for the Banks Boys: team, coaches, fans, and students. They couldn't come to our house and hang derogatory signs whether they actually did it or not.

Practice was fairly light that Monday and we were frisky with the chill in the air. Even so there was some pushing and shoving among our players. Tempers were running high. Acrimony of that sort at practice is just about always a good thing. When tempers were on edge, the team was getting ready.

During Trick or Treat week, football players got a note and a treat from their secret cheerleader, the one every player knew by now was his sponsor, every day. Monday, I got a Sugar Daddy, all day sucker, and a note that said, 'I hope this sweetness makes you think of me.' Well, that sure as heck wasn't going to get me ready for the BB's, but my secret cheerleader knew what I needed and it was not to be more fired up or tense. I needed to get my mind off all that for a minute at least. Thanks Andi!

The team, especially the mud-dobbers, like Mill and Tree, got ready by getting each other more and more pissed off. Quarterbacks have to stay cool, as much as possible. After practice Tuesday there were three reporters: local, city, state at practice, ready to interview Ivy, and Coach Drucker, who as he had promised, would be at every player interview. This was a good idea. For once Drucker and I were on the same page.

I drifted close to listen: 'And do you think you will break all John Savage's scoring records?' Ivy said, 'If I do, he may kick me out. You know he's letting me stay at his house while my granddaddy gets well.' 'Yes we heard about that. Wasn't there a fire?' asked the reporter from the state capitol. Ivy said, 'Yes sir. We think my granddad had a stroke while he was in the barn to milk the cows. He must have knocked over his kerosene lantern. Fortunately, some men saw the smoke and got him out, but they couldn't save the barn.' I thought, 'Or something like that. Smooth, Ivy, way to handle it.'

There were more questions about his importance to the team, all those leading questions that asked, 'Why don't you blow your own horn,' and he deftly handled them all. I think someone had been coaching him and I thought I knew just who that was. He didn't just live with the Hero, he was beginning to drink the kool aid. The Hero could do that to just about anybody. I knew because he'd done it to me since forever.

On Wednesday morning there was another banner. The caption in big letters read: 'Black and Blue' and underneath in smaller letters but big enough: 'We're gonna beat your blacks and you'll be blue.' It was not the wittiest repartee but the sense of it was clear. We were being told that we were nothing without Ivy and Jelly and all the BB's had to do was stop them and the rest of us were losers as usual.

Whoever was putting these things up knew how to get under the collective skin of a team. Even if it were our fans, as I was pretty sure it was, it made me want to play as hard as I could to prove that our team wasn't just about Ivy and Jelly, even though a part of me knew it almost really was. Without those two we wouldn't be getting messages from Howard Banks, who until this year, had barely acknowledged our existence. Being in the limelight had its good points but also its irritating ones.

On Wednesday night the seniors gathered at my house. Coach Oakes brought the teams 16mm play-back projector and the last two of Howard Banks' game films. He had Drucker's blessing for this meeting. It was customary for teams to share the previous two weeks game films with one another. Early on Saturday morning head coaches would drive half way between their schools and swap films, giving the phrase 'meet you in the middle' new meaning.

The coaches would spend most of Saturday breaking down those films and putting together a game plan. People who thought college football was more sophisticated than high school were somewhat naive. The plans made by high school coaches could be every bit as intricate and sophisticated as their collegiate counterparts. The breakdown in sophistication between the two levels of play was always the amount of time teams had in practice, implementing the plan and also the ability of their players to carry out the plan.

College teams had more time to practice and their athletes were better. But the basic principals of football are unchanging so a good game plan is not that difficult to put together no matter how complicated a coach tried to make it. Find the other team's weaknesses and choose plays to exploit them. Some wise coach had once pointed out, 'Every play drawn up on the chalk board scores a touchdown.' And that is true. The difficulty lies in getting flesh and blood players to perform like those 'x's & 'o's' on the board.

Real men are not chalk marks and transferring the ideas of the game plan into the reality of real time execution is the difficulty every coach faces. That is why we practice and practice and practice. Even with best laid plans, the 'chicken salad/chicken shit' metaphor is always in play. Each coach sent a team roster with his films. Looking at that roster reminded me that Howard Banks had a great deal of fresh chicken with which to work.

The smallest player on their offensive line weighed 215 pounds, the largest 235, and the average weight was

222. We had three players at about that weight: Jelly, the Mill and Tree. Our guards were about 180 pounds each. Our center weighed 165, a heck of a good player, but 165 pounds all the same. Their backs were big and fast. Our only advantage there was that Ivy was faster (and better) than any of them. Their quarterback was going to the state university next year to play football. Ours was going to the other university in the state, probably, but he wouldn't be playing football there.

Nobody on their team played both ways. Ivy, Jelly, Tree, and the Mill all played both sides of the ball part of the time, though they did have replacements to provide a breathing spell. The Banks Boys were well coached and extremely confident in their ability, but not overconfident. I placed no hope in them taking us lightly. They would come to our place Friday night, focused and ready to play. They were better than us, not so much this year, as in the past but they were still better, and every man in our locker room knew that.

Still, we thought we could win, somehow. We wouldn't be here watching this film if we didn't. As we watched the film, I thought that this could be any of the last three teams of theirs that I had played. They were big, not terribly fast but very powerful. They ran exclusively out of the I. Their fullback took you to the ball 95% of the time. If our linebackers followed Howard Banks' fullback, they would get to the ball. But even so, would they be able to stop their running backs? Nobody else had all season. They were 8-0 and only Midlands had come close to beating them but not really all that close.

Knowing what a team was going to do against you was often easy. Stopping them, if they were a good team, was another matter entirely. It reminded me of a story they told about Vince Lombardi, who ran a fairly simple offense at Green Bay. One season there was a team that continually cheated and illegally scouted the Packers. Finally, in exasperation, Lombardi sent them his playbook so they would not have to waste any more money traveling to surreptitiously scout. He put a note on the cover: 'Here it is, but you still have to stop us,' and they couldn't.

Basically, everybody knew what Howard Banks would do. That was the easy part. But stopping them was another matter. Even so, as we watched those monsters, a glimmer of hope began to emerge. There might just be a crack in their invincibility. It became apparent that their right guard was the weak link in the line and that their tight end was not a good blocker, a very good receiver, but not hard nosed as a blocker. I thought we might exploit those weak links.

On defense, coach pointed out to me that their safety was a gambler and their corners were not very fast. If the safety came up too fast, gambling on an interception, their corners would not have his help and we might be able to beat them deep. But the real weak link was their left linebacker. He was not as big as their usual breed and he was not fast either.

Coach Oakes remarked when I pointed this out, 'He's the coach's son.' And I thought, 'Who am I to criticize? I'm the principal's son?' I'm sure the Banksie's were licking their chops watching me at quarterback. Don't misapprehend. When I say there were weak links in the Howard Banks' lineup, we'd certainly be happy to have any of their average players on our team. Still it was helpful to see that even state champions have chinks in their armor.

Thursday, my secret sweetie put an Almond Joy in my locker with a note: 'Think about me.' With two almonds staring up at me in that chocolate covered coconut mound, how could I not? That day we all went out to lunch, the usual suspects: Jelly, Ivy, Tree, the Mill, Julia, Ronnie, Andi, Me, Rhonda, and Sally. It was the superior seniors as we thought of ourselves. Today we went to the Rib Shack and as our two cars pulled through the drive-in window, the cashier said, 'The meal is on us today. Go and check around the back.' When we got back there, a picnic table was set up and a sign was over it that read: 'Go Central, Batter the Banksies'. I liked the alliteration and the fact that they were not only okay with Ivy and Jelly being with us, but they treated us all.

It was private back there and the local constabulary was therefore apt to leave us be. Though lately I'd begun to think that their attitude toward us was less harassment and more protection. I saw them pass by our house at night more than I remember before. I guess I was thankful but it was not exactly a good feeling. Did we need protecting from someone for some reason? It was an eerie feeling, none the less, comforting to think that our local police had our backs. Sometimes it's good when big brother watches you, at least from a distance.

Friday morning came with brightness but also the usual chill of late October. This year Halloween ushered in our first frost, a little early for us. It promised to be crisp tonight, a good night for a football game. The best weather for football, in my opinion, was a temperature between 45-65 degrees, just a breeze and low humidity. It was especially good for a team whose best players had to play both sides of the ball. Heat and extreme cold provided multiple problems for two-way players. At least the Banksies would not have a weather advantage.

The day went quickly. I hardly remember the pep rally and then we were wrapping ankles and having our team meetings. My ankle was like new by now so I just got the regular wrap and no shots. The game plan was reviewed but I knew it by heart. Before you could say,

Beat Banks it seems, we were hearing the national anthem, saying the Lord's prayer and the Mill was shouting, 'Let's kill the bastards!'

We kicked off high and deep but for some reason their safety let the ball hit the ground. The unbreakable rule for fielding kicks and punts of all types is, 'Do not let the ball hit the ground.' But even the best teams make mistakes. Footballs are oblong, you knew that? When they hit you never know where they will go and this time it spun crazily past him as those oblate spheroids will sometimes do and he had to scramble back and field it at the three. We swamped him at the eight and that's a good place for them to start, I thought, their own eight. Eighteen plays and eighty yards later, I wasn't too sure it mattered where they had started.

They were on our twelve yard line, third and three. It had been one of those drives. Twice we had them third and ten or more and the quarterback hit receivers for just enough for a first down. They overcame two penalties, one a fifteen yarder. They fumbled and recovered it, barely. Any time it takes 18 plays to go eighty yards, you know there's been a heck of a fight by both sides. Do the math: eighty divided by 18 equals, about four.

But lots of those plays were for zero or minus yardage. Ivy had been all over the field, making tackles at the line, on the sideline, and Jelly was killing their left guard but still they moved inexorably down the field. They tried to run an inside lead on third down and their fullback wiped our linebacker out but Jelly slipped his blocker and slid behind our nose man and stopped the tailback for almost no gain.

So they called timeout, which was good for us, because our guys were exhausted. They had a great kicker but opted to go for the kill. The quarterback gave it to the tailback on the same play as before. Wait, no he

251

bootlegged back left and was looking to the corner of the end zone. We had expected a short ground play, what they usually did, but they made a great strategic decision to go for the touchdown. Our defensive back had come up and the wide receiver had him beaten to the corner. It was an easy throw but their quarterback tried to make too easy. The soft, slow pass allowed Ivy to come twenty yards from his safety spot. As the ball was coming down, Ivy leaped up and intercepted it in the end zone, falling down. It turned out to be a bonus for us.

The interception in the end zone resulted in a touch back so we got the ball on our twenty instead of the eight. Their drive had taken all but thirty seconds of the first quarter. We ran one play and the first quarter ended with score 0-0. Thankfully, we got a little rest as we walked to the other end of the field.

Ronnie went to tailback for one play so Ivy was able to get a very short rest. Our next play was 25 Iso out of our I formation. This year it had become bread and butter for us because Jelly was our tight end. We ran at Jelly and Tree who began a double team block together but then Jelly slid off that two-man block and hunted up the unlucky linebacker on that side, their weak link. The boy must have thought a car hit him in the ear hole of his helmet. What's the matter buddy, just a big ol' fat colored boy. Our fullback got the outside linebacker clean and Ronnie slipped between them for a twenty yard gain. I couldn't help thinking, 'If that had been Ivy we'd be kicking an extra point right now.'

Anybody who knew Drucker, and that would include the Banks coach, knew he was old school. Drucker's motto was, 'If a play worked one time, run again, and again, until they stop it.' How many times? 'Until they stop it.' Banks loaded their left side to stop the

252

inevitable 25 Iso and Drucker for the first time in my years on the team, did not run the same play again.

He called for a 25 Iso Boot, play action fake off of the Iso action and then a pass the other way. So both teams can play the strategy game and I'm in heaven but with my knees knocking. This will work if I execute. Ivy was back in the game and when I faked 25 Iso to him, it looked like the entire Banks team was waiting in the hole where he was to run. But then I doubled back still with the ball and Jelly was streaking against the grain, directly across from me. I've hit this pass a million times but this time I knew that I had overthrown him. As I was dropping my head in failure, Jelly jumped like I'd never seen, mitted it with only one hand and was off to the races. They finally caught him on their twenty.

It was hammer and tongs from there but after eight plays Ivy pounded it in from the one. Twenty yards divided by eight is two yards. It took us four to make a first down and then four more to make a touchdown but we did. And with four minutes left in the half we went up on the reigning state champions 7-0. It was the first time they'd been behind in a game in two years.

Each team had held the ball only once and the half was almost over, almost, but not quite. Unfortunately, we were so spent by our effort that I knew we'd have a difficult time keeping them out of our end zone before half. Ivy was gulping for air and the Mill was on his knees. They would need substitutes for at least a few plays but we could not afford to hold them out. Drucker held them out anyway and it was a good decision. We still had another half to play.

I stood on our sideline, praying they would make a mistake, a fumble, big penalty, an interception. Unless they imploded, the score would be tied at half time. We would not be able to hold them. But we had a lot of fight in us that night and even though they scored as I had feared, it took them the rest of the half and an amazing play by their tailback to squeeze it into the end zone as the clock ticked to zero. So we left the field for our locker rooms exactly as we had come out to begin the game. No one held the advantage but we had twenty-four minutes left to play and there would be a winner in the end. I don't think either coach would settle for a tie.

At the half there was not much to adjust. They were as predictable and methodical as always. We knew what to expect. We just had to put forth a super human effort in the second half; 100% of our ability would not win this game. If you have never played football what I just said makes no sense; 100% is absolutely all one has within himself. There is no more.

But if you have played, you know that there is more; 100% is simply all that you think you have. That extra little bit, the part that adds to 110%, that is the part you never knew was in there until you had to reach down deep and draw it forth. I promise you that extra 10% is there if you have the courage and the will to go looking. Champions can always find that extra 10%. It's what makes them champions. When we went out that locker room door for the final half of the game, not a man on our team knew if we had it in us. At the end of this half of football we would know exactly who were the Central Hornets of 1966.

The third quarter was a defensive struggle. Neither team was able to put together an effective drive. A fumble, a dropped pass, a fifteen yard penalty. Some things happened to stifle both offenses. But we were physically exhausted and that leads to mistakes. Finally, it happened. We had a breakdown in punt coverage. In a close game it's small mental mistakes that kill and one of our defenders veered out of his coverage lane. Their return man saw his chance and cut into that vacated spot and outran everyone 75 yards to score. So they went up 14-7 and kicked to us.

Our drive was classic: run, run, pass. We were like a machine, functioning on all eight cylinders. Everything we ran worked down to their twenty yard line. They probably were expecting us to run. Ivy had over a hundred yards rushing. He was carving them up. The Mill was holding his own against their stud and Tree and Jelly were annihilating the left side of their defense. Dizzy Dean, famous baseball pitcher, once said, 'Dance with the one what brung ya.' In other words, 'if it works keep doing it.'

That was normal Drucker football, like I told you, but he out-thought himself this time and called for a pass. Ronnie would circle in from wide receiver, find a hole in the coverage and settle there. Ivy would flare and I'd pass to the open receiver. It actually was a good call. They bit on the fake and were all over Ivy and Ronnie broke clean on his route. So I threw it to him, maybe a little high, but a catchable ball. Unfortunately, it slid through his fingers an incomplete, No! Their safety, the gambler had come up and over behind Ronnie. He should not have even been there. It was not his assignment but his misplay put him in the right spot. He intercepted on the run. He was gone before we could blink, eighty yards, touchdown. Now it was 21-7 with two minutes to play.

It should have been 14-14 if there were justice in the world. We did not deserve this after the game we had played. We assembled on the sideline to put in the special team for the kick return. Ivy shouted, 'It ain't gonna be this way. Coach, don't use the freshmen. Put in the starters.' Drucker was so shocked, he didn't protest. So rather than the young guys who normally played special teams, our first team offense took the field.

When we huddled, Ivy told Tree and the Mill, 'If you get the stud blocked, you don't need to block the other two. I'll be fine.' The stud was the all state tackle who still covered kicks his senior year. His coach would have taken him off the suicide squad but he stayed out of sheer meanness, I suppose.

Ivy had backed up almost to the goal line so that when he caught the kick at the fifteen, he was running full speed. The Mill stuck their stud with his best shot but that guy was a warrior. He was recovering from the Mill's block and almost back in his cover lane when Tree hit him full speed from the other side. You could hear it from where I was thirty yards away. I knew he was done for the game when I saw the block.

The inside cover man and the kicker were unblocked because we had shot our bullets on their stud. They both were coming at Ivy full speed. At impact the inside cover guy's helmet flew off and he dropped like a rock. The kicker held on for a second until Ivy shook him off his leg and after that he never broke stride. Their safety was running with Ivy step for step at the fifty, but when Ivy crossed the goal line, their safety was pulling up at the twenty. We kicked and now it was 21-14.

On the sideline Drucker called for the onside kick. If you are unaware of how the kickoff in football works, the kick is considered a free ball so that whoever recovers gets the ball. Onside is a short kick, meant to be recovered by the kicking team. Ivy and Jelly lined up beside one another in the kickoff line and our kicker punched the ball their way. It was heading toward a Banks lineman, but before he could touch the ball, Jelly hit him and knocked him upside down. Ivy fell on the ball and with one minute left we were in business just past midfield.

Ivy carried twice and we had a first down on their 39. We ran two straight isolation plays, one right and one left, and picked up fifteen more yards. With those runs Ivy went over a 150 yards rushing for the game, first to do that against Howard Banks in years. But then they threw us for a loss and stopped us for no gain on consecutive plays.

With 25 seconds left we were third and ten at their 33. Coach called our next to last time out, and when I went over he said, 'Any ideas.' I said, 'I want to run the hook and ladder.' Coach said, 'We have never practiced that play.' I said, 'Ivy, Jelly and I have practiced it out on the sand lot beside the country club. We'll tell the line to block it like a regular rollout pass which we run all the time. We can ad lib the rest.' Not having any other ideas he said, 'Okay.' The wide side of the field was left so that was our only option even though I preferred throwing to my right. Jelly was going to slide into the short flat and come back toward me and I would throw it to him at that spot. Then as everyone converged on Jelly, he would toss the ball back to Ivy as he arced by to the outside.

The big If on this play was that everybody had to converge on Jelly. If someone, like their safety, sniffed the deception out, the play would fail. As I rolled out to my left, I could see the safety closing on Jelly full speed from the inside and the corner converging from the outside. They were falling for the trick but I had to be quick with my pass. If I were too slow and they hit Jelly before he could toss the lateral to Ivy, the play would be over, so I fired. Jelly caught it and tossed to Ivy in one motion. Everyone hit the Jelly man. They were completely fooled so that Ivy ran into the end zone untouched. As we lined up to kick the PAT, Drucker motioned me to call our last time out.

After all my complaints about our coach, I was proud of him. He could have kicked the PAT for a tie and still been a hero. No one had beaten or tied Howard

Banks in three years. A tie would have been a victory of sorts for us. We were the smaller school and the underdog. We had fought toe to toe with the big boys. A tie would not be bad. But Drucker did not want a tie and neither did the rest of us. And so He said to me, 'Tell the boys I've seen their 110%, so here's mine. Let's go for two. We'll run 25 Iso.' Of course we would. It was our best play. When we got in the huddle, Ivy said, 'Sorry guys, but they'll be all over me. Run 25 Iso Boot.'

The stadium was so loud you couldn't hear in the huddle but we got it called. When I faked to Ivy and he made a great fake, everyone on the Banks team came up to hit him, except the safety. I expected he'd be the first to come up but he was actually a very good player and smart to boot. He was fooled once. He wasn't going to be fooled again. As I rolled out on the bootleg pass, the corner somehow got tangled up with Jelly and they both went down together in a pile. With no one to pass the ball to, I had no choice but to run to the corner formed by goal line and sideline as fast as I could.

Unfortunately, the safety was a lot faster than me. He hit me as I was almost to the goal line and I knew I was going out of bounds before I crossed the line. Then in a flash I saw Ivy's trick move in my mind. As I was sailing out of bounds, I extended the ball in my right hand back inside the boundary pylon. It hit the orange plastic marker as we both went down. The pylon was part of the goal line so the ball had crossed the goal with me still in control. Technically it was score. I was praying the referee was a technician. When I heard his whistle, I looked up to see both his arms extended over his head. It was in the record books. Central Hornets 22, Howard Banks Panthers 21.

We had to kick off, but we made a good clean play of it and they threw one desperation pass which, of course, Ivy picked off. When the gun sounded, I charged the field and lifted Ivy over my head and we danced on our 50 yard line. Then the others were all there dancing for joy, until Jelly said, 'Fellas, they played a great game. We need to shake their hands.'

We did. We shook every hand, and then both teams walked off the field together, tears and congratulations on both sides, well wishes for state glory all around. There are very few times like that in sports, when both teams play so hard that nobody loses. Games end like that once or twice in a lifetime. I saw Tree and the Mill walk arm in arm with Howard Banks' stud tackle all the way to the dressing room.

When I got in the dressing room, there was a phalanx of coaches surrounding Ivy's locker, waiting for the state reporter to finish his interview so they could shake hands with the best player to ever play for Central high school, maybe the best ever to play in our state. I heard him say, 'Our team won this game, because we just would not lose.' I saw the USC coach shake Ivy's hand and whisper something in his ear. And I saw a lot of very sad looking southern coaches watching.

When I had showered and was dressing, someone tapped me on the shoulder. It was the head coach from my dad's school. He and everybody's Hero had been teammates back in the day. He said, 'Son, your daddy couldn't have done it any better, great game.' And as I was leaving the coach from the nearby small college handed me his card and said, 'I want you to call me real soon. I'd like to talk to you about spending the next four years of your life with us.' Yeah, small school, but they played good ball.

When we got outside, the party was there in the parking lot rather than in the gym. Our fans were literally dancing in the streets. I found Andi and she gave me a huge hug and kiss right in front of her mom and dad and mine. The Hero leaned over and whispered in my ear, 'You were not too bad tonight, son, not bad at all.' Music to my ears.

When we finally did go inside to the party, the Mill and Ivy walked to the microphone and stopped the music. They said, 'This is a great party and tonight was a great win. But the road to the playoffs begins next week. From here on, it's win or go home.' We all knew what they meant. We were 8-1 and #1 in the state but Royal had no region losses, yet, so the winner of the game next week would win the region and the trip to the state. The loser would go home.

Football is a hard game to enjoy, because there's always one more game to play. From here on to the end in December it would be win or go home. Here is the irony and general heart ache of making the playoffs. There would be eight very successful teams in the playoffs but every single one of those teams except one would lose their last game of the season, all but one, the eventual state champion. You can have the greatest season in your school's history but if you don't win the finals, you have to live with a loss for a year. That's what makes it such a tough game. Every champion but one would finish with ashes in their mouth. So now the real season began.

CHAPTER THIRTEEN

If winning doesn't matter,
why do we keep score?

Vince Lombardi

On Saturday morning at 5:00 AM, I was still awake from residual adrenaline. Mom had listened to my replay of the game as long as she was able but had gone to bed. So I dressed and drove to Granddad's drug store where there was a state newspaper dispenser. How they got a paper printed and delivered from 100 miles away by this time of morning was a mystery to me but there it was. I slipped a quarter in the slot and opened the window.

There were 25 papers in there but I only took one. I was tempted, as always, to grab a dozen for my teammates but the 'Little Johnny' still there in me could not do it. I thumbed through the sections quickly and found the sports page but when I went automatically to page two, where the high school games are reported, there was no article about our game. 'Odd' I thought, 'Since the editor and assistant editor were both at the game.' Then on a hunch I turned to the front page, which was usually reserved for college and professional sports. There was the headline in the top right side, the spot where the day's lead story sits:

Greatest High School Game Ever?

It is impossible to put the label, 'the greatest ever', on a sporting event, especially a football game. So many great games have been played, who can agree on which of all the games ever played was the best. In our state thousands of high school games have been played through the years and many could be labeled great. That disclaimer having been made, I will say that last night it was my privilege to witness a great high school football game.

Last night I traveled to the small town of Central and attended the game between the Central Hornets and the Howard Banks Panthers and it was the best high school game this reporter has seen in twenty-five years of covering the sport. There' I said it and I won't retract what I said, greatest ever.

First of all, it was not decided until the final seconds of the game when JJ Savage launched himself, or at least the ball, into the end zone for an improbable two point conversion. It was sleight of hands magic, that I have not seen before, as he physically went out of bounds but managed to keep the ball inside the pylon.

Second, I saw a performance that may not be matched soon. Ivory York played what may have

262

been the best single game any player has played on Friday night in this state. Those were things that made the game great. What made it the greatest was that two superb football teams went at each other with unmatched intensity for a full 48 minutes. There were no losers in this game. I will go out on another limb and predict that I saw two state champions, in the making, go at each other last night with a ferocity that had to be witnessed to be believed. In the end both of these teams will go down in the history of this sport as winners, as champions.

It was a game of drama as these teams, watched by almost every college coach in the southeast, traded blows and touchdowns. The height of the drama was that as Goliath towered over David in certain victory, the little champion got up from the ground and smote his opponent with two, not one but two, touchdowns in the final two minutes of the game.

Howard Banks was the stronger team, as should be, since they are from a larger division. But Central on this night would not be denied. Much of that is due to the ability of two young men, who a year ago were not on the Central roster: Ivory York and Bertrand 'Jelly' Rolle. These two exceptional black athletes helped Central win. They were the difference between the teams.There can be no denying the fact that had they not been playing for Central, Howard Banks would have won this game.

But teams are not made up of one or even two players. Everyone on the Central team is to be commended for their play. The most interesting play of the game was the third Central touchdown, the old hook and ladder. I asked Ivy about that play after the game and how long they had practiced it.

Here is his comment: 'We never practiced that play at school. Me and Jelly learned it from JJ (Savage) over at the sand yard (a rough field near the tracks that adjoin the country club in Central where the three worked last summer as caddies together). We were razzing JJ about white man's football, you know, no razzle dazzle and fun. And that's when he taught us the hook and ladder. We practiced it for fun all summer, got a lot of laughs out of it, never knew we'd actually get to use it one day.'

I said, 'So you mean it was like drawing up a play in the sand?' He said, 'The blocking was the same for another play we run. Me, JJ and Jelly knew what to do. So I guess it was kinda in the play book and in the sand lot, both.' That sand yard miracle and the two pointer were the final scores of the game. But it was the game itself that was the difference.

I will go out on another limb and predict that the face of southern high school football will be changing dramatically over the coming seasons as more and more coaches realize there is a wealth of untapped sand lot talent waiting to be employed by those who want to win football games.

The article and the game it described pretty much completes the story I have been telling. It tells how two fine young men came to be accepted by a community, because they could play ball and then were accepted for who they were. If you want the final results of our season, if you want to know did we win it all, it's ancient history. You can look it up in old newspaper archives. If you want more details of what happened to our team personally, I'll have to tell more.

264

I am tempted leave that part of the story to your imagination. There are now some children's books where the child is allowed to read the beginning and write the end of the story himself. I am a preacher, as I told you earlier. In seminary my professor of homiletics (the art of preaching) told our class that the epitome of great preaching was knowing when to stop. He said, 'More sermons (I guess by extension stories) have been ruined by one paragraph too many than any other reason.'

Maybe I ought to stop my story here but I just can't do it. I can't stop quite yet. Though it might be a good place to stop, it's not quite the end of the story. The record books can only tell you the results for football in our state in 1966. But lots of stuff, good and bad, happened to us. I'm going to keep telling the story. If you are tired of my southern drawl, put this book down and go look it up. If the story so far has kept your interest, stay with me a bit longer.

The Mill and Ivy had said it all at the party last night. They warned the rest of the team and the entire student body that we still had four games to go if we wanted to make history. Royal, our big rivals from twenty miles away, had yet to lose a game in the region. We had to beat them if we truly were a team of destiny. To my mind this week they were in the exact place we were last week when we faced Howard Banks. No one thought Royal had a chance except, of course, them. They were a good team, they had a great deal of pride, and they knew that if they beat us, they would put themselves into our shoes.

I'm sure they had talked about the fact that if they could beat us, they could beat anybody in the state. This game could be their springboard into the record books. That is what I told the packed house at the Breakfast Club that next morning. I said, 'You are welcome to continue celebrating, I hope you will enjoy our victory but we have to come back down to earth, now! Out of the corner of my eye I could see the Mill nodding vigorously. I'm sure he was not the only one.

That afternoon, as we were watching the college game, the seniors put their heads together and came up with a list of every team we remembered who had lost a game after a really huge win. The list was long. So I asked them, 'What should we do to get mentally prepared for this game?' Ivy responded, 'I don't know about the rest of you but I ain't even cracking a smile again, 'til after we beat Royal. I am going to put my white man game face on and keep it on 'til then.' Voila! There it was, our method to get ready. Then and there our seniors made the no smile pledge, no smiles 'til it's over next Friday night. And then we postponed thinking any more about it for the rest of the day, because tonight the town of Central was having a Halloween party, one like never before.

The night started with trick or treating by the younger children and then everyone converged on the high school gym. It was decorated appropriately in orange and black. The older kids ran games and shows for the younger children. The football team and cheerleaders conducted the haunted hay ride. This was complete with haunted house along the way. We borrowed manikins from the local department store and the grocery gave us ketchup, tons of it. There were severed body parts along the way.

We had one segment where we charged the hay wagon with chain saws (the saws had the chains removed, of course, the Mill wanted real chainsaws). We had the cheerleaders dressed as witches. We had a black Frankenstein. You can guess who that was. We had Count Dracula, that would be Ronnie, and we had the Werewolf, also black. There has not been before or since, a scarier

266

werewolf. That wolf did not smile one time all night. The party ended with an auction and then a bust the Royal mobile, where for a dollar you got a whack with a sledge hammer at an old junk car. This was always Tree and the Mill's favorite thing. It was a great time and we raised over $1000 for our senior trip that May. Throughout the night not one of our seniors, boys or girls, smiled. And I'm not talking about just the football players. The word had gotten out.

The first casualty in the war on smiles was the Mill. It couldn't have happened to a better guy! I happened at the film session on Sunday. Drucker was in rare form and this Sunday he singled out the seniors. There was no winner in the Drucker pool that day. He fooled us all. Why he would focus on us, nobody had a clue. As I said before, he never criticized either Ivy or Jelly publicly. He had plenty to say privately but not in public. Ronnie and I knew that we would get blasted good for the interception, pick six. But he left us alone for the most part.

Drucker decided today that he would get under the skins of our twin all-state tackles. Well, they weren't all-state yet but the announcement came out in a week and we were betting we'd get five or six of our players on the all state team. For certain Jelly and Ivy, most probably Tree and the Mill.

So today Drucker decided to talk down the tackles. Tree had a pretty good game but the Mill had been blocking their stud hoss tackle all night, actually trying to block him. Every other comment from Drucker was, 'Great play Mill, missed him again Mill, you get the whiff award, Mill.' Finally, he shouted: 'Mill, did you ever get your britches back? This time he took your pants off in front of the entire town of Central.'

There was steam coming out of the Mill's ears, not because he was mad this time, but because he was trying

267

to keep from laughing. The rest of the team was suffering, too. Everyone had adopted the seniors' no smile rule. And it was becoming increasingly difficult for the entire room to not burst out in peals of laughter. Finally, the Mill looked at Ivy and whispered, 'Shit man, give me one, okay.' Ivy nodded and the Mill fell out of his chair laughing. As Drucker stood over him screaming, nobody else cracked a smile.

Ivy got a severe test of his will that week from none other than my sister Mandy. I don't understand how anyone so gawky in ninth grade could have turned out as well as she later did. At fifteen she was all knees and elbows and a mouth full of braces. And she hated me with a passion but loved all my friends with an equal passion, especially Ivy.

And she could make him laugh, that deep rumbling baritone laugh of his, just by looking at him and crossing her eyes. When we came down the hall upstairs that day after films, she was waiting to give him her crossed eyes look. He was breaking up but managed to make his room finally. All week she made faces at him over meals, in the den watching TV, in the car on the way to school. He managed to control himself, but barely, and it was painful. Finally, he said, 'Mandy, you killin' me, but I can't smile. We gotta win this game.' She crossed her eyes and stuck out her tongue, and he knew right then he should have just kept his mouth shut.

And I got in my first fight with Andi over the no smile edict. The one who had the most difficulty with the no smile promise was Andi. She did not have a frown in her repertoire. She grinned, she laughed, she smiled, sometimes she pouted, but it was almost like a smile. She did not frown. She didn't even have a straight, sultry look. So she really struggled that week.

268

As we were in her car going to lunch, just the two of us, she said, 'JJ, I want to make 'Impy' into a smile sanctuary.' Impy was her Chevy Impala. She wanted to laugh in the sanctuary of her convertible. She pleaded, 'Let's make a pact that when we are in my car, just you and me, we can act normal.' It was a reasonable request, considering I'd be the only who knew. But I said, 'Andi, I can't do that. It's important to keep to the promise until we beat Royal. It's an integrity thing, you know?' But it wasn't my integrity at stake and she knew it.

She pouted, 'You are the most superstitious fool I know. You are afraid if I smile, it will jinx the team. Like I could do that.' I shouted back, 'It's not about being superstitious. It's about getting ready to play Royal. And by the way, I'm not superstitious.' She grimaced, 'So how's that Tee shirt holding up? Mr. 'I'm not superstitious?'' I said, 'It'll make it to the end of the season.' She said, 'We need to stop this.' I said, 'Can't do it, Andi.' She slammed her foot on the brake and my head almost hit the windshield: 'Get out, you can walk back to school.' As she drove away, I was not smiling. I shouted, 'No smiling. You know the rule.'

By Tuesday a new thing to go with no smiles was all over school. Some freshmen had gotten the urge to be good fans and support us. They showed up in all black: black Tee shirts, black converse tennis shoes, black jeans. By Wednesday the entire student body was in black and unsmiling. When I walked in my Trig class, Mrs. Jenkins had on a black dress and black stockings. I'm not sure the no smile and, now, dress black movement did one thing to get us ready but it didn't hurt. It sure got our minds off of the Banks game. We had definitely put that behind us.

On Tuesday afternoon the coaches had black jerseys in every locker as we continued our black out week. Since the game was away, we did not have a pep

269

rally but when we got to school Friday, the entire building was streamed in black crepe paper. There was not a smile to be seen. It was like the whole school was behind us.

It really was exhilarating to see that the entire student body and our teachers were with us. The bus trip to Royal and the pregame meal were not a problem. Drucker did not allow smiling during that time anyhow. The Mill leaned over to me at dinner and said, 'If we lose this game, I'm gonna fall on the ground laughing, anyway. God, I miss it.' That night after the Lord's Prayer, the Mill's place to call for death to the SOB's, he changed his tune: 'Kill the mother fuckers, so I can finally smile again.'

That night Royal scored first but we never doubted or faltered. We answered their score with two touchdowns of our own and let 14-7 at the half. We scored two more unanswered TD's in the third quarter and were cruising by a score of 28-14. In the fourth quarter the Mill came out of the game with a big grin on his face. He said to the defense, going in, 'If you let them score, I'm gonna wipe this smile off my face and wipe your asses all over the field.'

He needn't have bothered. We scored again and they did not: final 35-14. We were 9-1, and we knew the one loss was without eight of our starters playing. We were undefeated when we all played. More important, we were still #1 in the state. We had three games to play for the dream season to be complete. On the way home we were all smiles. When we got back to the gym that night, Andi was waiting, with a frown on her face. I thought, 'Jeez, she must still be pissed at me,' but then she couldn't hold it anymore and a grin the size of Texas went from ear to ear. We drove home that night with the argument completely forgotten.

CHAPTER FOURTEEN

Sure, I know what basketball is,
the sport you play between football season
And spring practice.

Wallace Butts, University of Georgia

Most high schools were into basketball full speed but that was only because they had been knocked out of the football playoffs. Almost every team playing basketball now would have loved to be where we were. Since there were now only eight teams in each classification left playing, the state paper listed the rankings as well as the pairings for the upcoming playoffs. We were #1 in our class and Howard Banks was #1 in theirs. There were three classifications in our state, which was divided East and West, rather than North and South, like most states.

The schools were either A, AA, or AAA. We were AA and we, along with the seven other region winners, would face each other over the next three weeks. There would be quarterfinals, semifinals, and then almost on the doorstep of Christmas, the state championship. We had three games to win in order to win state, unlike today where 32 teams make the playoffs in each classification. In 1966 there were only 24 teams left playing in all classifications.

We were in the western division geographically. If we continued to win, we'd face two western teams and then the winner of the east. But that is enough of this diagrammatic analysis. The real and final analysis was simple. Cut it any way you chose, it was win or die. And from here on to the end there were no spaces to breathe deeply and relax. Every opponent would be a good one. We were facing Meredith in round one. They were an annual football power in the far corner of the western division. They were coming to play at Central, happy to miss that bus ride.

When the All-State results were posted in the paper on Wednesday, there were few surprises: Tree, the Mill, Ivy, and Jelly all made first team. Ronnie and I were second team. I might have been first team but the quarterback we would probably face if we made the state championships was ahead of me in the player rankings. And here was the real injustice. That QB was also Back of the Year in our classification.

Ivy was head and shoulders above every player in our classification, in any classification, in fact. And yet, he had not won the Back of the Year award. But here was the even more interesting thing about the politics of the end of season awards. There was one final award, not controlled by the coaches. It was the All Classifications Player of the Year.

This was the Heisman award for high school football in our state. It was without doubt the most prestigious award given in our state. The selection committee included former players from around the state who had won the award. Men like my dad, the Hero, made the choice. In other words it was an award given by

272

one's peers. There were twenty former winners from all over the state. The winner of the award in 1966 was Ivory York. Ivy had won the biggest award for the year, but had not been named Back of the Year in our class.

Here is the politics of why. As his coach, Drucker could have said the word and Ivy would have been Back of the Year. Drucker should have said the word. What he refused to do to honor his great back, however, turned into Ivy's source of motivation for the rest of the season. In doing less, Drucker could not have done more to inspire Ivy to end the year with a bang. But it wasn't all venality on Drucker's part.

I, for one, was pretty sure that Drucker had withheld his nomination of Ivy in order to challenge him to play hard in the last three games. Drucker was mean and nasty like that. Withholding a deserved reward to get what he wanted was Drucker's modus operandi with all his players.

Basically, without saying it, he had said, 'Prove it,' to Ivy as he had all season. The gauntlet had been thrown down. As a side note, Drucker had been named Coach of the Year in Class AA. He won the award for the first and only time in his career, principally because he had Ivy on his team and yet he refused to give Ivy the credit due. Life is not always fair.

There was a tone of underlying hostility at practice all week. Drucker did not say one word to Ivy. And Ivy had reverted to his 'I'll stare right through you, style.' I had hoped that we had settled this black/white issue way back after the first game of the season. I had hoped by now that Drucker would have realized what Ivy had done for our team, what Ivy had done for Drucker himself. The assistant coaches did all they could to mitigate the anger that was everywhere. I don't think there was a player on our team who was happy with what had been done.

Drucker acted as if he had no idea there was anything amiss. On Thursday when the starting lineup was posted Ronnie was back at tail back and Ivy was at wide receiver as well as starting on defense. It was the final slap in the game, not football, the other game, the two of them had begun to replay.

The game against Meredith turned out to be a rout but the way we walked over them was significant. Ivy ran the opening kickoff for a touchdown. In the films that Sunday there was not especially good blocking. It was pretty much Ivy doing it by himself. Then he intercepted a pass and ran through the entire Meredith team en route to his second touchdown. His third touchdown came on a pass from me as he continued to pad my statistics. It wasn't a particularly great pass and he broke three tackles along the way. Finally, he blocked a punt and ran it in for a touchdown.

He had scored four touchdowns: one on offense, one on defense, two on special teams. After the game a reporter asked him why he had not started at tail back and he said, 'Maybe Coach wanted to give Ronnie some time since he was the starter last year. Ronnie's a good man. I am happy for him.' We won, by the way, 28-7.

When we got home that night, the hero told Ivy he had played a great game.' I had never heard that man say anything more complimentary than, 'Not too bad.' I had not been aware that great was even in his vocabulary. I think those words made up for a great deal of pain.

Saturday morning at breakfast club Ivy asked, 'JJ, you and Andi want to go to dinner with me tonight? A coach is taking me out and said I could bring some friends.' I said, 'Sure; I'll give her a call.' Andi, as always, was game for just about anything, especially where pushing the envelope was involved. Ivy said, 'We will be leaving for dinner about three o'clock.'

I had no idea where we would be going to dinner at around six that involved driving three hours. We left our house at three and Jelly drove us out to our town's tiny airport. There a six-passenger plane was waiting on the single runway. I said, 'Ivy, I think I need to call my dad,' and he said, 'Relax, I talked to your dad and Andi's, too. They know and said it's okay.' Andi had flown before for vacations. I'd never been on a plane but apparently Ivy had. In fact he'd flown on this plane. It belonged to Jonathon Carver. We flew at about ten thousand feet to Atlanta. Having never seen the world from this perspective, my face was glued to the window all the way. Andi and even Ivy had a good laugh at my expense. Jelly cut me some slack, principally because he had never flown before either.

Before you get out your NCAA rule book, I can tell you that in 1966 a lot more things were legal than they are now. This trip was completely legal. After all, the hero knew about it and let me go and it had yet to be proven conclusively that he had done a wrong thing in his life. We landed at the big airport in Atlanta and were met in the baggage area by a chauffeur. He took us to a limousine where Ruth and her father sat, waiting for us.

We drove downtown to a restaurant called the Russian Tea Room. There wasn't a Russian in sight and we didn't have tea but we did meet Southern Cal's head recruiter who was hosting this get-together. The food was excellent and Andi and Ruth were the two prettiest girls in the restaurant, I think. Although I only had a quick glance as we passed through the main dining area to get to a private room. After a wonderful meal the USC coach basically told Ivy that he was the number one recruit on their list for 1967 and if he came to their school, a Heisman might be in his future.

It was the usual schmooze for recruiting, according to what I had been told. I had never been schmoozed myself. I was ready to sign, but Ivy seemed uncommitted at that point. By their presence it was clear that Ruth and Jonathon were in favor of this offer from USC so it was probably a matter of time. The only two other people who had significant influence on Ivy were the Hero and Big Joe. The fact that we were all here: me, Andi, Jelly, told me that Ivy probably had their blessing as well.

There were no early commitments in 1966 but I left the Tea Room fairly certain that Ivory York would be a Southern California Trojan in the not too distant future. My only worry was how that might affect the rest of his season with us? After dinner, Jonathon took us to a movie at the Fabulous Fox theater. I think we saw The Amorous Adventures of Moll Flanders. I didn't see much, though. We were seated, by choice, in the tallest balcony I'd ever sat in. I was afraid I'd stumble and fall right off into the mezzanine section.

Above us there was a night sky with moon, stars and clouds, moving overhead. At first, I thought the roof was open and it was the real sky until I realized that was not possible. What a bumpkin I was. I'm glad I did not ask anybody about it. During the intermission of the movie an organ arose 100 feet out of the orchestra pit and the organist played show tunes for thirty minutes.

We stayed over that night at the Carver's home. The one in Atlanta made Seven Oaks, out in the county where we lived, look positively shacky. This entire trip was so surreal that Andi and I stayed up all night in her room talking. Yes, I said talking. Leave me alone about it. Early the next morning we flew home, would not do to miss Drucker's movie. It would not be as good as the one we saw the night before and there was no organ in the locker room. But the Mill would be there, and he was always entertaining.

When we got to the field house, I went to take my usual seat beside the Mill. He said, 'I missed you last night, sweet lips,' and I laughed, 'You say that to all the boys, Milly.' As usual we had our crowd of underclassmen around us, soaking up the knowledge of the great and wise. Our latest exchange had them rolling on the floor. The windmill, sometimes he was much wind and very little mill, but I have to admit, he was funny as all get out. I noticed he had a cut over his eye.

'Get that in the game?' I asked. He grinned, 'Something like that, tell you after films.' When Drucker came in with the film, I swear he was limping. I'd never seen him limp. He was a tough man for sure, not one to give away his pain. He'd rather amputate a limb than limp on it. The films went surprisingly fast that day, as if Drucker needed to be somewhere else. When we finally got to our cars, I said, 'So tell me the story, Mill.' He grinned again, 'I went to see Coach Drucker to ask why Ivy was not starting. I think I hit my head on his door by accident.'

'But how did he hurt his knee, Mill?' I asked. 'Well, I think he might have tripped on the carpet coming to help me,' said the Mill with this stupid grin still on his face. 'Mill, did you two get in a fight?' I asked. He kind of brushed that aside, 'Well, we came to a meeting of the minds. We agreed that Ivy would start this week.' This was crazy. I asked again, 'Mill, did you two get in a fight in his office?' The Mill just laughed at me, 'I don't think, I'd call it a fight exactly.'

I said, "Jeez Mill, what if he kicks you off the team?' The Mill laughed, 'And what is gonna be his reason? That I asked him to put Ivy back in the starting lineup? I think I'm safe.' 'But still,' I said, 'We can't tell anyone else what you did because if he loses face, he'll kick you off the team for sure.' The Mill laughed, 'You can't tell anyone about nothing, JJ, because I never told you what went on in the meeting, you dumb ass. Who will you tell and what exactly will you tell them?' I think I'm safe. The rest of you may need Drucker to recommend you for college scholarships but I don't need his sorry ass for anything. I'm going to Viet Nam next year and when I get back home, I'm just gonna raise bird dogs. Julia will go to college and take care of me.' I have to say, 'The Mill he was a mighty man. And he feared nothing.'

All that week Ivy ran at tailback and Drucker did little in the way of criticism of anyone. He was remarkably reserved all week. Ronnie asked me in the huddle, 'What the Hell's up with Drucker?' I said, 'Ronnie, I honestly don't know. Maybe he's starting to miss us already, even before we are gone.' Ronnie looked over at the Mill, Jelly, and Ivy and said, 'I really doubt that, JJ. Even though he won't win the state, next year, I don't think he's gonna miss any of us.' The Mill and I kept our mouths shut and so did Drucker. On Thursday the starting lineups were posted and Ivy was back at tail back. When Drucker read it out loud, at practice, he was nothing if not redundant. The Mill smiled at me and winked.

We were traveling this week, so no pep rally. Since it was a small town team we were playing, we ate in the cafeteria before the trip. There was not a restaurant in that town that would let us come near them with Jelly and Ivy on our team. I thought that was a good thing to point out at pre-game: 'Well, boys we get to eat in our cafeteria because we are going to another backward town who wouldn't let a colored player on their team if they had to.' Of course, a year ago that would have been us. But what a difference a year makes.

I wish I could tell you we had exciting games in the playoffs but we had already faced the best team in the state, all classifications included. I was pretty sure Howard Banks could beat them all, all except us. Of course, if we played the Banksies ten times, we might win three. Without Jelly and Ivy make that a big goose egg. Jackson Heights was a good solid team. Nobody gets to the state semifinals without being solid. But they were a step slower than us and three steps slower than Ivy.

It was the Ivy York show again. The coaches were there, the press. Ivy didn't disappoint. He scored three in the first half. I hit Jelly for another in the second and Ronnie scored on a reverse. They had a great offense, so the final score was not that impressive: 35-21. But never mind the stats. We were playing for the state championship on the Friday after Thanksgiving. I happened to be near the coaches when they shook hands after the game. Their coach was a gracious man. He congratulated Drucker and said, 'Your back Ivy York is the best high school player I've ever seen.' Drucker didn't even say thanks. He just mumbled and limped, away.

CHAPTER FIFTEEN

Boxing ain't nuthin'
but 10,000 white men watching two black men
beat the Hell outta each other.

Muhammad Ali

After our semi-final game against Jackson Heights we were set to play in the state championship game which would be the Saturday after Thanksgiving. Since the Christmas season began about that time, our team had a plenty to deal with beside the championship game: Thanksgiving holiday break, and Christmas coming, all at the same time. I had never played football during the Christmas season before. It was definitely disconcerting to hear Jingle Bells and Drucker simultaneously. Christmas music had always meant I was safe from Drucker until spring practice.

I had always dreamed of playing deep into the playoffs but had never thought about the distractions that might occur. Distractions can be deadly in this sport. Football is a very routine oriented game. On Saturday you have a free day. Sunday is church and then films. Monday is school and a corrective practice. Tuesday is school and a preparatory practice. Wednesday is school and a fine tuning practice. Thursday is school and a situation practice. Friday is school and a game.

If you could set your clock by Drucker's schedule, you could also set your calendar by his practice routine. If we were in full contact mode, it was a Tuesday, etc. And game day had it own set of routine rituals. None of us needed a watch on game day. You knew the time without ever looking at a clock, I could tell you the time, by the particular Friday activity that happened to be going on.

But now in the playoffs, the routine had completely changed. First, only eight, four, and finally two teams were left playing high school football. Everybody else had started their basketball season, even played a game or two. And not only that it was Thanksgiving week and for the entire week there was no school and school was very much a part of the football routine. Actually, school was the center of the routine. So the routine was broken and with it our carefully groomed but fragile concentration. Football is such a demanding game that to be at ones best, the cherished routine is vital. Without that it is almost impossible to focus on the task at hand.

I talk about this from 25 years away as if we seventeen-year-old boys actually could articulate what was happening to us the final week of our season. For some of us it would be the last football game of our careers. That, too, was a distraction. Of course, we could not explain what was happening. We did not even realize how important our routine was. But every boy on our team was aware that something was amiss.

It was our assistant coaches who understood and solved our problem. Coach Oakes suggested that in lieu of the normal school practice routine we go back to summer mode. It was a scary idea but we voted as a team and asked Coach Drucker to let us practice two a day all Thanksgiving week. Coach OCD was more than happy to grant our request.

And so we reverted to two practices per day and a pre-practice film session and chalk talk before the afternoon practice. The morning practice was devoted to special plays for the game, situations that might arise, and special teams play. That practice was in shorts and was not intended to be overly rigorous. The chalk talk was just rehearsing the plays we would be using against Bishop Morris and looking at portions of their game films. The Battling Bishops were a private Catholic school and perennial power from the east coast. Though they had not made the finals in six years, they had been in the playoffs each of those years. They were an experienced playoff team and we were not.

The idea for filling our idle time during Thanksgiving turned out to be a godsend. I think we might have been mentally unprepared had we not filled our time with football. Coach Oakes, whose high school team had been in the playoffs every year, knew exactly what our team needed. Drucker, being the OCD clown that he was, never thought there was enough time to implement the game plan anyway. And so it all came together. School was out, so we had our own special school all week. Coaches know more about this mental preparation thing than players. So though they are a constant irritant to players, that's why we have coaches in this silly game. Even with all their faults, they know best.

When they heard what we were doing, the citizens of our town wanted to lend a hand. They planned a big pre-Thanksgiving dinner for the team and our families at the school cafeteria on Wednesday night. Since everyone would be eating turkey the next day, it was to be a fish fry. Suddenly, what had appeared to be an empty week of lying around watching TV, became incredibly busy. It's wonderful when a last minute plan works.

Everything we did that week helped keep our minds focused on the big game. The Bishops were undefeated, and we had that one early loss. We were ranked above them because they had not played as tough a schedule as we had, including three teams from the larger classifications and the top team in the state. We knew they had the advantage in playoff experience, but felt our schedule might have compensated us.

They were the team we had thought we'd be playing all along. They were the ones with the great quarterback. They were the most pass-oriented team in the state and their quarterback was the key to their offense. On the other hand, our team was built around the ability of Ivy to tote the mail. It would be run verses pass in the state final. At least two of us had tremendous motivation: Ivy had finished second to their QB as Back of the Year, and he beat me out for first team All State. Of course, he deserved to beat me for that award. He was better than me. Still, I tell you I was pumped to compete against him on that coming Saturday night.

After Monday morning's practice, Ronnie invited the rest of the seniors to a cookout at his house that night. We were to bring our girlfriends as well. This was special because Ivy and Jelly were invited, as they always should have been, but often were not. It was also special because Ronnie's dad was one who had not been in favor of Ivy and Jelly being on the team. He had difficulty with his son being replaced at running back by Ivy. Ronnie had not minded nearly as much as his dad had.

Fathers were often more bothered than their sons when the sons lost their position to another player. The only father I knew who was not his son's greatest promoter was my dad, every body's Hero. I suppose because he had been a self-made man, he expected his progeny to follow his example and stand or fall on their own two feet.

The Mill's parents were helping out with dinner that night and we really had a great and relaxing time. I think every one of us was beginning to feel some pressure. Andi helped me keep the pressure at bay, by saying things like, 'Even when you lose, I will still let you date me.' Or, 'Even if you throw three interceptions, I'll still tell everybody you used to be my boyfriend. Throw four, though, and I won't admit to anyone I ever knew you.' See what I mean? How about that for taking the pressure off?

On Tuesday, my folks and Tree's had us over at our house. Then Wednesday was the big community fish fry. For Thanksgiving it was just our family and Ivy at home. I'm not sure he'd ever had a big thanksgiving dinner. When dad asked him to carve the Turkey, he almost cried. Of course, he had never done anything like that before. With a little coaching, however, he managed. Thanksgiving had always been our family only. We would have a reunion of the extended family nearer to Christmas. Ivy was the first person outside the four of us in our family who'd shared big bird.

By now we were so accustomed to having him live with us, I was almost happy that his Granddad would be staying in Atlanta. I knew Ivy missed him but I think he enjoyed being part of our family. From what I had gathered from Ruth and her dad I supposed that he would finish his senior year, living at our house. He was truly becoming the brother I'd never had and the kind of brother my sister had always wanted. But that's just how little sisters are, I guess.

Saturday dawned bright and very cold, promising more of the same weather that night. We actually went down to the gym for a quick walk through (We'd had our usual two practices on Thanksgiving. What did you think? It was Drucker for goodness sake.). Bishop Morris arrived about two o'clock and went to the field for their walk around. We were just coming for pregame meal and taping so I got a good look at them. They were pretty big but we knew that. We also knew they were not as big as Howard Banks, nor as fast. And their tackles were a junior and a sophomore, good solid players, but no match I thought, for Tree and the Mill. I was pretty sure we'd be able to run our full offense but also sure Drucker would not pass unless and until he absolutely had to. At any rate, if he decided put some air in the pigskin, I intended to be ready.

That night our run through sign was broken by our permanent captains: Tree and me, believe it or not. Ivy without doubt was our best player but not as much a team leader. He didn't have any desire to be a captain. Jelly and the Mill liked to play around too much to be thought of as captains. Actually, Jelly had his serious moments but the Mill never ceased to play around. Nothing could keep him serious for too long. Ironic that the last state champions from Central had our dads as captains. I hoped that was 'omenic' or if that is not a word, something like that.

As I was heading for the glory of the run through, the Mill pushed me out of the way and broke through it for me along with Tree. I could hear him laughing in front of me. I guess that last move was appropriate. He'd been bursting my balloon forever. As we were jogging to the sideline, he dropped back to my side and said, 'You'd have never broke that big ol' thing, anyway, you little pussy.' After the Lord's prayer, everyone paused, and the Mill stood and said, 'Okay, sportsmanship, guys. Play nice.'

Then to the stunned silence, he shouted, 'Just kidding guys. Let's kill the mother-fuckers!'

Our first drive was as perfect as our playbook intended it to be. Ivy left, Ivy right, quick hitter straight ahead to our fullback, option right and I pitched to Ivy as I was being hit and we took the ball eighty yards in eight plays. It went so smoothly that we only ran four minutes off of the clock. That was not good. Our plan was to keep the gunslinger off the field as much as possible.

But he had offensive command now and he sliced us pretty finely the first time he had the ball. We were just a step from picking off two of his passes but he made the completions and steered them down the field, and they scored to tie the game. Usually, that is how first drives go for both teams as the defenses are getting their bearings. So, two quick touchdowns were not a surprise.

Our next drive, while significantly more difficult, was exactly what Drucker wanted. We ran a big chunk of clock, converted three third downs, one a pass to Jelly, two runs by Ivy. We scored with six minutes left in the half. But after taking our kickoff, they were moving again. It looked as if they might match us, until finally Ivy managed to get his fingertips on a third down pass. He didn't intercept it but he knocked it down.

They punted from midfield and we returned to the thirty. We immediately began to move the ball again but didn't have quite enough time to score. We went in at half up 14-7 but they were receiving the second half kickoff so there was plenty of playing left to do. It had been a good half for us but we missed an opportunity there at the end. I knew fourteen points were not going to be enough to win this game.

As we left the field through the end zone, we passed through two sections of temporary stands that the school had borrowed from the junior college in the nearby city. Those temporaries had raised our stadium capacity to 10,000, and the extra seats were sold out in four hours that week. Someone had said we were playing before the largest high school crowd in the history of our state. I don't know about that, but it was very noisy that night. There were lots of people for sure. The end zone section was completely filled with the negro community of Central. Up high in the middle of one section I saw Big Joe and I was pretty sure that was Yorky sitting beside him. On the other side of Big Joe were Ruth and Jonathon Carver. Ivory York had plenty of extra incentive to be great that night.

In the locker room at half I received some sobering news. Ronnie had injured his ankle. It was not a bad sprain. He'd be able to play on offense where he was in control of his cuts but he could not play defense in the second half. Coach had been using Ronnie and Ivy over our usual starters because of the Bishop's QB. But Ronnie would never be able to cover the Bishops best receiver on that ankle. Drucker looked over and nodded at me and I said, 'Yes sir,' but inside, what I said to myself only, was, 'Holy crap.'

Ivy slapped my back and said, 'Don worry JJ, we can do it. I'll watch out for you. I'm gonna Sam it all night, you only have to be Will. Sam was the term that meant that Ivy would be the safety coming up to the line to help with the run and being Will meant I'd be the safety playing behind him covering deep passes.

That was the easier of the two tasks. However, I'm not sure that would have be my first choice. Their one really good receiver was lightening fast and the gunslinger could heave it a mile. I knew that at some point they'd take a shot deep, just because I was in the game, not a comforting thought.

287

The second half started with them in possession of the ball. They completed a couple of passes in the flats to their wide receivers. Ivy had charged up and made the tackle both times and once, had narrowly missed an interception. In the defensive huddle, preparing for the Bishop's next play, he said, 'JJ, the gunslinger gone go deep this time. I feel it in my bones. See, I been baitin' him by jumping on the short routes. He thinks I'm coming up and he knows he can beat you. When he drops back to pass, you act like you slip down. Just, go on and fall. Don't worry, I got your back.'

As the play evolved their quarterback read it exactly as Ivy said. He looked directly to the flat as if intending to throw a short pass there and as Ivy appeared to take the bait and come up, he was watching me out of the corner of his eye. He really was a good player. When I slipped down, as instructed, he did not hesitate. He fired it long and deep to his good receiver who was streaking behind me. Through all of this, however, he had failed to take Ivy into account. He took his eye off our best player, not a good decision. He never saw Ivy plant his feet and come back hard and deep.

It was a perfect set up. Ivy had managed to drift out of his field of vision. Their receiver was good but he had never seen speed like Ivy's before. Maybe he would in college but maybe not. Ivy was one of the fastest high school players in the country that year. If they had been able to compare in those days like they do now, I'm sure he was right at the top. Their receiver was so intent on the ball, he never saw Ivy gaining on him on his right. He planned to let the ball drop into his hands without reaching up for it. That was a smart play when you were wide open. That way he would be full speed on the catch. It was sound thinking but he didn't reckon on Ivy who leaped high in front of him, picking his pocket as we say.

Everyone, including our fans, who had groaned when the ball was released, thought it was touchdown Bishops. When Ivy went up, the stands became completely silent. In that moment, that beautiful moment, was the picture of our season. One superb athlete reaching above and beyond what opponents and supporters had until then understood as possible. Ivory York was redefining football for ten thousand people that night.

The game we knew and loved would never be the same. Some decried the change but those who could appreciate beauty in motion, looked forward to the future portended in that leaping, one-hand interception. Ivy came down at full speed. I was back on my feet by then and doubled back and took out the receiver who was trying desperately to run him down, a very satisfying hit for a player who spent his evenings being hit by others.

Ivy strung the play out right, further and further, until it seemed he'd be trapped by the sideline. I knew exactly what to expect so I headed left, the opposite way, as fast as I could. When he reversed his field to the left, which I knew he would do, defenders were falling all over themselves trying to turn with him. No blocking was required with that move. As he traversed the field east and west, I moved north and south and was able to get between him and the quarterback, the last man with a chance. And the quarterback had done his job. He thought he had Ivy trapped on the left side line, his only chance for the tackle. This time when Ivy cut back, I hit the gunslinger from the blindside. He never saw me and Ivy turned on the jets.

That first scrimmage, remember, he had walked into the end zone. Not tonight. This night he treated the crowd to his 9.4 hundred speed. He was a blur the last forty yards. There was no noise in the stadium as he ran.

When he crossed the end zone, the place erupted. That incredible play broke the Bishops' backs. It was now 21-7. THE PLAY, as it has come to be called in the town of Central and in other places across the state, as well, has gone down in history as one of the greatest interception and returns of all times.

The Mill still swears that the real historical significance of the play was that JJ Savage, finally made not only the first block of his career, but the first two! I'll take it. No, I'll take them both. It was the highest praise I'd ever gotten from the Mill. I was sure I'd never get any again. The game ended 28-7. I threw a touchdown pass to Jelly, which meant I had out passed the gunslinger that night. Their only TD had been a run and the 'slinger' had mentally shut down after what Ivy did to him.

And so Central high school won its first state championship since the current captains' fathers had played. As we were walking off the field together, Andi said, 'When you slipped down on that pass, I thought I was going to have to tell everybody I was dating the Bishops' quarterback. Ivy saved you.' Then she asked, 'You two planned that whole thing didn't you?' Andi understood football pretty darned good, but I just smiled. It would be our secret, mine and Ivy's.

We had our awards banquet the week before Christmas. Since the team voted on our awards, Drucker couldn't screw anybody. We gave Ivy the Most Valuable Player Award. Jelly won Most Valuable Lineman, and I was somehow Most Valuable Back, only because Ivy could not win both awards. The Mill whispered, 'Don't get the big head, I didn't vote for you. I voted for Bishop Morris' QB. That pass he threw to Ivy was our best TD pass of the year.' Thanks Mill; thanks for nothing.

I did set a record with sixteen touchdown passes that year. Guess who's record I broke; 'Not too bad', the hero was later heard to say, not to me but to some of his cronies who were sitting around him. Drucker got a new car which was rolled in toilet paper that same night when he got it home. The rumor was it was a certain head cheerleader's idea. Mill started that rumor. He knew I did not have the guts to do it. And that, friends, is all I have to say about Central's incredible run to state in 1966.

Basketball went well that year. I started at guard and Ronnie at forward but it was the Ivy/Jelly show. Because of them we made it to the second round of the state playoffs. We won the state in baseball and Ronnie got a scholarship to pitch at the nearby U. He really was a good baseball player.

The state track meet that year, which we won, was the, Ivy/Jelly show, too. Jelly won shot and discus and Ivy won 100, 220, and 120 high hurdles. He anchored both relay teams which got first place. All our points were scored or anchored by the two of them. Me and the rest of the members of the relay teams just went along with Ivy for a ride.

He was magnificent in the turn of the anchor leg of the 440 relay. I have never seen the likes before or since. He took the baton in third place that day and finished ahead of the field by ten yards. All in all, we won four region championships and three state championships. There has never been and probably never will be a year like that for Central again.

It's not possible now anyway. There is no Central High School now. Central and Birney combined in 1970 and moved to a new, state of the art facility on the outskirts of town. That became the only school for our entire county. Ivy did go to tinsel town, as planned, to play for the Trojans. Jelly went to a nearby small school, more noted for academics than football. He played three years and then went on early entry to dental school, as he'd always dreamed.

The Tree and I went to the church school down the road, which really wasn't a church school anymore, to play small ball, and the Mill went to Viet Nam, exactly as he said. He survived, but lost a leg from the knee down. Eventually after coaching for a while, I went to a Presbyterian seminary and came back to serve the Central church where I grew up. Drucker was head of the search committee that hired me. I will never understand that.

We all came back home, except Ivy. His career went exactly as we thought it would. He shared time at tailback his sophomore year at USC, rushing for over 500 yards. His junior season he had the spot all to himself and gained over 1000 yards rushing. USC played in the Rose Bowl that year and he was MVP. Of course, there was talk of a Heisman in his future. He would be a first round pick in the NFL as well. There would be no stopping him.

But early in January that year, the hero called me at school: 'Son, I have some really bad news. I wanted to tell you, before you read it in the paper or heard it in the news. Ivory York died last night. He was killed in a car crash. He was coming home from a party and was hit head on by a drunk driver.' I was devastated, didn't say a word to anybody at school, just got in my car and came home immediately. The others, my teammates, coaches, students, they were all there when Ivy came home. When they brought his body home, everyone in Central lined Main Street as the hearse from the funeral home brought him from the airport.

The service was held in our church. Ivy had been baptized there his senior year and had been allowed to join, the first African American member of our congregation. His teammates from the '66 Dream Team were honorary pall bearers and the fated eight carried out the body. He was buried in the cemetery beside the church. Ruth was there, of course. Big Joe Driggers, the Hero, and Jonathon Carver spoke at the graveside. I spoke in church at the service. I cannot remember everything I said but I remember the end: 'Ivy York was a good friend. He stood by me in my fights. He had my back in the games we played together. He changed the way I thought about things. He changed my life. Maybe, he changed us all.'

Andi and I get Christmas cards from Ruth every year. We try to visit her in Atlanta and she is here some, too, since she runs the family businesses. Yes, Andi and I managed to stay together. She went to the U like her dad and mine and she was a cheerleader for football, of course. I was not too far away, playing small ball so it was not even like a long distance relationship. Our schools were an hour apart.

She tells everybody our staying together was lack of imagination on her part. She just couldn't think of anything else better to do. I tell everybody it was insanity on her part because she had plenty of better options. Tree's son and mine play football together, and Dr. Jelly's son plays, too. Guess what? Jelly's kid plays QB and mine is a lineman. The Mill only had girls and they are real smart like their mama. That's what I tell the Mill every time I see him.

My only regret is the Hero never got to see his grandson play. Dad died in 1993 at the age of 63. He was still principal of Central Consolidated at the time. Central, the town, is twice as big as it was. The interstate that came near town and the nearby city have made us just another large suburb. But some things never change. Jelly, the Mill, Tree, principal Ronnie, and I still have breakfast at the drugstore every Saturday, not just during the season, every Saturday. Andi calls that a lack of imagination, also.

The best time is during the season, of course. Then we talk to the players who are now on the team, our sons and the rest. They don't ask us much about our time on the '66 Dream Team. That is only ancient history to them. But they do want to know all about Ivy. I don't say much as I get teary eyed when I try to talk about him. But the others have great memories and sometimes an old timer with those good memories will tell our sons about the year when a black boy came from out of nowhere to change forever the game we'd always played.

EPILOGUE

*If there is any greatness to any of us,
it is because we stood on the shoulders of giants.*

It was January of 1993 and everybody's Hero was dying. The colon cancer had been slow at its onset and he battled gamely and without complaint for a year. But in the late summer of 1992 dad told his doctors that he would not undergo heroic treatments, especially since the prognosis, even with those treatments, was bleak. He was able to attend all the Central home games that fall and even went back to his university to be honored with his former teammates at homecoming.

Then the season ended, and the decline since, had been dramatic and rapid. When the first symptoms came at the beginning of 1991, he reacted in his typical fashion. He ignored everything. He assumed he was just having a case of stomach aches and then maybe the flu. Finally, things reached the point at which the symptoms could not be ignored. There was a colonoscopy and almost immediate surgery. That was followed by a round of chemotherapy and then a blessed year of complete remission.

But when the cancer reappeared, and with a vengeance, dad decided that enough was enough. He would live his last months with as much quality as he could for as long as the illness would allow. And he would die with as much dignity as he could maintain. With that in mind dad decided he would die at home.

Through those last two years of life, as you might expect from this story, he never uttered a word of complaint, never asked for an ounce of sympathy. He died as he lived, a true man. Only I knew the humiliation he endured. In the last months I had to carry him to the bathroom, bathe him and help him dress. I kept all of that to myself. He was the Hero after all. Nobody outside the family needed to hear the details.

In early January of 1993, he was near the end. He had made his 63rd Christmas as everyone knew he would. No one loved Christmas like my dad. It was his favorite time of all the year. But by New Years he looked like a punch drunk fighter hanging on the ropes, trying to get through the last the round. I called Mandi in Atlanta. She had just gone home after being in Central with us for two weeks but she turned around without even unpacking. She left her husband and children standing in the driveway and came home so dad could have us all together at the end.

That night, as Mandi was driving back, the hospice nurse told me that he couldn't possibly live more than a day or two longer. And so I determined that I would sit with him, night and day, to the end. Late that night Andi had gone home to take care of our kids, and mom and Mandi had finally gone up to bed, exhausted.

Dad and I were sitting, actually I was sitting. Dad was upright at an angle in the home hospital bed. I thought he was asleep when he said, 'Johnny, did your mom ever tell you about how I learned to swim?' I could not hide my smile. 'She said that you taught yourself by watching the older boys.' He said, 'That's true, but did she tell you I almost drowned that first day?' I said, 'She mentioned that, too, said you were trying to dog paddle to the dock out in the lake and that you couldn't make it.'

Dad asked, 'Did she tell you who pulled me out?' I said, 'No dad, she didn't mention any name.' Dad said, 'It was a black boy. In those days out on the farms in the country, black children played together with white children until they were twelve or thirteen. It was only after that we went our separate ways. The boy who saved my life that day was Ivy's uncle. He was, maybe nine or ten, I was five. He was a good enough swimmer to pull me out.

'No one even saw us but he came right over and saved my life. Then he took me into the shallow water and taught me how to really swim. Soon enough, I could make it to the dock on my own but he still kept an eye on me. He was a good friend to me, almost like a big brother. When I got older, I didn't see much of him but occasionally I'd see him around and we would talk.

One day when I was about twelve or thirteen my daddy and I were hunting rabbits on our land and we heard a commotion over in the field next to ours. We walked to the edge of the woods between our field and our neighbor's. I was about to step into that field to see what the noise was about when my daddy grabbed me and threw me on the ground hard. 'Hush boy,' is all he said.

Then we watched in horror from the tree line as men in white hoods hung a young black man from the lone oak tree in that field. After a while, they lit a cross on fire and left. When it was safe, daddy and I went and took down the body. Johnny, it was Ivy's uncle. He was named Ivory, too.'

We took the body back to his dad and we helped him bury my friend in the back yard. I asked my daddy, who those men were and why they had murdered my friend. My daddy was a good man and he had kept me fairly sheltered from the whole Jim Crowe mess. I'd never heard of the KKK.

But after what I saw that day, even though I was only twelve, daddy knew it was time for my real education about how the world worked. He explained to me that those men were members of a powerful organization called the Knights of the Ku Klux Clan. They were a legal organization, per se, so the local law enforcement agencies turned a blind to most of their doings. They were not illegal but they did some very illegal things. Even then the police left them alone. Some of our police, he told me, were rumored even to be members.

They claimed that they were in the business of maintaining racial purity but in reality they were using fear tactics to keep black men and women, too, in virtual slavery. Even though slavery had long since been abolished. Much of what they did had to do with what they considered sexual impropriety between the races. I later learned that what Ivory had done was smile at a white girl in town when he should not have even looked at her.

As dad continued his final story to me, I thought of my first swimming lesson with Jelly and saw again the fear in his eyes when he saw those white girls swimming in the lake. In a barely audible whisper, dad went on, 'Right then, son, even though I was only twelve years old, I decided that if I were able, I'd try to change things. I would do my best to avenge the death of my friend who had saved my life.

298

But also I made a promise to myself that I would do whatever was in my power to fight this thing my daddy called Jim Crow. When I became older and perhaps became more influential, I promised myself that if I couldn't do anything else, I'd keep the KKK out of our town. I might not be able to do much out in the county but I'd do my best inside our town limits.

'I made that a main purpose of my life. Of course, I never dreamed I'd have a chance to do anything really significant but sports gave me the forum I needed. I was a good football player and people respected me for that and they looked up to me some.' 'Yeah dad, they looked up to you some,' I thought. He went on, 'For a long time, I didn't do anything, but I made sure that neither I nor anyone close to me would do or say anything demeaning to the black race.' At least I'd raise my family to do the right thing.

'For a long time I had no opportunity to do anything of importance other than keep the KKK out of our town and off the police force. But the other thing I did, Johnny, I stayed. I stayed here in Central for Ivy's uncle and all the others. I could have left Central a half dozen times for what some would call better jobs but I stayed here, waiting.

'Times began to change a bit when we admitted a few black students to Central high. There were plenty of our good citizens who wanted to stop it but I told them that as long as I was principal, if a child qualified and applied legally, I would admit them regardless of race. Then a few black football players began to emerge in high school athletics around the state. I hoped that would happen here but I tried to not act with undo haste. I bided my time.

'One day in your junior year Beefy called me about two boys who were working as caddies at the club. We did

299

some investigating and by that I mean that we called Big Joe and asked his opinion. He told us that there would be no better athletes than Jelly and Ivy for many years to come. The time was right so I decided these were the boys that we needed to break the color barrier on Central's football team. But I could not just go and recruit them. Instead I sent you.

'You thought I was out of my mind, getting you a summer job as caddy with nothing but black boys. I knew how I had raised you, however, and I knew you would not go into the job with prejudice, at least not the kind of closed minded prejudice of most of your friends in Central. I felt pretty sure that you would get to know Ivy and Jelly. It's just who you have always been Johnny. Of all your classmates you were most open to new things, well Andi, too.

'Also, I forced you to compete for yourself from an early age. It was a great temptation for me on several occasions to jump in and rescue you but, thank goodness, I let you fight your own battles. Even though you probably never imagined it, you have always been a much fiercer competitor than I ever was. Things came too easily for me, Johnny. You had to fight for everything you ever got and you did. I thought that you would figure out on your own what an asset Ivy and Jelly could be for your team. When you came to me that summer with the idea of getting them in Central, half the battle was won. Of course, I'd get them enrolled. That was the door I was willing and able to open for you.

'But what you did to convince those two boys to come and what you did to fight against Coach Drucker's decision about Ivy, you and your teammates did that all on your own. I promise you that I never said a word to Coach Drucker. To this day I don't know how you mustered that kind of courage. I'd never seen it before, except maybe for the time you punched Mark in the nose.

'I had faith in you, son. I should have had more. You really always have been just like me. I got the ball rolling but you and your friends finished the drill. Well, Ivy York, of course, finished it with grand style. There were many in the supporting cast, as you know. Big Joe Driggers was vital to the process. Son, outside of Ivy he really was the best player to ever play in Central. He played at Birney shortly after I played for Central and I cultivated him as a friend when he came back to town. We have been friends for years, though few people knew.

'Of course, the Carvers were always a big help, too. It was the Carver family connection with the Kennedys and Lyndon Johnson that keep the FBI sitting on the KKK in this area. Son, there were many people who made the miracle of '66 happen. I promised myself that before I died I would tell you the whole story and now I have. Your part may have been the most significant, but you were never alone. It truly was a team effort.'

Dad took a deep breath and said, 'Maybe someday, JJ, you can write this story so others can see how a miracle happen. They happen when people understand the right thing and then join together and just do it.' And that was the last thing my daddy, my hero, ever said to me, to anyone.

I closed his eyes and I went to get mom and my sister. But before I left the room, I turned back to look at him there in that hospital bed. He seemed very much at peace. I knew in my heart that wherever he now was, he could hear me. I said, 'I will, Daddy. I'll write the story. But you have to do one thing for me. When you see Ivy, tell him we all miss him.'

Made in the USA
Middletown, DE
20 August 2017